The Ce
By Pa

To Henry Gaddis: Utah Beach, Rennes, and Brest, France 1944. Never forget.

To Margot Wolk, who provided the inspiration for the character of Sonne Becker: I wish I'd known you.

Acknowledgements:

Amy Mikell, you are skilled beyond compare. Thank you, my friend.

Karin Mauldin, I am grateful for the contribution of the von Bachelle name for this story. I took the liberty of creative license and changed the spelling. Thanks also for the history shared about your family's emigration to the United States.

Kim Boykin, thank you for sharing some author insight, and for your honesty and encouragement in the writing process! Your books are wonderful!

Author's Note

This is a work of fiction. While great care was taken to weave a story around as much of the actual history as possible, there are certain events that have been altered, primarily with regard to timing, in the interest of blending the elements of history with the timeline of the story. I tried to preserve as much historical fact as possible.

The food testers, the Jewish skeleton collection, Lebensborn, the Orly crash, and the Amber Room, and other events were mostly factual elements. The timing, specifically with regard to the food testers, was altered slightly to fit the story. They were not kept near the Wolf's Lair until after the "Valkyrie" 1944 attempt on Hitler's life.

Thank you for buying and reading this book! I would love to hear from you!

Patricia Brandon
patriciabrandon.com

Prologue

South Carolina Lowcountry, October 1975

My name is Rennie Easter. At least that was once my name. Everything I knew about my family, my past, and who I really am, shifted like a great seismic quake when I returned to St. Jude's Home for Children where I was raised since the age of twelve. I suppose I could have lived an unfortunate life after the tragedy that took my parents from me, but that was not true. My world was happy with the loving warmth of laughter and glowing fires on a dune-filled South Carolina beach. We feasted on marshmallows toasted brown, and found our way through the darkness with fireflies that sparkled in our jars and lit up the night with fluorescent beauty when released into sultry summer air. We were the best of family, the lost children, graced with the loving care of compassionate nuns and priests. We played, teased, fought, grew, and loved each other through the years as we readied ourselves for independence and migration into the world outside of the orphanage my parents had helped to build.

It is that love that reunites us now, as many have returned to celebrate the twenty-fifth anniversary of St. Jude's Home on this auspicious autumn day. During the long weekend away from my internship position at The High Museum of Art in Atlanta, I took advantage of my early arrival and walked around the beautiful stone buildings until I came to the familiar classroom of Fr. Geoffrey. Easily one of the most beloved of staff members, he had been both priest and teacher for us and remained in that capacity still. Though his hair had begun to gray, only the faintest lines of age and wisdom manifested in his face. Seeing him once again gave me great comfort as he meandered around his students. Much as he had done with us, smiling, encouraging, and teaching with pedagogical passion, he engaged each one with his proclivity for humor.

As I watched this familiar scene, my memory slipped back to a particular lesson in his classroom. I must have been around fourteen, just before going to public high school. How we had erupted with laughter when he caught Ethan Werner chewing gum. Ethan, the tallest and definitely the funniest of our rather awkward and small assembly of adolescents, had ambled to the front of the room, grinning and glancing between Fr. Geoffrey and an appreciative audience on his way to the wastebasket. I always wondered if Ethan knew just how much we enjoyed his occasional antics _ his care to push, but not cross, the boundaries between comic relief and outright disobedience. Under the omniscient eye of Fr. Geoffrey, he spit the wad of gum slowly and ceremoniously into the bin below, looking up only to deliver a mischievous smile. We had tried, unsuccessfully, not to laugh when the wad of gum dropped with a gentle thud. Fr. Geoffrey ignored our collective amusement and remained focused on his wayward student.

"Ethan, you can help us with this part of our lesson, now that I have your undivided attention. "Gravity", our word of the day, and specifically the "center of gravity" is what we're after." Fr. Geoffrey Radcliffe leaned against the chalkboard and gently rubbed his white clerical collar as he gave Ethan an amiable smirk. "Class, why did Ethan's gum fall to the trashcan?" He ran long fingers through his thatches of thick brown hair before raising his hands in the air, palms facing the ceiling, in great anticipation of our choral response.

"Gravity!" we all shouted in gleeful unison.

"Because what is gravity?"

"Gravity is the force that causes all things with energy to move toward each other!"

7

"Indeed, yes, yes, yes! Gravity gives us weight, causes the tides we love to play in, and controls the orbits of the moon, the sun, and the planets, too. Mr. Newton _ as in Sir Isaac _was once bonked on the head with an apple, remember? Ah, gravity!" Fr. Geoffrey began walking among us and tapped Ethan on the side of his head, smiling. He sent the now gum-less youngster back to his seat. "So, we know the definition of gravity. But what about the center of gravity? Thoughts, my young scholars?"

"Well, maybe the center of gravity means that everything is in its right place, or that it's all maintaining a balance?" I asked, trying to rely on a measure of common sense and deduction.

"Rennie, yes!" Fr. Geoffrey abruptly stopped moving, turned suddenly, and pointed at me. We were accustomed to the playful manner in which he recognized a thoughtful and accurate response.

"Hey, Fr. G, doesn't gravity mean 'serious' too?" Sean offered, donning a most serious tone of voice. "You know, like Hitler trying to take over Europe was a matter of great *gravity*." Sean Bennett, who always chose to sit at the back of the room, emphasized the word as he offered another less scientific, albeit correct, meaning. Sean always dabbled in the somber and scary.

"Ah, my young and brilliant stars continue to impress. Absolutely, yes, Sean! So my little scholars, Archimedes, the Greek physicist, told us that the center of gravity keeps people and objects balanced, or as Rennie said, in place. Witness the sun and the moon orbiting in perfection around each other, all due to the effects of gravity. And when the center of gravity is thrown off balance or out of whack? Why, a plane cannot fly if its load is not balanced. A racecar will topple over at high speeds if it is not low enough to the ground. There is also another center of gravity, a military center of gravity developed by a fellow named Carl Von Clausewitz, a Prussian military theorist." Fr. Geoffrey quickly made his way to the blackboard, chalk grinding furiously enough for dust to fly, and instructed us to think about the idea he read aloud:

The center of gravity is the source of power that provides moral or physical strength, freedom of action, or the will to act.

"So, what was the change in our center of gravity, as a nation, that plunged us into WWII?" Fr. Geoffrey examined each of us, issuing a challenge for us to think. It amped up the lesson to include not only science but history, as well. "What were the happenings we have discussed before, that we simply could not ignore?" He smiled at us all, and pointed to Hawaii on the wall map, which prompted a spontaneous eruption of knowledge.

"Pearl Harbor!" Mary Jacobs offered, her hand flapping in the air, as was her head full of thick blonde curls. I always wanted golden waves like that, but mine would be forever a light chestnut.

"And the Nazis rounded up Jewish people all across Europe, after Hitler gained power and controlled the government. We didn't want that to happen to them, or to us," Sean offered again, "so we became allies with the British and the Russians to go to war to fight the Axis powers."

"Correct again, my young protégés! So now, your written assignment, and you knew there would be one," Fr. Geoffrey grinned, "is to define your center of gravity. What makes you act, or react? What keeps you in balance? What would cause your center of gravity to change so dramatically that life, as you know it, would be forever different? You may start the assignment for the remainder of the period, then bring it to class tomorrow. I'm looking for good solid thinking and writing here. Extra points will be given for incorporating all aspects of the center of gravity into your paper. Of course, correct grammar and punctuation are a given, as I'm sure we all know. You may use the time we have left to begin your work."

Fr. Geoffrey had smiled knowingly as he motivated each of us to dig deeply into our life experiences to make meaning out of both new and old knowledge.

Looking back on that memory, I could never have foreseen the irony of that lesson, nor the impact of secrets past, or anything that could impact my life more than the tragedy that had brought me to this place. Regardless, the truth now haunts me, and my place of comfort and balance _ my center of gravity _ is forever changed. And so am I. But that is a long story, with roots that reach back to a time when Nazi terror was just beginning.

Contents

Chapter One

Berlin, Germany
Early 1933

Sonne

"Wake up, Oma! Mama, she's not dead. She can't be dead. Can she?" Nine-year-old Sonne Becker rubbed her eyes and stared, through tears and the soft light of pre-dawn, at the empty vessel that used to be her oma, as German children often called their grandmothers. She knew this day was going to come, but the knowledge did not alleviate the pain and loss. Now cocooned in thick blankets on the antique bed, the sickly woman only appeared to be sleeping, now resting in realms beyond. Rumpled gray hair framed the gaunt paleness of a once radiant face. Thin lips were apart, as though ready to speak, while one hand rested on the chest that no longer rose and fell with the labored breathing of pneumonia. Alsa Becker brushed a thick chestnut strand of hair behind Sonne's ear and reached for the hands of her only child. She whispered, preserving the quiet dignity of a life that had slipped away in the night.

"Do you remember when Oma nicknamed you "Sonne," after the brightness of the sun? She called you her little "sonnenschein." I can still hear her calling outside for you to come home from playing with your friends. You know the way she would go up an octave when she sounded the last part of your name. So-neeee! We stopped calling you by your given name of "Cotterena" and called you "Sonne" from that very day. She was so happy to be the one to give you such a special nickname. It will always be part of her legacy to you." Sonne saw the pools of sorrow that crested in her mother's eyes, bittersweet reflections of the timeless passage of the matriarch role from one to another. For a moment she felt the intensity of that kind of pain, the responsibility of having to become stronger and wiser, in the midst of overwhelming loss. Losing a parent must hurt no matter the age or time. Her arms encompassed Alsa's waist as she laid her head against her mother's arm.

"I know how much you loved her, Mama. Like I love you."

"Oh, Sonne, my sweet girl. She loved you more than you could ever know. We are sad that she cannot talk with us anymore or be here with us in body. But her spirit, her kind and happy heart, we can keep with us always. And she is well now, not frail and hurting. We will cry sometimes when we miss her the most, and that is as it should be. My heart is breaking now, and I know yours is too, my sweet girl. It only means we loved her as much as she did us."

Sonne snuggled against her mother's chest, her eyes closing as the memories and tears came flooding back. Oma teaching her to make German honey cookies. Oma laughing with abandon as they waltzed around the furniture to "The Blue Danube". Oma sewing clothes for her each year. Oma reading stories at night, her soothing voice exuding the comfort and warmth of unconditional love.

"Your father just got home," her mother whispered. "It's been a difficult couple of days for him with the burning of the Reichstag, and now this. I hear him stoking up the hot coals from last night. Let's close the door to Oma's room until they come for her. You can lie on the sofa with her quilt while we make the necessary burial arrangements. I will make us all something warm to drink, too."

"Leave her door open, Mama. Please?"

Her mother smiled at the tenderness in the voice of her daughter, who was caring but also headstrong, with a resiliency beyond her years. They made their way into the sitting room, where Eduard Becker coaxed the rekindling of the firelight that reminded Sonne of

15

family times spent on snowy nights, cuddled in blankets while reading or listening to the radio broadcasts. Sometimes she would play chess with her father, who was a master competitor, while Oma and her mother cheered and laughed whenever she made a stellar move. Now she watched as her father stood, rubbing the ache in his back, and reaching for his family. His face masked grief with weariness as he held his wife and daughter. The stillness of the early morning hours brought only a brief respite with the promise of another grueling day yet to come. Sonne knew that his job as both a munitions expert and an architect for the German government had caused him to be in more late meetings than usual these days. Such staffings were most often followed by dinner, for which he would apologize, though he had no choice but to be present. He had been sleepless for two days now as the investigation into the parliament building fire continued. Sonne watched every move her parents made, intuiting worry and sadness as her mother breathed her father's name with relief. She fought to keep despair at bay, but the tears rose once more as she looked into his sad eyes.

"Eduard. We're so glad you're home."

"I'm so sorry that I wasn't here with you when Oma died, my precious ones. God love her, she is finally free from the illness that wracked her body for so long." Alsa smiled through tears as he lifted a heavy blanket from a chair and wrapped it around Sonne, who had moved to the nearby sofa. Somehow the security of having both her parents close had allowed her to venture away from their arms. She stared into the now raging flames. They were the only color in a room still devoid of much light. She listened as her parents moved into the kitchen. There had always been great amusement in knowing that they thought she could never hear their exchanges when they migrated into the next room. She would not tell them otherwise, especially when she could sense the urgency in her father's demeanor. Oma's death might have been the catalyst that brought him home but intuition told her there was more on his mind. Sonne lay still and quiet, wrapped in Oma's favorite quilt, and absorbed the scene before her and the conversation not meant for her comprehension.

"On my way back here I saw lights on at the Gerhard's, so I stopped. Franz was awake, so he already knows about Oma's death and will take care of her as soon as he can. I'd have been here as soon as you sent for me if the fire had been anywhere else but the Reichstag, of course."

"Are there any clues as to who did such a thing, or why?" Alsa handed a cup of café to Eduard, and sat beside him, her hand resting on his arm.

"The Nazis arrested a Communist Dutch National, a Marinus van der Lubbe, who was found at the scene. Hitler, Goering, and Goebbels were quick to point out that there may be a number of other rabblerousers who could have been responsible. I heard them openly saying that the fire would serve as the beginning of a new day in Germany. In an instant, they locked down everything from the Brandenburg Gate to the river on the east, all secured by this new Nazi regime with mind-staggering precision and efficiency." Eduard lowered his voice and continued with caution. "Never repeat what I am about to say, Alsa. Promise me. You cannot tell anyone."

"I don't understand." Alsa's voice was fraught with concern. "What are you saying, Eduard?"

"Strange as it may seem, I am glad that Oma is no longer here to see what is happening in Germany now. It would break her heart. I believe there is more to this fire than what is being told in public. Something is not right."

"Eduard, you are scaring me. What do you mean?"

"It was too convenient, Alsa, too staged. All of them seemed as if they were enjoying the whole sordid disaster. They were especially ready to blame the Communists. I think this may well be the setup for a major power play. For all that we hold dear _ and especially for our Sonne _ I hope I am wrong. German liberties as we have known them may be on the brink of extinction. I pray that I am not right. If I am, God help us all. Promise me that you will say nothing of this ever, that you will discuss it only with me."

"Of course, Eduard. By all that is holy, I pray you are wrong, as well."

The adult conversation shifted to plans for a funeral in their hometown of Rastenburg. Sonne studied the flames as they lapped around the glowing logs. How strange it was that fire could provide lifesaving warmth and beauty, yet destroy with such rapid ferocity. As if she had a measure of her father's intuition, she knew that his plea for secrecy must be honored. For a fleeting moment she thought about telling them what she had overheard. No, perhaps after they had all said a proper goodbye to Oma would be the best time. Honesty might also encourage her parents to limit adult discussions to when she was not present at all. She had once confided in Oma that she overheard more than was meant for her young ears. Oma had smiled an endearing, all-knowing smile.

"Seek to understand, always, my little Sonne," she had whispered. "Ask questions, and find the answers with your own mind and with your heart."

Sonne stared into the flames once more. How she wished Oma was here to explain what she could not fully comprehend. Explain sickness and death, or how one was supposed to live without a beloved grandmother. Explain why her parents seemed so worried and afraid of these new people, these Nazis. Was it possible that they could take away German freedom? She fought the sliver of fear lurking behind the immense sadness of this day. For the first time she could remember, Sonne felt apprehension amidst the confusion that swirled inside her head. Then, she remembered something else Oma used to say. Time will tell.

Chapter Two

Like a fog that clouded both view and judgment, billows of thick smoke rose with the towering flames as masses of university students gathered in the square at the State Opera to burn any book that violated Nazi ideology. Festive music and singing highlighted the charismatic address of the dark-haired man who incited the crowd to destroy in the name of German superiority.

"Who is that little man screaming at the people?" Sonne raised innocent eyes to those of her father, as they made their way home from an evening walk past the downtown shops. His grinding jaw, a natural habit made worse by recent worry and stress, told her she was right to feel apprehension.

"That," her father said with a careful measure of disgust, "is Joseph Goebbels, Minister for Popular Enlightenment and Propaganda."

Sonne stared through the crowd at the small man who was barely as tall as her mother. He was even more diminutive in stature as he stood among the German police who surrounded the podium bearing the odious swaztika. He spoke with evangelical fervor, a high priest on a mission, with fire oaths and incantations summoning "action against the un-German spirit" and relegating detractors to eternal damnation. His voice burned with an intensity that matched that of the growing flames as he railed against the invasion of centers of learning by imposters who would corrupt German decency and morality. When he smiled, his eyes grew wide and his mood jovial. In that moment he could have been called handsome. But when the ranting about all that was not German reached a fevered pitch, he was a whirling dervish of demonic ugliness. His hands gestured in wild abandon to the appreciative crowd, who now seemed a part of him in a frightening symbiotic dependence. Brown-shirted storm troopers continued to feed books to the crowd, who relished every opportunity to toss them into a burning oblivion. The scene before them incited overwhelming fear and a desire to run and hide. Sonne slid a small hand into the reassuring grip of her father.

"What is happening? Why are those people throwing books in the fire? I thought everyone loved books, Father."

Young men and women, members of the National Socialists German Students' Association, were now wild with excitement, breaking into frenetic chants about degenerate influences and Nazi ideals. The youth grew more empowered with each book that was wasted in the inferno. Sonne watched her father, who inwardly grieved the magnificent texts now consigned to perish: Einstein, Freud, Glaser, Brecht, Remarque, Werfel. Sonne's favorites, Hemingway, Wells, and London, were not exempt from the wrath of the crowd. How she would cry if she knew the stories that had been read to her were included in this madness. She squeezed her father's hand, unable to intuit his thoughts as he struggled with how to give his young daughter a plausible explanation for the insanity happening before them.

Highly educated professors joined the youthful students bent on a cruel cause and embracing all that was the antithesis of Western Civilization. These learned men had abandoned their intellectual integrity to align themselves with the Nazi party. Her father knew full well that the expulsion of Jewish professors, deans, and administrators had opened up vacancies that were sure to entice many to fight for favor, like frenzied sharks among the bloody bait. Good men, once partners in pedagogical endeavors, now turned on

21

one another to curry Nazi favor. Gone were personal liberties and free exchange of ideas that had once defined the quality of a German education.

Sonne winced at the tightening of her father's brow, the strange expression on his face. Little did she know how helpless and complicit he felt in his inability to do anything but watch the scene play, as if it were a theatre production. The need to have his family survive had long overridden his conscience. His anti-Nazi sentiment was now deeply buried under obedience to the state, a dormant volcano of fear. There was no way possible to make insanity become reason.

"It's wrong to burn books, isn't it?" Sonne challenged, waiting for a reassuring answer. "They should read them instead, shoudn't they?" She searched her father's eyes for affirmation, but found none.

"Let's go home, Sonne. We will talk about it with your mother when we are back inside our house."

Confusion settled in with the smoke that now engulfed the city. Sonne squeezed his hand, looking up into his tired eyes, and wondered what thoughts were hiding there. As they made their way down Unter den Linden, away from the square and the Grand Opera House, her father hoisted her onto his back and locked his arms around her legs to carry her homeward. Sonne clung to the strong shoulders, her cheek against the warmth of his jacket, secure for the moment, but wondered in silence if the danger her father had predicted was happening. It had only been three months since Oma died, when he had whispered the growing concern about the Nazis for whom he was now inextricably linked. From what she saw tonight, they all had reason to fear the days and years to come. Little did she know that her father was pondering the words of poet Heinrich Heine, terrified of the prophecy they carried:

22

"Where they have burned books, they will end in burning human beings."

Chapter Three

Rainer

"What? No, c'mon, you are joking with me, right?" Rainer von Bauchelle brushed a wisp of brown hair out of his thirteen-year-old hazel eyes and stared at the rooftop of his church in the early twilight, looking for whatever it was that his Jewish friend, Josef Taffel, was talking about. Josef must have seen the questions and disbelief in Rainer's eyes.

"You really don't know, do you? Well, I guess we've never really talked about it. In Judaism, a pig is considered the most unclean of animals, so a judensaue is a depiction of a Jew, or several Jews, that are having obscene contact with a sow, or female pig." Josef paused, before adding, "You know, like licking its genitals, suckling, having sex with it, or even eating its dung. Look, there."

Josef pointed, in the least obvious way, by raising his eyebrows, and nodded his head upward to the small, sculpted stone scene. There it was, tucked in a corner, one of two gargoyles. Rainer had been oblivious to the presence of either, or more accurately, to their meaning. It would seem that the rest of the city was ignorant as well, as they hurried by the magnificent gothic church, with its yellow sandstone facade dotted with occasional pink or red variation and crowned with diamond-shaped tile roofing. How could a sanctuary of the holy, with its beautiful altars, Baroque organ case, and stained glass images of love, forgiveness, and glory, display such pieces of ugliness and cruelty? Rainier stole another hesitant skyward glance,

24

almost wishing that the architectural wonder with its massive pillars and high apse windows might come crashing down. Yet, there it was, in painful detail.

His family had attended services here at the Eglise St. Martin for all of his life and he had never noticed, nor had anyone ever mentioned, the judensaues. Rainer looked yet again, reluctant to believe that which had been there all along. He tried to erase the images of what were indisputably Jews in their traditional caps engaged in these horrible bestial acts, but they would not disappear. Both the sculpture above the portal and this one of the gargoyle-sow were as horrid and graphic as Josef had described. Why were they here now after centuries? For a certainty, he did not think his family would ever endorse such as this.

"Judensaue," he whispered aloud, as if articulating the word would ease the feelings of sadness and erase the sin now present on this place of worship, his own church.

"See. I told you they were there. Did you think I made it up?" Josef shoved his hands deep inside the pockets of his work pants and shook his head at Rainer, who was staring at their reflections in a nearby window and wondering what was so different about the Jews to cause anyone to want to create, or tolerate, this kind of ugliness. He and Josef had never cared about whatever might separate them. They had far more in common, becoming instantaneous best friends as soon as Josef's family had moved into their idyllic medieval town two years ago. Josef's father, Abner, had fought as a patriot for France years ago in the war and brought his family to Colmar because of its peaceful beauty and ample opportunity. The Taffel family ran a respectable shop selling hosiery and work clothing in the marketplace. Life was harder for them now since Sarah Taffel had died in childbirth, leaving Abner with four children, three younger than Josef.

Rainer loved helping out in their shop when he was able, and being a part of the brisk market business. He also relished working in the von Bauchelle winery and vineyard, which was a different kind of busy altogether. Established by Rainer's father, the winery was arguably one of the best on the Route des Vins d'Alsace. When they were not working in the shop or the vineyard, both boys could be found sharing a prank and a hearty laugh, or trekking through museums and the halls of notable buildings that provided great hiding places for youthful curiosity and imagination. Josef tolerated the passion Rainer had for cultural beauty in a way that none of his other friends would.

"Josef, you know my family had nothing to do with those judensaues. "Come inside my church, you will see. Those judensaues don't mean anything now. You are welcome there. If you say you will come, I will go to a service at your synagogue first, what do you say? I will even put on one of those hats that you always wear for church. I mean, for synagogue. I can even mumble along and pretend to understand all that Hebrew and such. You've taught me a few words, at least. What do you say? Come to my church, you know I won't feed you to a lion or anything. You might even like it there. We drink real wine at communion. The inside of the sanctuary is really something to see. Maybe they can take the judensaues down. Besides, you know I would go inside a synagogue if you asked me to go." Rainer could not contain his excitement when he spoke of the opportunity to show off the inner beauty and fine art within his church, and also to visit the Jewish temple.

Josef pulled his cap down low over a head of thick dark hair. A few curls peeked out from underneath and framed the brown eyes that betrayed his reluctance. The caution was evident in his voice as he leaned close to Rainer to whisper. "Some people in your church do not want us here, even now. It has been like that in Europe since the Middle Ages. My father says there are Christians who do not like Jews, more so in Eastern Europe than here, which is one reason my family settled in Colmar. But a judensaue on top of your church proves that we are not completely accepted anywhere. Yes, it has been there a long time and we know that your family did not put it there, but it is there, just the same. Why do you think you and I have never really talked about going to our places of worship together?" Josef did not wait for Rainer to answer before quickly adding, "It's just one of those things that will not change. It's not important for you and me, I know. But it's important otherwise."

Rainer studied his best friend's sturdy face, with only mildly Semitic features, searching for clues of emotion in either Josef's eyes or his words. There were none. There was, however, an abundance of absolute resolve, and it was clear that Josef would not be attending any service at St. Martin's Catholic Church. "Will you at least come inside my church? We can go explore whenever you say. If you lend me that gold star you always have around your neck, if you can bear to part with it for that long, I'll even wear it. You know, the one you Jews like so much, with the six points." Rainer grinned at his own small attempt at comic relief and punched Josef across the shoulder in a boyish gesture of affection.

"Put your word on it, then," Josef shot back, smiling and not backing down as he removed the cherished Star of David from around his neck. In a brilliant execution of stealth, he moved to stand beside Rainer and slid the sign of his faith into the front pocket of his friend's coat. "Wear it, I dare you. But I still can't come to your church, at least not to a worship service. Perhaps we will explore inside tomorrow, you and I, on one of your crazed excursions to places where I'm sure we're not supposed to be. Or at least where I'm not supposed to be." Before leaving to return to the Taffel shop in the Market Hall, Josef reached into the burlap sack hanging by his side and handed Rainer a packaged work shirt. "Don't forget to give this to your father. He's already paid for it."

Turning his collar against the coolness of the approaching night, Rainer tucked the work shirt inside his jacket and began running down the Rue de Marschands, past the burgher houses on the canal toward the edge of town. His thoughts drifted back through what he knew of the history of the region. Both his father and grandfather had told him of the uniqueness of their homeland. With Alsace having been alternately under both French and German rule, every aspect of Colmar, from food to architecture, was rooted in the traditions of both countries with other cultures blended in. It was not uncommon, therefore, for many in Colmar to have both German and French influences in family names. His own was no exception. For the most part Jews, as far as he knew, were living and working in the same manner as his family, though he knew of a few folks that occasionally made disparaging comments about them. He could not help but wonder what had happened, and when, to cause hatred deep enough to warrant atrocities such as the judensaues. Why had they not ever been removed but rather allowed to remain on a church, of all places? As he approached the warm lights of home his fingers wrapped around the Star of David inside his pocket as if to protect it from the unknown. There were far more questions than answers.

Chapter Four

Colmar; Alsace, France
1933

"What took you so long? Your brothers are already washed up for dinner and everyone is downstairs now. The evening meal is ready for us." Albert von Bauchelle, tall, sturdy, with piercing eyes that resembled those of the awkward one bounding through the cottage door, was barely home from a day's labor in his vineyard and winery. He reproached his youngest child with feigned sternness as Rainer hustled in from the growing darkness.

"Your work shirt, Papa," Rainer offered quickly, "from Mr. Taffel." Tossing the garment to his father, he took the stairs two at a time to reach his tiny room in the uppermost part of the house. Removing his coat and laying it on the single bed, he retrieved the gold necklace from its hiding place. He studied the six-pointed star and traced the edges with his thumb before clasping it around his neck and securing the chain safely under his shirt. The aroma of simmering *choucroute*, a mainstay of sauerkraut with sausage and dumplings, served as a reminder of the family waiting below and the meal to be consumed. As he made his way back downstairs and seated himself for the blessing, Rainer wondered what Jews mostly ate, if they did not consume any pork. Thinking back on the times when he and Josef had taken a meal at the home of the other, he had never given much thought to the prepared kosher foods being served, rather only to the pleasantness of the visits. Josef would tell him, of course, if he asked.

"What prosperous work happened today at the von Bauchelle winery? How did my husband do, eh, Albert? I hope you got a good day's labor from all." Giselle von Bauchelle, Rainer's grandmother, or Memere, as the children often called her, smiled as she brushed a strand of silver hair away from kind, knowing eyes. Tucking the unruly strand behind an ear, she passed a tray of warm, crusty homemade bread to her son. Appreciative of hard work in any form, the stately matriarch was unabashedly thankful that Albert, a superior vigneron in the Haut Rhin region, kept their grandfather active and occupied in the harvest and production of the family gem, cremant d'Alsace rose.

Rainer had often heard his grandmother boast of the exceptional creamy feel of the wine, due, as he knew, to the use of lower carbon dioxide pressure in the making. Though not yet a fully appreciative consumer, he knew of the perfections of their cremant, with its muted salmon color and crisp, dry, minimal notes of white peaches and berries that rounded out the palate with a nice clean finish. With a cellar life of two years, as opposed to the five of champagne, the von Bauchelle cremant was an exceptional, yet cheaper, option for aficionados of sparkling wine. Marthe, Rainer's mother, and Gisela, his sister, also worked with Memere, to make Alsatian honey spice bread, along with their signature artisan jams, that were also served at the vineyard. With its own intoxicating aroma of aniseed, dried orange peel, and ground spices of cloves, ginger, cardamom, and cinnamon, the bread rivaled their wine in purchases made, rendering the von Bauchelle family business one of the most successful in the village. Rainer inwardly smiled as he reminisced on long but rewarding days when Josef and a few of his siblings were allowed to assist in harvesting their grapes. The memory made him wonder all the more why ugliness such as judensaues existed today.

"Rainer? Rainer, where did you go, *mon petit*? What are you thinking about?" Rainer winced as his grandmother noted the temporary lapse into daydreaming. His brothers, however, were unforgiving in their teasing.

"Yes, little one, where did you go? Skip school and go to the museums today?" Alain, barely sixteen, and the younger of the two brothers, badgered Rainer often about the beyond-his-years love of all things cultural and artistic. Alexandre, who favored himself a man at seventeen, tried not to succumb to the temptation to join in the fray, but grinned as Alain poked him under the table. Only Gisela, at fourteen, was nonplussed by the brotherly behavior and made a face at both siblings, as she mounted a defense for Rainer.

"Leave him alone, Alain. He isn't boorish, like some who should know better, and he always does his fair share of work around here, doesn't he?"

"Rainer, Memere asked you to tell her about your day. What did you do at school and after?" Marthe von Bauchelle, holding a place of tenderness for her youngest, who shared her appreciation for the beauty of art, reached a gentle hand to touch his wrist as if she could sense the troubling thoughts he battled.

"Why do we have judensaues on our church, Maman?" Rainer stared at his mother, hoping he would be rescued with a kind response. For a moment, there was rare silence at the dinner table. Albert laid his fork firmly with a loud clinking noise against his plate. He swallowed an admirable sip of wine to wash down a morsel and studied his youngest son.

"Where did you hear that word, Rainer?"

"I bet Jew-sef told him, didn't he?" Alain leaned toward his younger brother and whispered, then grunted like a pig.

"Shut up, I wasn't talking to you, you fat sow!" Rainer held back angry tears, as he spat the words out, regretting them instantly, as he saw the surprised faces around the table. He especially did not want his grandparents to think him rude.

"Oh, the little one is angry now, he's going to cry!" With a forefinger shoving the end of his nose upward like that of a pig, Alain leaned toward Rainer and gave a loud snort, while looking for approval from Alexandre, who could no longer repress a smile.

"That's enough!"Albert raised his voice above the growing melee, while his eyes remained fixed on Rainer. For a moment, no one spoke, but all looked around the table at one another, unsure of what would happen next. "The judensaues have been there for many years, Rainer. They were part of the architecture of the church before any of us ever drew a breath, Son. We pay them no mind, and they mean nothing to us today. Nothing."

"But they do to Jews. They do to the Taffels. And they do to me."

"The boy speaks with a strong heart, Albert. It is a good sign." Rainer's grandfather chuckled as he regarded his grandson with a measure of pride, while reaching for the bottle of wine in the center of the table and brushing a crumb from his manicured beard. "Today, Jews in Germany do have cause to believe that they are being persecuted. Now that President Von Hindenburg has succeeded in appointing that odious Hitler as Chancellor of Germany, I fear it will not bode well for all of Europe, but especially for the Jews right now in Eastern Europe. Those in Poland, the Soviet Union, Romania, and Hungary are most at risk for his irrational thinking. The man is an imposter."

"But, Pepere," Alexandre addressed his grandfather with affection, "I read that Adolf Hitler proposes shared wealth for Germany, prosperity for all. He is an artist, too, and wants to expand everything cultural for all people. Many say he is a brave new thinker."

"They are wrong, Alexandre! Mark my words. They will rue the day this bastard came to power! He is evil incarnate. The Jews there have every reason to be apprehensive. He hates them, as well as gypsies and the Negro race, Poles, too. And, as for culture, no! He was denied entry to art school in Vienna more than once. He is a charlatan with little talent. He is a dangerous man, masquerading as a savior. Loons, all, if they believe this maniac without carefully examining his ideals. They must think for themselves. He will steal their homes and their very lives."

"Enough of this talk of politics!" Memere admonished as she reached for a glass of cremant. "Let us enjoy this sumptuous meal that we ladies have prepared and have blessed family time."

Thus, the evening banter turned to more talk of the daily winery routine, happenings at school, and the toils and pleasantries of the day until the meal was consumed. Later, as he lay in bed cocooned in a thick blanket, Rainer stared at the wooden ceiling above and relished the simple beauty and security of the home he loved. What would his family do if they lost everything, like his grandfather said could happen to the German Jews? As he snuggled deeper into the safety of the covers, Rainer strained to hear the male conversation that was taking place in the smoking room amidst a cloud of sweet smelling tobacco and cigar smoke. Though he could not comprehend all that was being said, this Hitler person seemed to dominate not only Germany, but also the thoughts of the men here this evening. Pepere spoke of rumors of a new kind of camp near Munich called Dachau, though it did not much sound like a fun place from the serious tone in his grandfather's voice. The thought of anyone hurting Josef and the Taffel family was enough to keep him awake for much of the night.

Chapter Five

Colmar; Alsace, France
Eglise St. Martin
1933

On this morning Rainer arose, grabbed a small loaf of spice
bread and some fruit, completed his requisite chores of tidying up
the courtyard and gathering firewood, and bounded out the door to
meet Josef. They rambled with giddy abandon through the Grand
Rue and up the Rue de Marschands toward the park and the
renowned Musee Unterlinden. Formerly a 13th century Dominican
religious convent and later a public baths building, they had often
wandered through its Isenheim Chapel and gazed at the daunting
Isenheim Alterpiece: Grunewald's best work, as Rainer would
explain when they were older. But when they reached the Place de la
Cathedrale, Rainer paced in front of his Catholic church.

"Rainer, what are you up to?" Josef asked as if he did not know
already, tilting his head and twisting his lips into a gesture of
uncertainty.

"You know, exactly!" Rainer grinned, taking a step toward his
friend, never breaking eye contact, and retrieved the cherished Star
of David from underneath his shirt and jacket. "I did my part. I will
wear it until you want it back." He motioned toward the sanctuary.
"Hey, 'Jew' want to go check it out, see if there are any snake pits
inside?" While Rainer outwardly pushed and teased in a way that
only best friends could, he knew that he needed Josef to come inside.
Surely the mere presence of his friend would transform the small, yet
gargantuan, ugliness on the exterior of the gothic structure into the
compassionate place of goodness and healing that was supposed to

be the Church for all time. Josef stared at him, thrusting one hand deep into the pockets of old tattered pants and reaching atop his head to tip the traditional black Jewish cap that he wore on Saturday, the Jewish Sabbath.

"I can take this off, Rainer," he offered, glancing momentarily skyward and back, "but you cannot destroy what is up there, what has been there for centuries."

"The hell I can't!" In one forceful motion, Rainer bent low to pick up two large pebbles in the road and threw the first at the depiction of the Jewish man portrayed in a pointed cap, licking the genitals of the squealing beast. As he released a low, unintelligible scream toward the heavens, Rainer heaved the last rock, squinting into the sun to watch as it struck the side of the stone sow and ricocheted back to the street below."Jesus was a Jew like you, was he not? Doesn't the New Testament say we are supposed to love everybody, right? Treat others the way we want to be treated?"

"Okay, okay! Besides, I wouldn't know about all that Jesus, New Testament stuff." Josef shot his friend a bemused glance, shaking his head as he removed the black cap. He stuffed it inside his white shirt and buttoned a portion of his black jacket for added security.

"Jews know your Old Testament, the Torah. All that New Testament stuff is Christian. So ask some of your Christian brethren_ the ones who made the judensaues_ about loving everybody. Your Jesus probably loves you, I suppose. Personally, I think you've had too much of your family cremant, my friend. This is going to get us in trouble for sure."

"Hurry!" Rainer commanded, laughing heartily and already running. "This way to the side of the church, for interlopers and sinners!"

35

Before the arched portal doors under the sweeping tympanum could close, they had escaped into the great transept and stood in the center aisle before the congregational rows of heavy brown chairs that spanned the length and width of the sanctuary. Even in the relative dark of the unpopulated interior, the altar and choir seemed to glow with a soft gilded ambience that was both tranquil and majestic. They crept through the quiet holy place, with its many stained glass windows and intricate carvings and statues. Josef was fascinated with a large statue of the *Virgin and Child.*

"I think that is definitely a Jewish baby. Do you see those curls? Now, the nose is not an overly Semitic nose," Josef laughed softly," but I think that could have been me as a baby if the hair were darker and the nose just a bit more grand in stature. What do you think?" Josef opened his coal-dark eyes with wide abandon, lifting his chin with pride, and brandishing the barely Jewish nose. Rainer rolled his eyes and shook his head as he gestured upward.

"Look there." He pointed to a large circular stained glass window, with striking rounded red interior panes and an image of the face of Christ, with golden yellow hair, elongated eyes, and no apparent beard, and smiled at his friend's playful enjoyment, glad that they were inside the church together. "See, you know you like it in here, admit it. The real Church does love everybody, even you Jews who don't believe who Jesus really is."

"Once again," Josef offered glibly, "He has no beard. I thought Jesus was supposed to have a beard. And blonde hair? No, you Christians don't even know your own man!"

Rainer attempted a sarcastic response as priestly voices grew stronger and echoed through the interior, and he knew preparations were about to be made for worship services. With great fanfare, he motioned for Josef to follow him. They found their exit closest to the exterior circular clock, set high under a gothic arch in a bed of soft red color, with a turquoise border and golden Roman numerals. There was a Latin inscription of *Memento Mori* underneath. Rainer pointed upward and shouted to his friend, as both boys careened around a yellow sandstone corner and slid, laughing and tumbling over one another, onto the walkway below.

"It means to remember that you are mortal! That you should make your life count for good while you can!"

"Good advice," Josef guffawed aloud, rolling onto his back and stretching his arms out, as if on a cross, "Seeing as how we almost got crucified in your church. I think my synagogue is safer."

"Sacrilege! To the lions with you!" Rainer yelled, tackling his friend and sending them both rolling off the walkway onto the softer grass. A large flock of mistle thrush that had descended, looking for bits of berries and leftovers from passersby, now scattered to the sunny skies, as the boys rolled across their feeding ground. What a warm memory, this one. Rainer would treasure it through the many years when life turned cold and hard and full of more hatred than he ever thought possible.

Chapter Six

Berlin, Germany
Summer Games of the XI Olympiad, Olympic Stadium
1936

Sonne

Seated between her parents in the honorary viewing box for German dignitaries and guests, Sonne Becker listened as the United States National Anthem permeated every corner of the grand Olympic Stadium. She thought the music sounded majestic, as did the appreciative throng of cheering spectators. The Negro man for whom it was played must have thought so too, as he made a proud military salute. He looked happy wearing the crown of an olive wreath and the newly won gold medal for the 100 Meter Sprint that now lay against his USA garment. He held a young potted oak tree, the gift of the host country of Germany to the winning athletes. The idea behind the unique gift had been the notion that an oak tree could grow anywhere in the world and was, therefore, a symbol for strength and resiliency. This dark-skinned athlete must possess both of those traits, having faced insurmountable odds to even be present in these games according to all she had been told by her parents. Sonne leaned close to her father to ask his name once more.

"Jesse Owens," Eduard Becker whispered. "An incredible athlete. We are witnessing history, my sweet."

" Will the Fuhrer be angry that he won? Because he is not a German, and is a Negro man?" Sonne whispered back, fearful of what might happen, as she remembered the burning of the books. At twelve years of age, she was beginning to sense the measure of cruelty that was Nazi Germany. As an expert in German munitions and renowned for his skill as an architect, she knew her father, and thus her family, had experienced a layer of protection within the Third Reich despite their Catholic faith, though even that was becoming more frowned upon with each passing day. While Hitler had already outlawed Jews and disliked Negroes, Roma gypsies, and Poles, there were many other groups that were now deemed as being against the tenets of the Nazis. Sonne was often perplexed by what she heard in this regard. She thought about the few children in her neighborhood, those with whom she was not close friends, but would never treat them unkindly. She could not think of anything that the two Jewish families she knew could have done to deserve being ostracized by their own government. Of a certainty, the streets of Berlin were much more pleasant, more welcoming, since the ugly signs about Jews had been taken down for the Olympics. She had heard her father say they would go back up when the Games were all over. It seemed a cruel and dishonest maneuver, like pretending to be a friend but in reality, being an enemy. Her friend Greta had once intentionally left her out of a game at school, after having pretended to be her friend when they played together at home. She never forgot how it felt to be betrayed by one she trusted.

"Shhhh, no, Sonne. The Fuhrer wants to display a strong, unified presence at the Games. He will not like this man winning, of course, as he wants Germans to dominate these games, but the presence of the world in Berlin will offer the visiting athletes some protection."

When they had watched the Parade of Nations from the same viewing box where they now sat, Sonne had been reminded about the Olympics being televised live for the first time ever and was glad to be a part of giving people the chance to see the welcoming Germany that was her home. How thrilling it had been to be among the color, pageantry, and sheer numbers of different countries and cultures. What blight on the large world stage, to demonstrate beauty

39

and humanity, only to revert back to cruelty afterward. It had been previously rumored that a few Jewish athletes would not be allowed to compete, despite the training and years of preparation. Sonne could not imagine the hurt they must feel, after having given so much effort to compete for a country that now turned against them. There seemed to be an ever-growing list of those the Nazis chose to ostracize. She wondered if it were only a matter of time before church attendance of any kind would be disallowed, as well. Swallowing the gnawing taste of fear in the back of her throat, Sonne focused on the celebration before her.

As the medalists walked from the podium to the area just below their viewing stand, the Negro athlete, Jesse Owens, made a quick dignified bow in front of the Fuhrer. It was a brave and courteous gesture. All eyes were on Hitler, who stood stoic and stiff with lips pursed underneath the tiny mustache. Only those seated close to him could see the simmering disdain. Germany was faring well in the Games thus far, as was the United States. Such a display of superior athleticism demonstrated by this gifted man, no matter his race, would surely be recognized now, even by Adolf Hitler. Aware of the attention he commanded in the entire worldview, the right arm of the Fuhrer rose in a brief Nazi salute as he forced a smile and took his seat with haste. Sonne guessed this was his way of recognizing the man who was now the champion. The humble gold medalist was greeted by an otherwise appreciative throng and media presence. Only those in the Fuhrer box remained polite but quiet. She wanted to show her admiration. More than that, she wanted to match his courage and spirit, to join him in the victory celebration that was about far more than she understood but could somehow sense. She wanted this man to be embraced by her Germany, the one that still recognized the dignity of all humanity and displayed only the most courteous of manners.

A palpable pall settled over the Fuhrer's box like a wet woolen blanket. Jesse Owens smiled; his white teeth that gleamed against his ebony skin seemed expansive as Olympic Stadium. They reminded Sonne of the keys on the old Hohner piano that belonged to Mrs. Greiner next-door. He moved away from the Fuhrer box, closer to the admiration of the crowd. The dignitaries stared in flat stoicism at the visiting athlete. A few clapped their fingers in obvious gratuitous display for the cameras. The gestures were enough for Sonne, who mistook them as permission to congratulate the winner. She cheered and clapped her hands in innocent abandon. Her father gripped her hand in an instantaneous vise, glancing at her mother, who returned his concern with her eyes.

"Sonne, stop this minute!" he hissed aloud and grabbed her arm with a ferocity that brought tears. "You can't be vocal for anyone but a German!"

"I'm so sorry, Father, I ..."

"Do not speak!" Eduard's raised and angry words could be heard by all seated nearby, as his pointed finger was pressed repeatedly into her chest. "We will deal with this when we get home, do you understand me? Do you?"

Sonne nodded, real tears of confusion pooling unabashed in the corners of her eyes. She could feel the stares of Nazis burning into her skin and dared not lift her head. One of the officers reached for her father's shoulder.

"Sometimes we have to discipline our children publicly, Eduard, so they know they are proud Germans who never question their superiority and heritage."

Eduard smiled, turning a stonefaced gaze to Sonne. "Indeed. My strong-willed daughter thinks she's an ambassador for Germany, welcoming all to the best country on the planet. A bit overzealous, though. At home tonight, she will be reminded of her duty as a German youth."

From his seat on the front row of the box, the Fuhrer took note of the distraught girl sitting with her family. She had the makings of a pure and strong Aryan beauty. With more strenuous training, perhaps she would one day make great contributions to the Third Reich by producing many pure German children. He made an obligatory smile for the television cameras.

Alsa pressed her leg against Sonne in a silent gesture of reassurance, as she whispered into her daughter's ear. "Your father had to do that, Sonne. Don't be afraid of him." Sonne kept her eyes on the track and scene in front of her and tried to steady her trembling hands. Her father was the least of her worries, as she knew his true sentiment. What terrified her was the power and fear that the Nazis imposed on all of Germany. And now her father, whether he wanted to be or no, was part and parcel of it all.

Chapter Seven

Berlin, Germany
The Reich Chancellery
1937

Eduard Becker raised his head from the desk in his modest office, rubbed exhausted eyes, and checked the time. 6:45 P.M. He must have fallen asleep. It was now as dark outside as it was inside the spartan office space. He had locked the door around 5:00 P.M. or so, when most were leaving, to finish revision on more details for what would eventually be the new chancellery building, which was being designed by Albert Speer. Of late, his time had been divided between this project, as well as the further development of a recoilless gun design for Luftwaffe paratroopers, under the supervision of Hermann Goering, with whom his group of munitions people had just met. He smiled, gathering his papers and satchel and picturing Alsa, who would gently scold him for the lateness of the hour and the demands of life as a dual expertise worker in the Nazi government. She was right, of course, as he had been required to work harder and put in more time since Hitler had come to power.

Walking down the vacant and dark hallway beside a small conference room wall, he heard voices coming from inside, some raised and insistent in tone. Instinctively he froze, trying to decide whether to round the corner to the front of the room or not. There had been no meetings scheduled for this hour, as far as he knew. The ominous sense of apprehension grew stronger as he tried to identify the voices inside. Hitler, Goering, and von Blomberg, for sure. Hossbach, Hitler's military adjutant, was also there. Could that be Gen. von Fritsch, Commander-in-Chief of the Armed Forces?

Another was not readily identifiable, though there did not appear to be many men in the room. He strained to hear the rise and fall of the voices amidst the steady debate of conversation. What was clear was the immense military importance of those he could identify. Laying his cheek against the cold, smooth exterior of the conference room, he listened again. Could it be that the heads of the entire German military were all in attendance in a clandestine meeting? Whatever it was, this was no informal affair and was intended to be of utmost secrecy. As words began lacing together and seeping through the wall, understanding dawned. Eduard Becker felt panic set in like a relentless storm. He could scarcely believe the phrases he could pick out of the hum of discussion.

A policy of needed aggression to provide living space for a Germany faced with substandard economic conditions, or Lebensraum... autarky... seizing Eastern Europe in order to even consider war against the French and the British...

Touching his forehead, he felt the flushed sense of fever and cold that began to radiate throughout his body. There was no need to hear more. He needed to find safety before the pounding of his heart gave him away. Scanning the darkened hallways, he moved with slow but deliberate purpose to find an obscure exterior door. There it was, a back entrance for ancillary service personnel. Making an escape into the night, Eduard Becker exited the rear door of the behemoth that was the Reich Chancellery and ran, without looking back, toward the residences on the other side of Wilhelmstrasse. Only when surrounded by the safety of dimly lit homes did he slow his pace to a rapid walk and check his watch yet again. 8:15 P.M. By now, Alsa would have stored his plate of food away, and she and his precious Sonne would be lying beside a warm fire. It was just as well. He felt far too sick to eat. The time had come to get his family out of Berlin if he could. Even if he had to stay, he must convince them to leave.

Perhaps it was time for Alsa and Sonne to reclaim Oma's house in Rastenburg until he could figure out a way to get them as far away from the madness he knew was just on the horizon. Getting her house in final order would suffice for an excuse to have them make the move, temporary or no. Walking into the comfort of home, the scene inside was as he imagined. Sonne called to him from the sitting room.

"Father, finally, you are home! Can we play some chess this evening, after you have eaten?"

Eduard leaned against the front door, steadying his nerves and reestablishing a measure of composure. "Not tonight, my sweet. You would best me for sure, as exhausted as I am. But I will come talk with you and be the one to kiss you goodnight when it is time. You still aren't too old for that, are you? Alsa, I will take a strong drink and would request the company of your presence in the kitchen for a moment, my love."

Sonne put down the book she was reading and nestled the blanket under her chin. She had become accustomed to the tone of urgency in her father's voice, which occurred with more regularity of late. For a moment she lay quietly, trying to piece together the snippets of information drifting from the kitchen, as she had done since early childhood. Tossing the cover aside, she stood in the kitchen doorway with arms braced against its sides and faced them with the boldness of adolescence. "I'm old enough now, I'm not a little child, you know. Whatever is going on, it's my future, too. Besides, I've been listening in on these adult conversations for way longer than you'd want me to, I'm sure. Don't you think its time to let me try to be more grown up?"

Alsa and Eduard exchanged surprised glances before acknowledging their only progeny. In many ways she was mature beyond her years. Though reluctant to include her in the discussion, Eduard motioned for their precocious girl to join them.

"All right. Come sit, Sonne. There is much to talk about, and it will indeed impact all of us, I'm afraid."

Chapter Eight

Colmar; Alsace, France
Taffel Home
1937

Rainer

"Hello, Mr. Taffel." Rainer forced a smile as he reached through the doorway of the Taffel home to shake the hand of a now pale and withering shell of the man that was once a tower of strength. Poor Abner Taffel had grown progressively weaker each year until he was forced to relinquish the family business to Josef, who had become accomplished in the handling of every aspect, despite his youthful eighteen years.

"Ah, here is our grown young man, our Rainer, off to the university at last. *Mazel tov*, Rainer!" Abner coughed violently and wiped his mouth with a handkerchief as he leaned against the open door and motioned to Rainer, who instinctively grasped the arm of the sickly man and assisted in steadying his gait as they walked into the family room.

"*A sheynem dank*, Mr. Taffel, thank you very much." Rainer smiled at the fatherly man he had grown to love almost as much as his own. "I've come to see Josef before I leave for Strasbourg in the morning, Sir. Here, let me help you sit down." Rainer gently helped the wheezing patriarch into a worn, soft leather chair that sat adjacent to the family radio. The rousing strains of the Charles Trenet tune, "Je chante," filled the darkened room with a pleasant air of comfort. He smiled as Abner Taffel clutched at his sweater with one hand and tried to wave with the other in time with the music.

"Rainer, you are a fine boy, a hard-working boy. It is good that you are pursuing your love of art and culture. You go make this world more beautiful and make lots of money, too." Abner attempted to pat him on the shoulder, as Rainer bent to move a hassock under the aging man's feet for support. The labored wheezing and breathing continued for a moment as Abner reached for his glass of water and wiped his mouth once more. "Your family should be proud of you. We will miss you very much while you are away learning to be a _ what do you call it? _ expert in fine arts history and restoration?"

"Yes, Sir, you are correct. And I will greatly miss seeing you, Sir, and your equally hard-working *zun*, Josef. Father is so happy to also have help in the vineyard and winery from your Ben. He needed to hire some extra help, with me gone. Alexandre and Alain are already immersed in the winery. Even Gisela is learning to be a vintner of sorts, although she still loves to help Maman and Memere with the bread making. I will be back to visit on occasion, though I will strive to finish my studies as quickly as I can so that I might also get to work as soon as possible."

The elder Taffel grimaced as his eyes reddened. "If I am still here, Rainer, yes, we will drink your father's wine and have a toast." Rainer frowned at Abner, assuring the frail man that his health would hold out long enough to allow them to see each other yet again, though he knew that might not come to pass.

"He means the Germans, Rainer." Josef appeared in the hallway, rolling the sleeves of his gray work shirt after just washing up from a long day in the market. Regarding Rainer and his father with only a hint of a smile, he ran sturdy fingers through unruly brown hair that seemed to curl even more as he tried to tame it. "You know after they invaded the Rhineland, Hitler and Mussolini formed a Rome-

Berlin Axis. Father does not believe it will be long before they decide to invade France."

"And that Fuhrer and those Nazis have now opened an internment camp called Buchenwald." Abner Taffel spat the words as if they were poison and began to weep in silence as Josef placed a hand on his slumped shoulders and faced Rainer. "Where can we go?" Abner wailed, as he lifted shaking hands in the air. "What will become of our family business if they make it to France? Jewish doctors can no longer practice in Germany. And now, Jews are no longer considered citizens of Germany. Then there is the Entarte Kunst." Abner raised his eyes and directed his gaze toward Rainer.

"The so-called Degenerate Art show. I have heard of it," Rainer said slowly. "Yes, the Nazis have taken thousands of pieces of valuable and beautiful art from museums and exhibited them in Berlin. They do not like anything remotely Modernist. They prefer only conventional, traditional art forms. No Matisse, Picasso, Renoir, Beckman, for starters. All forbidden. What they have not stolen outright, they have cheaply wrangled to build their collections. I have heard of Hitler's perverse interest in denigrating Jewish art, as well as anything from what he calls 'negroid culture.' Mr. Taffel, I know you are fearful. We do not want this. You know my father will help, if it is ever necessary. But let us hope we never have to face that in France."

"Where are my manners? Here, young Rainer is embarking on a momentous journey and we must celebrate and wish him well. Josef, get that bottle of von Bauchelle cremant, and let us send our beloved friend off in style and keep our good friend Albert in business!" With that, the elder Taffel and Josef made a series of glorious toasts to Rainer before he embarked on the journey to the University of Strasbourg. Afterward Josef got his father settled for the night and walked outside for one last conversation with his best friend. Rainer was seated on the bench beside the front door, staring out into the peaceful beauty of a calm Alsatian evening.

"Father is right, I'm afraid." Josef shoved his hands deep into his pockets. "You know the Nazis may not stop until they control all of Europe. No one will be able to save our business, Rainer. Or even this family." For a moment, both were quiet, as if absorbing the uncertainty that lay ahead and coming to terms with the distance that would separate them and forge their futures.

"I used to think that all of this Nazi talk was just the musings of my grandfather and Abner. But I fear it might, indeed, become much more than that for France. Thus far, Hitler has broken every treaty he has entered, and it appears he will not be satisfied until he has built an empire. Josef, you know my family will help in any way that we can, should that time come. It may be that we need to find a way to get you all out of here. Of course, you and I will maintain contact, and I want you to call on my father often. Please promise me that you will. He wants that, too. I dare you, as you once dared me, remember?" Rainer maintained eye contact with his friend and waited for the reply, knowing that Josef could be as stubborn as he. Somehow the judensaues still haunted him, even now, and today they seemed more alive than ever.

"I tell you what," Josef offered thoughtfully, "I will keep an eye out for your family and mine and will act on their behalf, to keep them all safe. But I will fight, Rainer. If I have to, I will fight. I will be damned if I let them take our business, our lives, without shedding every ounce of blood I have to give."

Once again, silence seemed to reign as each pondered the possibility of a German invasion, loss of freedom, and the imminence of real danger, especially for the Taffel family. Rainer knew his friend would be willing to die before giving up all that they had worked so hard to achieve. In the deepest part of his soul, he felt guilt at not being able to alleviate the sin of inhumanity and regret that his best friend was Jewish and there seemed little he could do about their futures and that of France as well.

"Josef, if a fight is what is to be, I will fight, too. We will do whatever we have to do, you and I. But, our families," Rainer hesitated, "our families, we must find a way to keep them all safe, and that would be no easy feat, I know. The planning for such dire circumstances as these will be considered when the time is right. We can also hope and pray to God Almighty that none of this comes to pass."

Josef regarded his friend thoughtfully, watching him fingering the Star of David underneath his shirt. He knew the risk and the burden Rainer took on by wearing it in a show of solidarity. "You know that could cause you some serious trouble."

"It could," Rainer smiled slowly. "Sometimes, one has to make a stand, act on his beliefs. 'Jew know what I mean?"

"Safe travels, Rainer. I will miss you badgering me all the time, with those incessant trips to museums and such sad attempts at humor." Josef lifted his hand to return Rainer's outstretched grasp as both embraced the other with the affection of years of camaraderie, secret confidences, and boyhood memories.

"I will miss those times, too, my friend. Let us hope France is spared from such atrocity. *Memento mori*, Josef."

"And to you, Rainer. Go with God. Stay out of trouble, if that is even possible." Josef smiled, trying to mask the underlying fear that hid in the farewell to his childhood friend, who he was certain could feel it as well.

Chapter Nine

Rainer arrived at home, expecting to spend the remainder of the evening with his family, but his father requested a short walk through the village with his youngest son. The night air was brisk as they donned jackets and hats before stepping into the quiet quaintness that was Colmar. Rainer could sense the need the elder man had to talk, which was quite the contrast to his usual tendency toward brevity and sparce expression of emotion, as the self-proclaimed and otherwise acknowledged head of the household.

"You are a man now, Rainer, my youngest, now grown. I am a proud but old father." Albert smiled warmly, looking away as if recalling every memory of his son's childhood. Rainer knew him to be a stern but caring man, one who never spoke unless he intended the words he chose. He decided to remain quiet in the wake of his father's display of unusual affection. "While I once entertained thoughts of you helping your brothers with the family business, I am now confident that Gisela and her fiancé will do well in helping to keep the winery and bakery successful, and that makes me very happy, indeed. I hope you will one day add a dimension of art and culture to this place, while you curate and teach in a grand museum, somewhere of historic significance, of course."

Rainer felt an instant pang of guilt, though he knew that was not Albert's intent. "Father, you know Colmar is home, and I will continue to do all I can to help here. Perhaps we will incorporate even more possibilities into the von Bauchelle winery. I promise, you will be proud of this place, always. I will be a part of this place, in whatever way I can, I promise." He wondered, momentarily, if his father in any way doubted his appreciation for the work that had sustained him since childhood. His intention to always be involved in the family business, regardless of his dedication to the art profession, was paramount in reassuring his father that von Bauchelle wine would exist long after the elder patriarch was gone. Rainer attempted to say more about how that effort might play out, when his father became somber and spoke with an air of secrecy.

"Rainer, I am afraid that your grandfather may be right about this Hitler and his party. I hope and pray he is not, but if the political climate changes in France and life for the Jews and all of us here becomes more difficult, we will do all we can to help the Taffels and others. I won't discuss my thoughts now, but I have been planning for the worst."

Rainer froze, unable to walk, and stared at his father, astounded at what he had just heard, though he had harbored those same concerns. Hearing his father give voice to the possibility was a shock, and he felt the similar visceral fright he had as a child when waking from a nightmare. For a moment both remained silent, looking anywhere except at each other.

"Son," Albert finally continued, "while you are at the university in Strasbourg, it is imperative that you not talk overmuch about our family being sympathetic to the Jews, and especially to the Taffels. Try not to talk about it at all. Anything said that aligns us with an anti-Nazi cause puts our family, the Taffels, and other Jewish friends in grave danger and will render us less likely to be able to provide aid to them, should that time ever arise. I'm not asking you to profess allegiance to Hitler or that cause, ever. The prudent strategy for us all now, will be to remain as un-antagonistic and as vigilant and diplomatic as possible while doing what we can to help. Do you understand what I am trying to tell you?"

Rainer stood quietly, gazing into the cloudless beauty of a starlit sky that showed no indication of the gathering storm and pondered what his father had just said. While he understood the reasons for care in his words and actions, how could he remain quiet about such injustice as this? If his father really believed that Hitler would attempt to oust the Jews from France and punish anyone who might help them, then they were all at risk for a danger like none they had ever imagined.

Albert spoke again, as if able to read the confusion inside his head. "Your grandfather once said that you were a young man with heart and courage. He was right, I'm afraid." Albert smiled. "It is a most honorable compliment. I trust you will discern when to speak and when to remain less forthcoming, Rainer. It is a skill that will serve you well in many areas, you will find."

It was a statement that required no response. Somehow, Rainer knew this night would mark a defining moment in his ascent to an adulthood that would test every aspect of his character. He anticipated life at the university with both excitement and reservation and hoped that those years would be devoid of fear and harsh change. As the two made their way back home, Rainer wondered what the immediate future held for those he loved and for France. He would study as tirelessly and diligently as possible, both for his family and for the preservation of the culture and artistic beauty that defined his childhood and which would now be his chosen profession. But now, worry sat on his shoulders and threatened to disrupt every aspect of life as he had always known it.

Chapter Ten

Rastenburg, East Prussia
1938

Sonne

Sonne had remained silent for most of the evening meal, feeling more like an invited guest in their new home that had once belonged to her grandmother. This was a requisite dinner to welcome the family of a colleague of her father's, who was also skilled in munitions design. The Hirsch family was in Rastenburg to see their son assume a position established by Propaganda Minister Goebbels, that was, as her father had painstakingly explained, designed to assist in the control of town communications and to promote Nazi ideals. Having been made aware of the Hirsch family affinity for Nazi political leanings, she had also been schooled in the fine art of tact when it was necessary to entertain such guests. Her father was obligated to make the dinner invitation, he had explained to her and Alsa, to help alleviate any suspicion of disloyalty to the Nazi party, who now wreaked vengeance on any potential would-be dissenters.

Frau Hirsch was pleasant enough, but her husband's demeanor was fraught with pretention. Their son, Anton, whom Sonne guessed to be perhaps a year or so out of the university, had also joined them for dinner and appeared to be a replica of his father in every conceivable way. Both were tall, striking, well coifed, and overly eager to discuss the expansion of the German Reich by any means necessary. Most of the conversation meandered around mutual interest in current munitions development, local issues, and the prospect of military conflict, although the women occasionally tried with little success to steer the men toward less incendiary topics.

Now they were discussing the game of chess as a metaphor for war strategy.

"This conversation must bore you, Sonne." Anton Hirsch stared in a way that made her want to leave the room. There was an air of unsettling sensuality in the way he had sipped his wine and now smiled at her, his tongue gliding casually over his lips. Now approaching fourteen, Sonne was aware that she was on the brink of womanhood, her body looking more grown than not. Her feminine beauty was accentuated by the intriguing sea green eyes and softly curled chestnut hair that framed her face. What remained unrecognized by her, but not to Eduard and Alsa, was the extraordinary beauty she was becoming. Everyone seemed in suspended animation as they waited for her response. She dabbed at the corner of her mouth with a napkin. The honey pink lipstick that her mother had given her made a pouting outline on the soiled cloth.

"No. Not bored at all. Just listening to the discussion. I am used to adult conversation in our home, of course." She smiled at her parents and then at Anton Hirsch, who never took his eyes away from hers. "I actually love the game of chess, as my father taught me to play when I was younger, though I could not speak to its usefulness in strategy for battle, of course."

"Well then, perhaps the ladies will excuse the men from the table after this delicious meal and allow us to borrow you, young Sonne, for an impromptu chess match with my son. He will be gentle with you, rest assured." It was more of a statement rather than a request, as the elder Hirsch smiled in the same disconcerting manner as that of his son. Alsa gave a nervous wince and glanced at Eduard, who was devoid of emotion except for the grinding jaw that belied his discomfort. He responded with swift certainty.

"My Sonne is quite the warrior, despite an understandable lack of military knowledge. I'm certain she can hold her own in most any arena."

"Well then," Anton Hirsch smiled, as he poured another glass of wine and raised it toward Sonne, "to the battlefield, little Fraulein."

Sonne studied her father, who remained expressionless. She understood the message he was trying to convey. Show no fear, no sign of weakness. Play to win. Concentrate on the board, not the undermining tactics of an opponent. Laying her glass on the dining room table, she pushed the sleeves of her blouse to just below her elbows and smiled with newly minted confidence. Anton Hirsch continued the campaign of intimidation.

"As my father said, I will indeed attempt to be merciful when playing against such a sweet and lovely young lady such as yourself."

"Then you will lose." Sonne returned the gauntlet with a defiant smile, as she rose from her chair and readied herself for the ensuing battle. The surprise on the faces of both Hirsch men, in addition to the occasional faint smiles from her father, only served to steel her resolve.

As the contest worked its way to the hour mark, the women finished their toils in the kitchen and now joined them in the sitting room. The drone of their feminine banter was soothing to Sonne but proved an obvious source of irritation to Anton, who openly scowled at the ladies. He leaned forward with elbows resting on his knees and tapped his lips with interlocking fingers in an effort to bolster concentration. This girl had proven to be more than a worthy competitor. He would not allow himself to be beaten by a female, particularly one who was at least ten years younger than he. The space around the chessboard was laden with captured pieces from both opponents, and they had each maneuvered their way out of a check situation. As the match appeared to be waning, all were gathered around the two opponents, watching intently as Anton made what he presumed to be the final move.

"Checkmate." He whispered the word as if he had conquered an empire, raising his eyebrows and upper lip into a sneer and settling back into his seat. Sonne remained silent, studying the board with eyes that blazed as they darted left and right, searching for that which he could not see. There it was. She rubbed her fingers across the ragged edge of the white rook, not yet moving it, but reveling for a moment in the cool softness of the marble piece and in the perplexed look on the face of her opponent. Removing a captured pawn and sliding the rook into place, she met his eyes with an unspoken challenge. Anton's father swallowed the last of his wine and reached down to pat her shoulder.

"I believe we have a stalemate! Neither loses, neither wins. Well played, young Sonne, well played. Your father has done an admirable job in his instruction, especially for a girl. You are a tribute to the superiority of German women above any other."

Sonne ignored both the obvious sleight and the radical statement as she stood to face the younger Hirsch. "Anton, you are a most formidable opponent."

"My mistake for second-guessing you, Sonne. It would seem that you are both intelligent and beautiful. One day, you will make a fine wife, if your cooking is anything like your gamesmanship."Anton smiled in the same condescending manner that had defined his behavior for the duration of the evening. Sonne felt the simmering desire to reduce him with sarcasm but knew that would not be a prudent move.

"Ah, lucky me, then. My cooking is even better, with the exception of my honey bread, which will never be as good as my grandmother's but is very close. Perhaps you would like a rematch of sorts, this time in the kitchen, if you think you can handle it?" Sonne shot him a beguiling smile, as her eyebrows raised in question.

Frau Hirsch quickly came to the aid of her son, who now floundered in his inability to be the clear victor."Oh my, no! Anton now has far more important things to do than cook, dear. I hope he will soon find a wife that can attend to the tasks in the home. One such as yourself, perhaps one day I'm sure, Sonne."

Eduard, with his usual penchant for resolution and diplomacy, raised his glass to the guests, not wanting the restraint of his daughter to be further tested. "What a lovely evening, then. Welcome to Rastenburg, Anton. We are assured that you will be successful in all your endeavors and that my family will be safe and secure with you here. Your father and I journey back to Berlin for the tasks ahead, thankful for this brief respite. Alsa, Sonne, and I wish you the best in your future."

"Yes, congratulations on your new position," Sonne said, without smiling. "It was nice to meet you all." She crossed her arms in deference to her father, a smile crossing her face as their guests were leaving at last. As the Hirsch family made their way down the sidewalk, Sonne watched with disdain until they disappeared into the night while expressing her desire to never again see such a loathsome individual as Anton. Her father shook his head.

"With his political ambition and full immersion in the philosophy of the Reich, I'm afraid you will most certainly see him again one day, my dear one. And you will need to handle him with great care, always. But you played _ battled _ with great heart tonight. I could not have been more proud, Sonne. Sit with me and your mother in the kitchen awhile before time for bed?"

An intrusive late-night knock at the door startled them all.

"One of the Hirsch family must have forgotten something. No one else would visit at this hour." Sonne called loudly enough to be heard by the outside visitors who knocked yet again, as she moved to answer the door. Two men, each clad in otherwise plain long coats with military hats never smiled, but asked for Herr Becker.

"Just one moment," Sonne said, sensing an almost tangible apprehension. "Would you like to come in?"

"We will wait for Herr Becker outside."

Eduard appeared behind Sonne. Alsa was beside him, clutching his right arm and looking suspicious of the late night callers whom he immediately recognized. "What can I do for you, Gentlemen? It isn't often that I receive a visit from the Kettenhunde," he offered, referring to the nickname of "chained dogs" given to the Feldgendarmerie, a part of the Reich military police.

"Herr Becker, your services are needed within the Wehrmacht. We are here to accompany you to report for duty, as per the orders of the Supreme Commander."

"Supreme Commander?" Alsa asked, her hands wrenched together in a nervous knot.

Eduard stared at the men sent to retrieve him while putting an arm around Alsa's shoulder. "The Fuhrer himself ordered this? I'm afraid I don't understand. I am currently working under the auspices of War Minister General von Blomberg, by special assignment of General Goering, to assist in the further development of munitions for our paratroopers."

"Then you must not be aware of General von Blomberg's resignation amidst a most unfortunate personal scandal, it seems. You are hereby notified of your conscription into official service in the Wehrmacht and are to report at once to the new Oberkommando der Wehrmacht General Wilhelm Keitel."

"Eduard!" Alsa grabbed his shoulders. "What does this mean?"

"Father?" Sonne placed a hand on his back and the other around her mother.

Eduard turned to face his wife, removing her hands from his shoulders and holding them tightly in his own. He knew exactly what it meant. The Nazis, fighting among themselves for power, had taken an opportunity to eliminate yet another of their inner circle who was now deemed unworthy. Because von Blomberg had been his administrator, his own loyalty was now in question. No doubt that the Hirsch men might also have contributed to his demise. Unbeknownst to either Sonne or Alsa, conscripted service in the German military meant that his professional services to the government of the Third Reich were no longer needed. He was now a soldier. He must help his family to absorb his leaving with no designated end date to return. He could not let them panic. He looked at Alsa still holding her hands, as she now openly wept. Sonne stood behind her parents, burying her head between them and silently praying for strength. Eduard knew this was the moment that would forever change his daughter from child to adult, and that she would meet that milestone with strength and grace. He knew, too, that Alsa had been blindsided by the news and was terrified at losing not only her husband, but their relatively safe status within the Nazi party. Eduard and Sonne both could feel her trembling, swallowing gasps of air that threatened to become outright sobs.

"Could you at least give me a moment to gather a few necessities and say my goodbyes?" he asked, with a hint of disdain.

"Very well, be quick about it."

Eduard led his family to the confines of the kitchen for a moment of temporary solace, as he held the hand of each. They had always gathered there to talk about important issues or create a plan for the future. This moment must be no different, as he and Alsa had planned for the possibility as much as they could, but the immediacy of his leaving had caught them both unprepared. One thing was certain. Hirsch must have assisted in notifying the Nazis of the most appropriate time to secure him. He must make his women believe that he was coming back, though he was not even sure he would survive the night. The Nazis had a way of making unnecessary people disappear without a trace.

"Listen to me, Alsa, Sonne. We don't have much time. Money is in the hidden safe. There is enough to keep food on the table. I need you both to be strong, to take care of each other until my return. Promise me this."

"Father," Sonne hugged him tightly, feeling barely able to breathe, but knowing she must maintain strength. "I will watch over Mama and help her. Do not worry about us. Take care of yourself and try to find a way to let us know where and how you are. I love you so much."

"You will always be my little sonnenschein. Alsa, my love, keep me in your heart as I will you."

Sonne held onto her mother as the armed soldiers escorted her father down the walkway into a deadly night. She could feel her mother's shoulders begin to ripple once more, small tremors at first, then uncontrollable shaking and crying. "Mama! Mama, it's going to be all right! Come with me back to the kitchen. I will make us something strong to drink and we can sit by the fire. We are going to find a way to make it through this war. I hate these Nazis for what they are doing. I hate them all. But we are going to be all right, Mama! Together, for Father." Alsa held onto her only child and sobbed in waves of emotion as Sonne whispered stronger words of reassurance. "Mama, stop. You and Father have taken care of me all these years. Let me help take care of you and the house now. We can do this. One day this nightmare will be over. We will find a way. We must make Father proud of us."

But somewhere deep inside in a secret place where she could admit it to herself, Sonne was terrified.

Chapter Eleven

Clermont-Ferrand, France
1941

Rainer

"Ah, here is my favorite scholar. Come in, Rainer von Bauchelle, please sit down." The esteemed Dr. Reynard Renault, Professor Emeritus of Fine Arts at the University of Strasbourg, motioned for his most exceptional senior student to take a seat in the typically disarrayed office. Rainer readily accepted a steaming cup of café, as the cold rainy day had brought a deep chill to the afternoon. The distinguished teacher ruffled a wayward stack of papers on his massive, cluttered desk and attempted to focus his attention on the moment at hand. It seemed that he had not yet recovered from the upheaval that had faced the university in light of the ongoing German onslaught. When the French declared Strasbourg to be a military zone in 1939, all of the faculty and students had been incorporated into an existing facility that housed medical and law schools, as well as science and art programs, in the central town of Clermont-Ferrand. Much was still in disarray from the hopefully temporary move.

Rainer smiled as he settled himself in the large leather chair offered by his favorite professor. For a moment he allowed himself to revel in the knowledge that he had performed to the best of his ability throughout his university stay, and his academic tenacity would soon result in recognizable dividends. "Dr. Renault, I cannot say enough how happy I am to accept the intern position at The Louvre in Paris. I know that it comes largely at your behest, and my family and I are most grateful. I promise, this university will be well-represented there."

"Rainer," the distinguished teacher sighed, shaking his head, and spoke in a hesitant, quiet tone. "I'm afraid I bring most unwelcome news today. It is my unfortunate duty to inform you of that which will greatly impact all of us, but no one more than you, I fear." Rainer set his cup on the side table and leaned toward the aging professor, listening intently as Dr. Renault continued in a litany of apology.

"The Germans, as you know, have invaded France, and it is anticipated that we will soon be annexed as a part of the Third Reich under Hitler. It is also whispered that Robert Wagner, a most brutal man, will be appointed as the gauleiter of Alsace. When that happens, the Nazis will recruit the unwilling volunteers, the *malgre nous*, to either fight on the front lines or to work as German civil servants. The Nazis are seeking the best and brightest for their plans to create their supposed superior empire. Their affinity for fine art is known far and wide, as you are already keenly aware." Professor Renault rubbed his forehead as if to force the impending evil from his mind. "Rainer, your achievements here have been second to none. Your command of fine art history and new restoration techniques, coupled with your initiative and enthusiasm, has not gone unnoticed by many in the art world. Your passion for this work is unmatched in any arena, and you are light years ahead of your peers in your knowledge and level of professionalism."

"Thank you, Sir." Rainer remained still, knowing there was dismal news to follow as Dr. Renault took a deep breath and continued.

"Let me be frank. Hitler and the Nazis are vitally interested in acquiring the world's most acclaimed art by any means necessary. They also want the most qualified and dedicated workers in their commensurate fields of expertise, as long as they are Aryan, of course. You are young. Highly intelligent and gifted. Passionate, as well as strong. You would be desirable in any artistic venue in the mindset of anyone. Your talents may be demanded elsewhere in the near future."

"I won't work for Nazis, if that is the implication, Sir." Rainer rose from his chair, looking past the venerable professor onto the streets below, as he thought of Josef and his family.

"I'm afraid you will not have much of a choice, Rainer. The Nazi machine has quickly become more evil and powerful than anyone thought possible. If you are to survive, help your family, and preserve valuable works of art, you will go where they dictate and do what you must to live and help those you love. At any rate, your position at the Louvre no longer exists." Dr. Renault paused momentarily, studying Rainer's stunned expression before continuing. "But we French love our art also," he said, with a hint of stealth, "and great care has been taken to virtually empty the Louvre, as well as other museums, of our treasured pieces and distribute them secretly to locations all over our beloved countryside. The Mona Lisa. Venus de Milo. Winged Victory of Samothrace, and more. All secure and safe, for now, so not to worry. So, then, now that I have dispensed with this most unpleasant business, I do have at least a semblance of good news. I hope you do not mind, as I have taken the liberty to contact your father and request a visit so that he might be present when you are presented with a departmental award for excellence and the offer to teach here, under my mentorship, which I hope you will now consider thoughtfully and accept. More importantly, I suspect you and he will have much to discuss in private with regard to your future." Dr. Renault stared resolutely at Rainer and maintained eye contact for what seemed an hour. His words hung like the thick fog that wafted inland from the French rivers and canals. "Your father should be arriving within an hour or so, Rainer. He will meet you on the Place de Jaude, at the statue of Vercingetorix. Please give him my sincere greetings. I must be about the business of attending to my next class of aspiring art stars. Until tonight, then. Good day."

With that, Dr. Renault picked up his satchel, jacket, and hat and made his way down the hall to the auditorium, as Rainer headed into the now cold and damp air. A light snow had begun to dust the city. The walk in the brisk air would help to alleviate his troubled mind, which ran amuck with possibilities from reasonable to ridiculous. As he sat waiting for the arrival of his father, Rainer pondered the fate of his country with all of its picturesque villages and genteel beauty. What terrified him most was the danger that now seemed imminent for his family and friends. How could he work for the very regime that would put them all in peril? Try as he might, he could not rid himself of the images of the judensaues or of Josef's face. On this day, they haunted him with a frightening reality that seemed larger than any of his childhood memories.

Chapter Twelve

Clermont-Ferrand, France
Place de Jaude
1941

"Father, over here!" Rainer frowned in mild surprise at the figure moving toward him among the streams of people that scurried across the square. Albert von Bauchelle appeared more gaunt and worn than his age should allow, even on this gray afternoon, when the weather necessitated the wearing of additional gear. No doubt the journey, as well as the perilous state of affairs, played a role in the downtrodden demeanor of his father. The two embraced more warmly than usual, and Rainer thought he detected a melancholy tone in the fatherly voice as family greetings from Colmar were relayed.

"You look well, Rainer. I believe that university life agrees with you. We are all so proud of you, my son. Dr. Renault tells me of all your hard work, and how you are becoming quite the young expert in your chosen field. Maman and Memere cannot help but smile at the mention of your name these days. That is a most welcome respite from the remainder of the news of late, I fear."

Rainer gazed at the imposing statue of the warrior Vercingetorix with sword brandished for battle, then gave his father a wistful smile as he read the inscription beneath. "J'ai pris les armes pour la liberte` de tous. I took up arms for the liberty of all. This was sculpted by Bartholdi, who also was the creator of the American Statue of Liberty, you know."

"Well, I did know but had forgotten," his father shook his head, "but I had no doubt that my art expert son certainly knew."

Rainer felt momentary relief at his father's humorous attempt, as he guided him through the square and the gentle swirlings of snow, toward a row of shops and eateries. "We have time to grab a morsel or two and something warm to drink before this evening. You have had a tiring journey. We can talk more in a few minutes." Rainer placed his hand under his father's elbow to steady his gait and the two chatted about the events on the home front as they made their way to one of several bistros that punctuated the landscape. When they were seated with steamy espresso, warm croissants, and cheese, Rainer smiled appreciatively at his father while sampling the fare laid before them. "Not bad, huh?" He gently shook a croissant at his father. "Of course, none of these delicacies can match the loving care that defines a von Bauchelle specialty made by our women, no?"

A small grin appeared for a brief moment on the face of the elder man. He regarded Rainer thoughtfully before choosing words that were almost whispered amid the hum of voices. "Let me speak freely in the interest of time, my son. Dr. Renault knew it would be important for us to talk privately now, because events beyond our control may happen in the near future. He believes with a certainty _ and I share that belief _ that you may be required to provide assistance to the Nazis in your chosen field, as art is of great interest and value to them. You have mastered techniques and knowledge beyond your ken. You are young, strong, and educated. And you are not a Jew, Pole, or Negro."

"Father, I am coming home to Colmar to help, if I have a choice. I know you could use the help, since Pepere and Memere are no longer able to be as helpful in our family business. We should all be together now. Besides, I know Josef and the rest of the Taffels require much assistance as well now that Abner is bedridden, may God help him. I know that Elena is caring for him, so she can no longer assist in the shop. Times are hard for everyone. My work can wait for a bit, like everything else. I'm coming home to help, now that my schooling is almost done."

For a brief moment, Albert stared out the window past Rainer, perhaps to another place and time, wiping tears out of tired eyes. Only a hint of sadness was evident as he spoke, now facing his son and lowering his voice to an almost indiscernible level, though his words were resolute. "You should not return home, Rainer. For your safety, as well as ours. There has been a great deal of change. Now that France is coming under the control of the Third Reich, no Frenchman is off limits, and the Germans are already recruiting massive numbers of our young men to serve in their Wehrmacht. Alexandre has just been conscripted, and Alain was only allowed to remain because the business would die otherwise. The Nazis are desperate to advance their empire."

Rainer stared into the blackness of his café, unable to speak. His own brother now a Nazi soldier, required to defend those who took away freedom. Fighting off the nausea that roiled inside, he listened as his father continued with the dismal news from home.

"It is newly rumored that Josef has been providing aid to the Resistance, to Marcel Weinum. I strongly suspect that this is so, though Josef will not speak of it, as I am sure he has our safety in mind. He has all but halted any visits to us. I greatly fear for his life, since he may have chosen the most dangerous of paths to take."

Rainer swore under his breath as he fought with his own anger and helplessness. Marcel Weinum was the driving force behind the Alsatian Resistance, known as "La Main Noire," or "The Black Hand." Anyone in allegiance with him would face certain death if discovered, but Rainer knew that Josef had always insisted he would fight. If only he had half of Josef's strength and courage. Guilt rose inside and squeezed his lungs taut until he felt unable to breathe. "Father, I have to help, I have to."

"No." Albert was definitive in his response. "Your reappearance in Colmar and especially the reestablished camaraderie with Josef would only alert the Nazis to greater speculation about your intentions, as well as those of our family," Albert continued. "Your presence at home would draw unnecessary attention, as Professor Renault feels that you are already being considered for recruitment. You must let us manage the home front, Rainer, as if nothing were amiss. It will be risky enough and we are already having to work against time and great odds to do what we can."

"But what will become of the Taffels?" Rainer beseeched his father for an acceptable answer, knowing that there was none. "I can't just watch this madness happen!

"Elena and Abner are out of France and have been reestablished in England, theoretically to be with relatives and doctors who can assist with Abner's declining health, though he will likely die there. We ran out of time to get Ben and Ian out of the country, however. For now, they are safe but are being moved to more secure quarters. Keeping them from harm is an endeavor that carries an ever-growing risk for all. Jews who cannot escape are now being rounded up like sheep and sent to the labor and death camps." Albert took a sip of café and swallowed the last morsel of a croissant. "Josef and his brothers maintained the shop as best they could. When we hid the boys, the business simply dissolved, a casualty of this unthinkable insanity," he offered softly. "The Germans have overtaken it, as they have other Jewish mainstays. As for Josef, he refuses to leave. He remains hardheaded and stubborn, albeit noble and brave. Not unlike his best friend, I often fear." Albert remained expressionless as he watched Rainer clench and unclench his fists and struggle to retain a measure of reason.

"I have to see Josef! Perhaps I can convince him to leave now, or to at least be hidden before it is too late. You know I can't be here, not doing a damn thing to help, when my family and my friends are fighting to survive!"

"No!" Albert was defiant. "It is imperative that you not attempt to contact Josef! It is too dangerous for all involved! You must be far removed from this ugliness. Our lives and yours may depend on it. Do you understand what I am saying to you, Rainer? Go where the Germans choose to send you and do what you must to survive. You will know when it is the right time to act with conviction. If you attempt to find Josef now, we are all in danger, him most of all! He has chosen this path. While I pray for his safety, we both know that he is in grave peril already, and so are those caught providing any aid to him. That includes our women. The less you know, the better. We are doing what we can to discourage rumors and keeping up appearances, which is another reason I made this trip."

For a moment, neither spoke as they gathered their overcoats and hats and ventured into the cold wet evening air. As they walked, Albert issued instructions with the authority inherent to a family patriarch. "We will receive your award, of course, and celebrate your new position here at the university. Perhaps dinner later, and I will leave in the morning. You must wait to receive word from us about events at home. All communication must appear normal from this point on, and without arousal of suspicion of anything covert, ever. Letters, or any possible telephone conversation, should only be general in nature and about family matters. The Nazis have access to everything now, damn them. So say nothing political, nothing controversial, or anything that could be misinterpreted or twisted to their purpose. Rainer, I know you feel as if you have not done your part, or that you are somehow betraying us in Colmar. In truth, it is the exact opposite. If you are one who is recruited by the Nazis, if you gain their trust while holding to your morals, you are now helping to shield all of us from their wrath. You can gain invaluable information as one working behind enemy lines. Things are much too far-gone now to do otherwise. The acting with conviction will come in due time. You will know when. And I will try like hell not to worry about my son, my youngest boy."

Albert brushed away a stray tear that he did not want Rainer to see. Though he wanted to argue, Rainer took small comfort in knowing that his father was right in his assessment of the madness that threatened to engulf them all. He would honor Albert's wishes, as a good son should, by recognizing the wisdom in his father's words and the care taken to convey the immensity of it all in the most loving way possible. But on the inside, he screamed with rage at the Nazis, at those damned judensaues, and at his own inability to help his friends and family. Taking his father's arm once more, he promised that which he struggled to accept, and began guiding Albert back across the square. When they arrived at the Fine Arts building and the office of Dr. Renault, his father paused, as in afterthought.

"Before I forget. Josef said to tell you that the dare is off, and he releases you from a childhood promise made by two foolish boys. His words. He said you would know. Be careful, Rainer. Promise me that much, at least." Albert glanced at his son inquisitively, but Rainer remained silent as he forced a smile and quickly hugged his father. He watched Albert climb the stairs to Dr. Renault's office until his father was no longer visible. Reaching inside his shirt, he clasped the Star of David that pressed against his skin.

"I can be stubborn too, you know," he whispered into the early evening air.

Chapter Thirteen

Clermont-Ferrand, France
Place de Jaude
1941

Throughout the celebratory dinner with Dr. Renault, other faculty members and students, and his father, Rainer could concentrate on little but Josef and all that was familiar and sacred to him in Colmar. How gracious Dr. Renault had been to offer for the elder von Bauchelle to stay at his own home this night, knowing full well that university accommodations for students would be less than desirable for the comforts and necessities of a more mature adult. While happy to see his father, Rainer was thankful for the reprieve that allowed him to fully reflect on all that was happening. He buttoned his overcoat and walked with brisk intention past the pale warmth of light that emanated from the remaining shops in town. They were one of the only semblances of normalcy in the midst of war. A young boy on a bike, weaving his way across the street, careened to a stop next to the sidewalk and called to Rainer.

"Excuse me, Sir, s'il vous plait."

"Yes?"

"This is for you."

Rainer accepted the sealed envelope with a curious frown, ripping it open to reveal a few scribbled words with recognizable penmanship. The boy on the bike took his leave as quickly as he had arrived, riding down a side street and into the growing darkness as Rainer read the note. *Place de Jaude, Vercingetorix. 20 minutes. Memento Mori.* His heart beat quickened as he read the note once more, and looked wildly up and down the boulevard taking in every shadow of light and examining all who were in his line of vision. Could it be? He hurried as fast as his feet would go without drawing attention to his movement or destination. Stopping only for a large cup of café once within sight of the massive statue he perused the plaza once again. The freezing night air grew heavy with dampness and more intrusive as the minutes slowed to a crawl. He sat in the middle of one of the unoccupied benches in one of the more unpopulated areas. Buttoning his overcoat around his scarf, he waited for the unknown to be revealed as he scanned the square for anything recognizable and scrutinized any who strolled past. There were a few passersby, but the rain, snow showers, and cold had kept most safely indoors. Nazis were not as prevalent as usual on this kind of night.

"Would you like something a bit stronger in your café?"

Rainer turned and stared at the man that appeared from nowhere, now taking a seat beside him. Gray hair flecked with streaks of brown peeked out of a carefully placed woolen fedora, and a matching trimmed beard brushed the top of the red scarf thrust around his neck. Black rimmed glasses framed coal-dark eyes that were familiar as Saturday romps through Colmar. Despite the clever exterior there was no way he would mistake the identity of his best friend.

"Josef." Ranier breathed his name like a prayer, barely above an audible whisper. He could not help but grin at the disguise as relief flooded his mind. Sliding across the cold bench, he patted the vacant spot beside him. "Jew - wanna have a seat? The hair does not become you, by the way, but the beard might be a step up in the enhancement of your masculinity. Perhaps you should just give me the bottle of whatever it is you are imbibing, as it has clearly impacted your sense of style."

Josef removed a small flask of Cointreau from the inside of his overcoat before taking a deep drag on a half-smoked cigar. The combination of pungent spice that seemed woven into circular puffs of smoke and the fleeting aroma of sweet orange from the liquer reminded Rainer of autumn nights on the balcony with the men in his family discussing the musings of the day. Josef leaned toward him, tipping the flask toward his cup.

"I see that the remainder of your university training has not included gentility nor manners. Is that an affirmative on the Cointreau in your café or no?"

"Yes, thank you, my friend. I have a feeling I'm going to need it." Rainer extended his cup toward the proffered elixir, gently shaking his head and whispering. "I'm quite sure you shouldn't be here, according to all the rumors."

"Ah, rumors, those insipid little irritants." Josef took a lingering sip of Cointreau, carefully wiped the stray liquid that trickled down the bearded chin, and stared up at the towering Vercingetorix. Raising the flask in a feigned toast, he turned to face Rainer. "To Liberty! Perhaps one day, she will return."

"Damn it, Josef! It's dangerous for you to be here. Hell, it's dangerous for me to be here with you."

"And yet you came, my secret Christian friend, with his *verboten* Star of David."

"How do you know I still wear it, seeing as how you released me from that obligation, according to my father?"

"Because," Josef said, relishing the familiar comfort of the verbal jousting that had always marked their interactions, "I needed to assuage my guilt for giving it to you. However, I also know that you are as stubborn a fool as I am."

"Duly noted." Rainer raised his cup in return.

"You might be amused to know," Josef continued, holding his overcoat open just enough to reveal the cross that he now wore around his neck as part of his attempted disguise, "that the visit to your church and all that I learned there saved my Semitic ass when I was confronted one night by a soldier. I had to convince him that I was indeed a Christian from the Eglise St. Martin, just out and about to minister to sick parishioners. Perhaps your Jesus really does love even poor Jewish souls."

Rainer found himself momentarily unable to respond as he held his cup for more Cointreau. Knowing that his friend had to pretend to be someone so fundamentally different than who he really was just to survive another day, wracked his soul, pricked the guilt wound until it festered. "I'm sorry, Josef. I'm so sorry for what is happening to you and your family. May God damn this all, I'm so sorry that I haven't helped you more."

Josef poured another hefty round for them both and leaned toward his friend. "Didn't you just break a commandment or something?"

Rainer shook his head and smiled at the bearded man beside him. "Good Lord, now I have a Jewish guardian angel. *Mazel tov*, my friend. You are a better man than I will ever be."

For a moment they reveled in the solace of silence, lingering momentarily between the warmth of childhood memories and the rawness and reality of war. Joseph took several sips of Cointreau, leaned back against the bench, and crossed his ankles. "Perhaps Albert told you already. Abner and Elena are safely out of Colmar, now living in Wolverhampton, outside of London. I'm surprised he survived the journey, that grizzled old man. I know I won't see him again, but at least he will die with his dignity. It was much less obvious to smuggle them out first without any other male passengers along to raise suspicions. Not to mention that able-bodied men are now either conscripted into service, or if they are Jews, taken away to work or to die. Ben and Ian are safe for now, as of today, thanks to your parents. By the way, this will also make you happy. They are hiding in the attic of your church, up there behind the damn judensaues."

"In the attic?" Rainer repeated. He could feel his own incredulous smile expanding like spilled wine. "Of Eglise Saint-Martin? My church? Are you serious? Old Albert did not share that bit of information. How in the hell did they pull that off?"

"Apparently, the priests and a nun or two were willing to have them. They had to adjust to sleeping during the day and being quietly about the place at night, perhaps just reading, to ensure that no one else knows they are there. Your mother and the nuns take fresh food, clothes, and cremant to them on Sundays under the guise of a church event, and Ben and Ian also scavenge at night in the kitchen for food and other items left by those inside. It is a meager existence for now but better than the alternative. Your father has a secret wall prepared in the winery made with aged wood on which he and your brothers and sister added touches of spider webs to enhance the authenticity. They were hiding there until they were moved to Eglise St. Martin. If the need arises, they can be moved back to the winery, via the von Bauchelle business deliveries and transactions. Both hiding places are quite clever, really. Very dangerous. And probably the most loving act ever shown to us. Your father wants you as far away from this as possible. He's proud of you, you know, and worries for your safety. So don't tell him I told you any of this. I'd hate for him to disinherit his almost adopted and favorite Jewish son."

"I'll be damned," Rainer shook his head, grinning yet again. "In the church, behind the damn judensaues? And camouflaged spider webs in the winery? I'll be damned!" A small measure of redemption seeped into his soul.

"There's more, Rainer. I am officially underground now and have had a fair amount of training with the network of Resistance forces. I suppose Albert might have shared that rumor. I won't give other details, but it's enough to know that much. It was my choice, and I would do it a thousand times again." Josef took a long sip from the bottle of Cointreau and a deep drag on the cigar. "I have never hated in my life, until now. I don't believe I will live to see those Nazi bastards rue the day they ever came to be. But I dream of killing them slowly, one by one, and derive great pleasure from those thoughts. They have stripped every bit of charity from me. I must agree with your assessment. May God indeed damn them all to hell for what they are doing to Jews and all those whom they have persecuted in their reign of terror." He ground the last words out slowly, controlled, but barely containing the venom.

Rainer contemplated the depth of his friend's grief and anger. This was not the Josef he knew, but the man he had been forced to become. His home, his livelihood and family, all uprooted and threatened, for no other reason than being Jewish, while the rest of the world was only beginning to understand the scope of inhumanity and barbaric cruelty that was spreading across Europe like a plague. It was frightening to see Josef this way. Perhaps more frightening was the beginning of a hellish need to help his friend destroy anything Nazi. He feared becoming as cold and cruel, with no compassion, but the growing desire to protect his friend and both their families was sharpening his lust for vengeance.

"I wish we could go back to the museums, Josef. Remember the days of our youth when we roamed carefree among the masterpieces, and the horrors like crucifixion and even those godforsaken judensaues were supposed to be artistic representations of past

79

injustices, not the present? As if we had all evolved to that place where reason and humanity reigned with malice toward none. Now, the unbelievable is insanely real. Josef, I hardly know how to tell you adequately enough that I'm so sorry. I'm so sorry." Now the tears rose in Rainer's eyes once more. This time he was unable to contain them any longer, but quickly wiped them away.

Crushing remains of the cigar against the coldness of the iron bench, Josef was stoic as he stared at the imposing statue beside them before speaking. "Rainer, you and your family have been the best friends we could have ever asked for. Like old Vercingetorix here, you took up arms, of sorts, for us. Your father and brothers have risked much to help when they did not have to do so. My being in your church that day gave me the information I needed to save my life and the lives of others. Who knows? Perhaps one day I might break down and attend a church service with your family after all. Guess I would owe you that much. As long as I don't get sacrificed or fed to the lions, or snakes, or whatever strangeness happens in there. So there it is. And I should go now. I needed the visit, Rainer. I needed to be reminded of better days and of the goodness in men. I needed to remember the happiest times of my life just for a moment. Don't attempt to contact me, no matter what happens. You will not be able to do so, anyway. I will be able to find out what is happening with you, rest assured, though not always in a timely manner."

Josef stood slowly, adjusted his hat and coat, and extended his hand toward his beloved friend. The time of reminiscing, of innocence and boyhood, had gone for them both, faster than either thought possible. Rainer tilted his head and took a last long sip from the dregs of café and Cointreau, eyes closed and skyward as if to force another onslaught of tears back to a place of pre-war solace. Standing, he grasped the hand of his beloved friend, before embracing him firmly.

"Go with God, Josef. I love you, my friend."

"And I, you. *Memento Mori,* Rainer."

Rainer stood, silently watching his friend until the outline of Josef had faded into the darkness. He wondered with inescapable sorrow when or if he would ever see his best friend again.

Chapter Fourteen

Rastenburg, East Prussia
Late 1941

Sonne

Sonne Becker stared at her reflection in the antique hall mirror. Thick chestnut hair gathered into an elegant bun at the nape of her neck, while soft, wispy pieces fell about a winsome face. Light sea green eyes, eager and bright, were accentuated by her mother's favorite silk scarf wrapped with care around her neck and secured with a cameo brooch, a gift from her grandmother. Tiny pearl droplet earrings completed her classic look. Reaching underneath a light brown wrap, she smoothed the darker green dress hanging fashionably just below her knees and fitted with a belt of the same color that cinched her waist. Today, at almost eighteen, the smiling image in the mirror was the embodiment of the woman she aspired to be, though she remained oblivious to the attention her beauty garnered from eager suitors. She fussed momentarily with a beret before deciding to fold it in her handbag. Turning to face her mother, she spread her hands and raised her brow in a playful question of approval.

"So, would you hire me to work in the burgermeister's office, Mama? And should I go by 'Cotterena' now as an official adult, or keep 'Sonne' as my name of record? After all, the new burgermeister does already know me, even if he does not remember our acquaintance."

"Rest assured, Anton Hirsch will certainly remember you no matter which name you choose to use. But you are used to being called Sonne, so perhaps keep that. You look mature and professional beyond your years, I must say. Where in the world has the time gone?" Alsa Becker gave a wistful smile to her only child, trying unsuccessfully to hide the rush of emotion at seeing the once little girl transformed into a confidant woman who was willing to lay aside her own dreams amidst the tumult of war, to help her family. The Nazis had appointed the younger Hirsch to the position of Burgermeister of Rastenburg and were no doubt grooming him for services beyond even those of a town mayor.

"Your father would be immensely proud of you wanting to contribute like this, when we are faced with adversity. If you get this job, I will alter some of my dresses and skirts to be a better fit for you."

Sonne turned toward her mother with gentleness, knowing how hard it was for the elder woman to be without her husband or to have to reckon with the possibility that he may no longer even be alive. Alsa needed to believe that Eduard would come home one day. Her strength was inextricably tied to that belief, and Sonne tried to be supportive of her mother in that regard. These days Alsa mended garments and ran menial errands for those more affluent, as she attempted to scratch out a living in the midst of war.

"Mama, I wanted to work. You know we have talked about all of this more than once. It will be good for me, too, you know on my resume, when life is easier and I can go to the university. All those little side jobs I did during free days and after school, helping with the books and managing in Mr. Riker's shop and in the library should pay off now, yes? Besides, it is done now, and that is how it is going to be. I will have to flatter that pompous ego of Anton's a bit, but that should not be too hard. Besides, he thought I was pretty then, and you know some men are just stupid when it comes to women." Sonne smiled, rolling her eyes and making a silly face at her mother to lighten the moment. Alsa remained firm.

"Your father and I wanted to see you fully educated, Sonne."

Sonne raised both open palms to her mother, this time showing a measure of frustration. "Stop it, Mama. Stop. No more whining, isn't that what you always told me?" She softened her tone as she wrapped an arm around Alsa. "Besides, it is done. Now, we make the best of it during these terrible times and move along. We will be fine. Besides, if Herr Burgermeister Hirsch remembers playing chess with me when I was barely beyond childhood, perhaps he will also remember that I played him to a stalemate, and that I am intelligent enough to be of good service."

Her mother wiped away her tears and smiled at Sonne. "All right, all right, no more sad talk. Besides, by chance some wonderful, kind, and handsome man is sure to want a witty, intelligent, and caring girl for a wife, I hope. I do so want little grandchildren, you know. Perhaps Anton Hirsch has changed. You certainly have."

"Ah, here it comes, the ever-present husband endeavor. Perhaps one day, Mama, I will choose to marry. Not to Anton Hirsch, of that I'm sure. He and his father are conceited bags of putrid air." Alsa smiled at the imagery conjured up by her daughter's lighthearted reference to the Hirsch men. "Besides," Sonne continued, "he's probably in a torrid relationship or two now, anyway. I doubt he's married. I don't think he's the kind to be faithful to either a girlfriend or wife. Now, I must go convince our new burgermeister that I am the best choice to handle all of the office needs. It may be a long shot, but I can do this, I know! I just hope that Anton Hirsch doesn't hold too much of a grudge."

Her mother stood silently, bracing herself against the door and the weight of a now cruel and frightening world. Watching her daughter moving down the sidewalk, smiling and waving joyfully, Alsa offered a silent prayer of thanks that Sonne had always been such a driven and happy girl. Still, the intrusive sense of foreboding now seemed a constant in their lives, a part of the relentless nature of war. How she wanted so much more for her little girl. Now that life seemed long gone.

Chapter Fifteen

Rastenburg, East Prussia
Office of the Burgermeister
Late 1941

Walking briskly through the streets of Rastenburg toward the government office buildings, Sonne smiled as she greeted an occasional passerby. German soldiers in their stark uniforms now routinely occupied the streets and meandered into quaint shops, as Rastenburg was now a garrison city. She pretended not to notice their presence, though they most certainly noticed her. Instead, she remained focused on the task at hand and took a measure of satisfaction in knowing that her calm demeanor, level head, and ability to troubleshoot, combined with a solid work ethic and good references, should make her a viable candidate to work in the office of the burgermeister despite her youth. While men had been of primary consideration for all government positions, war now dictated the necessity to consider more women to fill needed vacancies. She remained hopeful that her skills would be strong enough to be chosen. Perhaps she might even be able to ascertain news of her father, or at least to more quickly discover what was happening outside of Rastenburg.

Entering through the cumbersome doors of the old and dreary building, Sonne gave her name to the attendant in the waiting area and smoothed her dress once more, as nervous anxiety began to build. She glanced once more at her reflection in a nearby mirror and swept a loose strand of hair back into place. A quick perusal of the room confirmed her suspicion that she might be the youngest applicant for the position of office assistant. The vacant position had attracted many wanting to make ends meet for their families, all of whom shared similar prospects as those of Sonne and her mother.

"Cotterena Becker? Burgermeister Hirsch will see you now."

Quickly, Sonne gathered her handbag and wrap and followed the attendant down a short hallway to the open door leading into the mayoral office. Anton Hirsch had the reputation for efficiency and brashness, as well as a proclivity for beautiful women. It was also rumored that he engaged in exchanging personal information with Nazis about the citizens of Rastenburg, though he deflected any who might foolishly dare to make such accusations. Anton Hirsch publicly professed nothing but concern for citizens. For the moment, Sonne was glad his back was facing her as he barked an order over the phone to a no doubt distraught underling.

"Yes, today! See that it is done and report back to me immediately."

"Herr Hirsch?" The attendant whispered softly, attempting to capture his attention without raising his ire. Sonne placed a hand on the woman's arm.

"I can wait until he is finished. I know how busy the burgermeister must be." She spoke in a quiet tone to the attendant as the formidable man on the phone forcefully placed the receiver down and turned to face her. For a moment no one spoke as his eyes hovered over her from head to toe and back to her eyes. She found herself struggling to not look away, though she inwardly admitted that she felt intimidated by his deliberate and aggressive manner. He was more handsome than she remembered. His light brown hair was cut close to the scalp and framed a chiseled face with eyes of piercing blue that still had the ability to disarm. They reminded her of ice crystals on a frozen pond that reflected the brightest of skies. A well-appointed suit accentuated the formality. She knew him to be approximately thirty years old now, though he looked older in his newly official capacity as burgermeister. His eyes softened as he regarded her, though he maintained an air of superiority.

"You are familiar. Do I know you?"

Before the attendant could utter a word, Sonne stepped forward, offering her hand and never losing contact with his intense gaze. "I am Cotterena Becker, Sir. Yes, we have met, almost four years ago. You might remember me as 'Sonne'. It is an honor to be reacquainted. Your family brought you to our home for dinner when you first moved here. We played a quick game of chess. You hadn't been here long then. Our fathers knew one another from work in the field of munitions development. My father is Eduard Becker, and he was a munitions expert and also an architect. Currently, we believe him to be serving in the Wehrmacht at the pleasure of the Third Reich."

The eyes of Anton Hirsch narrowed as he studied the striking woman before him. His memory flashed back to the evening in question, which he remembered in vivid detail, including the budding beauty of Sonne, now in full bloom, and how she had challenged him. He recalled her father, as well, who had been placed under alternate supervision upon the Nazi set-up dismissal of his former superior. Eduard Becker was one whose allegiances had been deemed not altogether clear, but his skills in the munitions field were proficient. Still, he had been relegated to serve in a reduced capacity. The man had become an expendable entity in the Reich hierarchy.

"Ah indeed, yes I do remember that evening. Your father at one time was called upon to provide assistance to Hermann Goering and Albert Speer in the Reich Chancellery, I believe? He was also a subordinate of Werner von Blomberg, before the general's unfortunate demise. It would seem that you have become an even more accomplished young woman in addition to being a formidable chess opponent. Please be seated, Miss Becker. Mrs. Schmidt, that is all for now. If we need anything further, I will let you know. Otherwise, I will inform you when the interview is concluded. Thank you."

His voice was deep and commanding, falling just short of frightening. Both women complied immediately without speaking. Sonne found his manner condescending almost to the point of arrogance. If she had not needed the job so badly, she might have changed her mind about working for him. If he were to hire her she would have to find a way to achieve a tolerable working relationship with him.

"How old are you now, Miss Becker? Sonne." He remained standing, and glanced at the paperwork Sonne had given him. She swallowed hard and prepared to plead her case with as much passion and determination as she could muster.

"Yes, please call me Sonne. I'm eighteen, Sir. I have had plenty of bookkeeping and management experience, and I am qualified to do this job. I'm energetic and a quick study. I can do anything given to me and will work hard to learn whatever I don't already know, much in the same manner as I learned to play chess. I love people and work well with them. I brought good references, also. I'm not afraid of hard work, Herr Hirsch. You wouldn't be sorry if you chose me. I need this job, badly." Sensing that she had been far too needy and verbal, Sonne closed her eyes and grimaced as Anton Hirsch strolled to the back of her chair. Silently chastising herself, she attempted to regain composure and began speaking again with slow and deliberate assertiveness. "I know I would be a good hire for you. I want this job very much."

"Do you, now?" Anton Hirsch smiled, reveling in his position of superiority that he believed kept her confidence at bay. She had become a stunning woman and appeared to be well skilled. "You are not married, Sonne?"

"Married? No, no Sir."

"Please, call me Anton, for now. We are, after all, old friends, are we not?"

Sonne winced, but responded with all the requisite diplomacy she could muster. "Yes Anton, we are friends, I hope. With my father involved more intimately in the war effort now, I still live with my mother. Like many, we are doing the best we can. This job would allow me to help my family as much as possible. My father has given me the best of parental advice with regard to office management and dealing with business protocol."

"I am certain he schooled you quite adequately. Very well, tell me what you know of my job requirements, Sonne."

With a signal to proceed, Sonne explained all of the requirements as listed in the advertisement and gave pertinent examples of why she would be the best choice to fill the permanent position. She had just begun to initiate a series of questions regarding the efficiency of production in his office when he held up a hand, motioning for her to stop.

"Sonne, as my assistant you would periodically be required to accompany me to certain affairs of state and be discreet in sharing any private information with the public. At times, you would not speak unless spoken to. You would be sure that in all ways and in all matters, this office appears impeccable."

"Yes, of course, whatever you need." She struggled to sound like she was not groveling. "I have been to a state affair or two with my father and understand about formalities for such events."

Anton Hirsch came to stand directly in front of her. Reaching for her elbow, he assisted her in standing and slid his hand down the length of her arm to her hand, which he now held with affection. Her eyes widened with surprise as he leaned closer and whispered.

"Sonne, you are clearly a competent young woman. I must say, you are more beautiful than I thought possible. This position could be extremely beneficial for us both, if you are willing to work closely and intimately with me. I can reward quite handsomely for your services, and you and your mother never need go without. What do you think about this proposal?" Without waiting for a response, Anton Hirsch leaned closer, his eyes searching hers.

"What? I _ I, uh…" Sonne withdrew her hand, trying not to acknowledge what had just occurred and to find the right words. She had been prepared for the possibility of not being selected for the assistant office position, but never for this. She felt exposed, vulnerable and weak. "I don't feel very well, I'm afraid. I'm so sorry to end this interview. I must leave now. Please excuse me. Good day to you, Anton." She rushed for the hall, leaving all of her papers behind as she searched for a back exit.

This was worse than anything she could have imagined. What would she tell her mother? Could she reveal what had happened? Alsa would be heartbroken and angry, not to mention scared, about what repercussions might follow her refusal of his advances. Any possible relationship the two families might have had would be forever severed. Would her refusal of him hurt her father in any way, if he were even still alive? She tried to corral her racing thoughts as the afternoon cold exacerbated the tears that were at the ready to fall. She would tell her mother she was not the best candidate for the job.

In his office Anton Hirsch did not hesitate before reaching for the phone. The young woman had her opportunity to be cooperative and to thrive during a time when others did not have such an advantage. Besides, most women found him more than desirable. Though Sonne would have been quite the prize on his arm, now there would be consequences for her dismissal of his generous offer.

A heavy German accent answered on the receiving end of the call, and the burgermeister smiled as he relayed the relevant information.

"I have the perfect replacement for your project. She is an excellent physical specimen and in the appropriate age range, with suitable family dynamics. She would be more than adequate for a number of needs. I can have her ready for you in the morning. Yes, I look forward to seeing you again as well. My best regards to all." Looking out the large window in his office onto the streets of Rastenburg, he caught a quick glimpse of Sonne, her wrap pulled tight across her body and her handbag swinging rhythmically with her rushed pace. A beret was positioned low across her forehead. For a fleeting moment he thought of her in his bedroom, eager for his affection. Anton Hirsch smiled a slow victorious smirk as he considered her refusal of his advances and now her impending fate. He reached for his phone once more.

"Mrs. Schmidt, please contact that last applicant immediately. Miss Becker, I believe was her name? You will likely reach her mother. Please offer my sincerest apologies. This position was not suitable for her, but there is a special government operation that is more appropriate for her skill level. She will need to spend time away from home, but the pay is commensurate and she will be working alongside a group of well-trained women to assist in the support of Rastenburg. Let them know that a bus will pick her up in the morning. Give her family my warmest regards, again with apologies that this position did not work for her. Take care of this now, and let me know what the response is immediately. Yes, that is all." Placing the receiver back on the phone, he glanced once more out the window, smiling.

Checkmate, my beautiful Sonne.

Chapter Sixteen

Rastenburg, East Prussia
Somewhere in the Masurian Woods
Late 1941

Sonne straightened her beige skirt and pulled a piece of lint off the soft blue cashmere sweater that accentuated her eyes. She turned to wave at her mother one last time before approaching the run down school bus that waited outside her home. Alsa was proud though Sonne saw the tears brought on by the necessity of temporary separation. Her thoughts ran rampant. Why had Anton behaved as badly as he did, only to have an important job waiting for her before she had even returned home from the interview? Her mother had been waiting for her on the sidewalk, happier and more hopeful than Sonne had seen her since the removal of her father. How distressed Alsa would have been, had Sonne told her what really happened in the office of the burgermeister. Perhaps the offering of this position was an incentive to discourage any discussion at all, maybe even intended as a true apology? Regardless, she smiled as she boarded the bus with her suitcase and handbag. It was important work and she was grateful for the opportunity to have a job that allowed her to be with other women, despite meaning time away from home and her mother.

But apprehension soon replaced excitement as she boarded the bus. There were roughly a dozen women scattered in their seating and only a few sat together. No one spoke or smiled. Most avoided her gaze, choosing instead to stare out the dirty windows or down at their hands. A Nazi soldier stood at the front of the bus and two in the back. They seemed somewhat oblivious to the women, chatting in German to one another. Sonne thought it odd that they were on board. How insulting that they inserted themselves into every aspect of their lives now. She quickly sat beside a woman she surmised was close to her age as the bus pulled away and headed east out of Rastenburg.

"Hello. I'm Cotterena Becker. My friends and family call me 'Sonne'. What do you know about this job? All I know is that Burgermeister Hirsch said that it is important. Seems a bit clandestine in nature, though, especially with these soldiers on this bus." The woman continued to stare out the window. When she finally turned to face Sonne, blonde strands of hair crept out of the brown linen scarf wrapped around her head, and vacant eyes filled with despair stared back as she spoke barely above a whisper.

"Burgermeister Hirsch is an evil Nazi sympathizer, Sonne. You are now an employee of the Third Reich. An official tester."

"A tester? For Nazis? What are you talking about?" Sonne felt the panic rising from the pit of her stomach and coming to rest deep inside her chest, making it difficult to breathe. She gripped her suitcase and purse.

"Bitte schweigen!" One of the officers issued the stark command for silence as he moved across the length of the bus with a menacing glance at each of the women. Sonne stared at the black swastika set in a patch of white on his left armband of red and peeked down at the black knee-high boots that passed her seat. These were Schutzstaffel, or SS uniforms of the German protective police. She placed a hand on the back of the seat in front of her to steady the growing uneasiness. No turning back. She felt sick, as fear mounted. *Deep breaths, think!* She tried to remain calm while the bus continued out of Rastenburg and finally down a nondescript road, winding its way deeper into the woods past a series of lakes until the abundance of pine and spruce trees seemed to overtake the landscape. Suddenly, a behemoth of massive cement walls covered with barbed wire and moss appeared before them. German soldiers scurried like ants as the bus passed through extensive rings of security and then came to a grinding halt. There was a myriad of cement bunkers, flat-roofed and camouflaged on top with grass, trees, and bushes. Thick netting was suspended between the buildings, and the windows had metal shutters that served to make the fortress more impenetrable. It was a city unto itself. The women were commandeered, ushered off the bus, and made to form a line for inspection. The blonde girl with the brown scarf whispered behind her.

"My name is Lida. Do not show them any fear. They will be merciless in their taunts so whatever you do, do not cry in front of them. If you have a drop of Jewish, Polish, or any other blood in you, never tell them. It will be much harder for you. It could cost your life if you are not careful."

The soldiers gathered all of their handbags and rifled through their belongings. Then each was made to step forward for a security search conducted by two officers at once. Sonne winced as their hands felt every curve of her body, the sexual innuendo abounding as they smiled and laughed at the torment they caused. She kept her eyes open wide, holding on to her anger toward Anton Hirsch for this revenge and letting the emotion fuel her will to remain stoic and strong. She breathed hard, once in and out, and forced a demeanor of quiet stillness despite the inescapable fear. Upon completion of the searches, the women were escorted to a small bunker on the far side of the compound opposite the kitchen and dining area. An SS officer stepped forward to give succinct instructions.

"These are your quarters for as long as you are here. You have twenty minutes before dining. You will be escorted to your work shortly."

Sonne clutched her belongings and stood frozen in place as the other women each claimed a metal cot and a small accompanying side dresser. How could this be happening? Intuitively, she knew that being duped by Anton was only the beginning of the terror that lurked in the compliance and reticence of these women. She began to feel the panic that grew inside and threatened to erupt in sobs and pleas to return home. She also knew she could never allow the soldiers to see the fear.

"Sonne." Lida placed a hand on her shoulder and stood close, recognizing the familiar frozenness of being captive and having to face the unknown. Telling the girl the truth would bring more fear, but at least she would be better equipped to fight for her own sanity amidst the unthinkable. "Put your bags under the cot beside me and sit down. You need to know everything." Sonne did as she was told in silence, shoving her suitcase beneath the bed and placing her open handbag on the small bedside table before sitting next to Lida.

"What is happening? Why are we here? What is this place? It's not what that bastard Hirsch told me, is it? Did he trick all of us? I swear, I will kill him, I will!"

"Sonne, stop!" Lida grasped her hands and squeezed them hard, fully understanding the panic this new one must be feeling. There was no time to allow for gradual accommodation to horror. The girl had to be prepared before the next meal. "Listen to me very carefully. When you are scared, take slow deep breaths and think about something that makes you happy, or think about how much you want to best these monsters. Draw on whatever gives you strength. Do you understand? Trust me, it sounds simple, but you will need every mountain of courage you can muster to stay sane and make it through this ordeal. Stay strong. You have to be more courageous than you ever dreamed possible." Sonne nodded and began to breathe with deep and slow precision. Of course Lida was right. She held her hands in return and nodded her head.

"You are in the Wolf's Lair, or the Wolfsschanze. It is the secret primary Eastern Front command center of the Third Reich. It is highly fortified, with steel-reinforced concrete bunkers everywhere and three zones of armed protection and gates around the central complex. You are now an official food tester. All of us are. We eat the same foods prepared for him when he is here."

"For him? You mean Hitler?"

Lida paused, noting the disbelief evident in Sonne's eyes, before continuing. "You must pay attention to everything I'm telling you. If you want to survive, do exactly as I say." Sonne nodded without speaking, fighting back the urge to run, knowing that leaving was not possible. "After we are forced to eat, we wait for an hour to be sure that none of the food has been poisoned. If we all manage to not get sick or die, the same food is given to Hitler. He has a fear of being assassinated. Hell, I'd kill the son of a bitch myself, if I could. There are fifteen of us in all now, including you. At first, we did not live here. They took us to an old schoolhouse for the meals, but now they want us kept here in this hellhole with constant supervision. You are a replacement for someone who found out, shortly after recruitment, that she was sick and expecting a child of Polish heritage. At least that is what we were told. No one knows what really happened to her. For some reason, they wanted a specific number of testers, it seems. You were the next unwitting victim."

Sonne felt the tears seeping from her eyes and tracing their way down her cheeks before dripping onto the hands that were folded across her lap. They shook in tandem with her body. Lida leaned close and whispered. "Let some of those tears escape now, but you don't want to cry in front of Nazis. You will never be allowed to forget it." Sonne spoke through controlled sobs, trying to retain a modicum of rationality while warding off the terror that threatened to erupt in screams.

"Human guinea pigs, lab rats, all of us?" She stared, eyes opened wide, at Lida, who placed a hand on top of her own.

"Yes, that's pretty much how it is." Lida was brutally honest. She did not wait for Sonne to ask questions. "Soon, they will take us to eat. Despite your fear, stay composed. Pray for strength. And do what you must. The food is delicious, of course, as the same will be served for Hitler once we are done. He is a vegetarian, so there will be no meat. Each meal is frightening, to be sure. Some of the women cry like abused dogs and huddle together afterwards. They are the ones the soldiers taunt the most. Focus on the trees outside, your family, anything that makes you smile, and hang on to your faith, if you have such. The more calm and still you are, the less likely they will make fun of you. Perhaps you will even earn respect. Some of the officers are more kind than others, but trust no one and try not to make them angry. You must do everything I'm telling you."

Sonne was going to ask if they would be allowed to correspond with home, only to be interrupted by the six officers appearing in the doorway.

"Mach schnell!"

"Remember, Sonne. Survive." Lida whispered.

The officers commanded them to move more quickly, some laughing aloud at their growing helplessness. Only a few of their words were unintelligible, but Sonne easily discerned their disdain. They walked a short distance before being forced into a makeshift dining room, void of any décor except one long table and the appropriate number of chairs that lined both sides. Along the only wall that contained a row of high windows were chairs for the attending SS officers. All but one sat with casual aloofness, speaking with one another and seemingly disconnected from the plight of the women. The standing officer was less than accommodating, relishing his position of authority. Sonne imagined him to have been quite the bully as a boy, and found herself growing angered by his unprovoked hostility.

"Setzen!" he commanded loudly, followed by a degrading "Schwein!" to a slower moving woman, putting his hand on her shoulder and shoving her downward into a chair. Some of the officers laughed at the pig reference. As if on cue, double metal doors opening from the kitchen swung wide and white-coated staff made haste to place heavy plates before them. Sonne stared at the sumptuous meal as others received their food. Steaming hot noodles, freshly prepared peas, cauliflower, and peppers, along with fresh bread and a cup of seasonal fruit were served in ample proportions. The aroma would have been both enticing and appetizing had circumstances not been both cruel and terrifying. She thought of her mother and others in Rastenburg who could not eat this extravagantly in time of war, and felt the queasiness rising in her stomach. This meal might be the last or cause wretched sickness and permanent damage. One of the women began to make soft whimpering noises followed by sobbing tears.

No! You are now a warrior, like your father! Let the anger and fear drive you to be tougher than these soldiers! Sonne silently chastised herself as she felt her jaw instinctively tighten. *Survive! You must survive. And if not that, then die with dignity and honor. Deep breaths. Focus.* Looking out the window into the tops of the trees that towered over the bunkers, she pretended to hear her old spaniel, Klara, her favorite dog as a child, barking with affection as she jumped up to play. Briefly, she closed her eyes and began to pray a blessing as she always did at mealtime. The voice of the standing officer sounded sarcastic and mocking as he addressed the distraught woman.

"Ah, the weeping begins. And, look, the new one is praying. It won't help you, Fraulein." Cruel laughter emanated from the officers while the women's expressions reflected pity and shared kinship. Sonne kept her gaze on her plate as she took a sizable bite of the fresh bread. It took gargantuan effort to refrain from vomiting or to speak at all, much less to keep her tone devoid of emotion.

"I pray at every meal, Sir. This one is no different. It will help me whether I die or no."

At once, the room grew uncomfortably quiet as all eyes came to rest on her. Sonne steadied both her breathing and vacillating resolve, chewing the bite of bread with exaggerated slowness. She felt Lida tap her leg underneath the table, pleading with her eyes for Sonne to be quiet. At first, the officer in charge stood without moving. Then, the rubbing sound of leather boots on the cement floor got closer as he approached her. He appeared stoic, then mildly amused, as a sliver of a smile sneered across his lips. Strolling past her chair with hands clasped behind his back, he turned abruptly to stand close and bent down beside her. She could sense the scrutinizing eyes underneath the dark SS hat examining every inch of her body. His hot breath was warm and moist against her cheek as he insisted on unwelcome closeness. He smelled strangely clean and fresh, like the Scotch pine that was indigenous to the forest around the Wolf's Lair.

"Then let us all pray that you, Fraulein, live to see another day. Enjoy your food. Heil Hitler."

More laughter from the officers as they joked aloud, unsympathetic to the terror of the women in this moment. Sonne ate the remainder of the meal without a word, praying that she would indeed survive and vowing to never let these monsters see her cry. The rest of the day and those to follow would be carried out in similar fashion. Nights vacillated between sleeplessness and overwhelming fear and sadness, or temporary respites from emotional exhaustion with only fleeting dreams of all that she held dear. Silent tears, merciless and plentiful, came as she lay in bed, when the longing for home became unbearable. Sonne wondered if she would ever make it out of this place alive.

Chapter Seventeen

Clermont-Ferrand, France
1941

Rainer

"Are we limited to paintings, or may we include other works of art in our critiques?"

Professor Rainer von Bauchelle paused before responding to one of his fledgling students, all not much younger than he, as the massive wooden door to his classroom creaked open. A university administrator entered followed by a dark-haired clean-cut officer with penetrating eyes and thick brows. The man was unremarkable except that his overcoat was that of a Nazi, with the red swastika band emblazoned around his left arm, and he was carrying his military hat. The school official spoke with an air of urgency.

"Our pardon, Professor von Bauchelle, for the interruption. May we impose upon your last class for these remaining minutes and speak with you afterward?" Rainer motioned both men inside and regarded them with irritated aloofness as they seated themselves in the back of the room. He continued his lesson, while monitoring the presence of the visitors in his class.

"The assignment is to select and defend your choice for the ten greatest works of art of all time. Before our interruption, the question was whether your preferences are confined to paintings or no. Indeed, works of art are found in a variety of media, and your selections are limited only by your astuteness in evaluating and defending them. I am confident that I will be amazed with your convincing acumen. Questions?" Rainer smiled broadly at his eager students as he noted the discomfort of the university official and the steely attention from the unknown visitor, who suddenly spoke aloud with a heavy German accent.

"Perhaps, Professor von Bauchelle, you will entertain a possible assignment choice consideration from one who is not your student?"

"By all means," Rainer responded with quiet reservation as he began to feel the uneasiness in the room. "A proper education should most assuredly consist of free thinking and rational discourse, not to mention a possible assist with an assignment from a guest, correct, class?" The visitor smiled only slightly along with the students, though he was insincere in demeanor. He leaned forward to stand, pursing his lips and rubbing a smooth chin, and directed his attention to Rainer. He articulated each word with an air of challenging authority.

"What do you know of the Amber Room, and would you consider it to be one of the greatest works of art?" Rainer hesitated with an appropriate amount of wait time, allowing his students a moment to consider the prospect of his response, which he intended to be a masterful tour de force of expertise and memory.

"Ah, the Amber Room, yes. I believe original construction began in 1701 in the Charlottenburg Palace home of then Prussian King Friedrich I. I think the German baroque sculptor Andreas Schluter was the designer, assisted by Danish amber expert Gottfried Wolram, if my knowledge is correct. In 1716, the King of Prussia at that time, Friedrich Wilhelm I, presented it to Peter the Great as a gift to enhance an alliance between them. It was then assembled in the Winter House in St. Petersburg. In 1755, Czarina Elizabeth had it moved to the Catharine Palais, the Summer House, Tsarskoye Selo, or "Czar's Village". At that time, the Italian designer Bartolomeo Francesco Rastrelli redesigned the room to fit into a much larger area using additional amber that was shipped from Berlin. The room now covers approximately 180 square feet and consists of semiprecious stones along with six tons of amber, reinforced with gold leaf backing. It is said to be worth countless millions and to 'glow a fiery gold' as if illuminated by hundreds of candles. It is often referred to as the 'Eighth Wonder of the World'. I suppose an argument could indeed be made to consider the Amber Room as one of the greatest works of art of all time." Rainer stopped to address his class of young students as he noted the time on his pocket watch, a gift from his grandfather. The German stranger noted his every move. "Until next class, then, please craft your carefully thought-out choices. Extra credit consideration may be given for eleven works of art, including the Amber Room. And you may thank our esteemed guest for a gracious and noteworthy contribution to your academic endeavors."

As students made an uncharacteristically subdued exit from the class, Rainer stood quietly, resisting the urge to touch the Star of David that hung around his neck. He met the gaze of the German visitor with a calm but guarded defiance. The school administrator could barely contain his nervousness, his hands wringing as he glanced at Rainer, then back to the visitor.

"Professor von Bauchelle, this is Herr Albert Speer. He is the Chief Architect for the Nazi Party." Rainer regarded the man before opting to address him at all. So this was how it was going to happen, this assimilation into the dreaded German machine. He had heard of the man standing before him, but never imagined ever meeting anyone who was part of the Hitler regime command.

"Speer. You are an architect of considerable reputation, Sir." He stared into the eyes that observed his every move. It was the most civil and honest statement he could make.

"So they tell me," the dark-haired official replied casually, with no hint of a smile before continuing. "That was quite an impressive spiel, in your own right. Your knowledge of the Amber Room is most admirable, remarkable really, for a young teacher such as yourself. It is reassuring to know that you are cognizant of the German origin and history as well."

"And why is that, Sir?" Rainer turned to face the Reich officer squarely, holding his breath and dreading what was most assuredly coming next.

"Rainer – may I call you Rainer? Yours is a fine German name, you know. As learned as you are, I am sure you are keenly aware that France is now part of the German regime. It is only a matter of time before all of the French, including those in your own Alsace region, are elevated to German citizenry." A smile crept across the face of the Reich architect as he reveled in both his insight into Rainer's background and implied superiority referenced in the assimilation of the French people to German citizenship.

"So, let us be frank, shall we?" Albert Speer spoke slowly, with a deliberation and finality that underscored his inherent belief that Nazis had the right to steal whatever they chose. "Being an undersecretary of state, I am authorized to assist in many matters, including arranging the acquisition of cultural goods of immense priority. As such, we are returning the Amber Room from the Catharine Palais in Russia to a more fitting exhibition and its rightful place in Germany, along with other select pieces of art. As we speak, meticulous arrangements are being made for transport under the auspices of Art Protection Officer Count Sommes Laubach, who is also an accomplished art historian and expert. For now, they will be kept at Konigsberg Castle and Museum where a grand and glorious exhibit will later take place. The most esteemed Dr. Alfred Rohde, the international amber expert and the director of the art collections of Konigsberg, will supervise and be in charge of the task at hand once the Amber Room is safely in Konigsberg Castle."

"You have the Amber Room now? Six tons of amber, mosaics ensconced with countless jewels and gold? How?" Rainer could hide neither his surprise nor wonder at the words of Albert Speer.

"Ah, it seems I have your attention, young Professor Rainer, as you are aware of the value of the Amber Room." Albert Speer waved a dismissive hand, moving aimlessly about as he continued in a condescending, almost preening manner. "The details are intricate and ingenious. More than I have the inclination to explain now. The Russians desperately tried to hide it under flimsy sheets of paper, but of course, to no avail. Regardless, it is ours now, as it should be, and will be re-created in splendor once in Konigsberg." It seemed to Rainer that the face of Albert Speer contorted into that of a hideous clown, as the Reich officer smiled broadly now at his captive and incredulous audience of two.

"So, Rainer von Bauchelle, our new art genius, your services are required, under the direction of Dr. Rohde and others, in this monumental undertaking at Konigsberg Castle. Your family in Colmar is being notified, and an officer will be arriving to escort you to procure your belongings and then on to Konigsberg, via rail. I am certain that you are aware of the importance and honor that has been given to you as an art procurement and restoration assistant. Other arrangements will be made by the administration for your classes and work here, so not to worry about your students and their German education." The Nazi official paused briefly, noting the dual surprise and horror on the faces of both men before continuing with unbridled sarcasm.

"By the way, did you know that the former institution in Strasbourg is now The Reich University? Indeed, it seems that the University of Strasbourg has now received an upgrade as well, no? Good day, gentlemen. I must be about other important business in the area. Until we perhaps meet again, young Rainer." Albert Speer did not wait for the university escort but left as abruptly as he had arrived, letting the door close behind him.

"My God." The school administrator breathed heavily and grasped at his tie as if to loosen the grip of fear that was the Nazi regime. "Our university, under Nazi control, under Nazi nomenclature. What will happen to us?"

Rainer did not respond to the desperate question but rubbed the area around his neck, feeling for the Star of David underneath his shirt. The growing weight of foreboding was an albatross in his chest. "I should go see Dr. Renault to discuss the transition for my classes." Inside his own head, he fought for control, but the judensaues came alive, squealing and snorting with delight, their stench now overwhelming. He was now officially an enemy of the very country he had loved since childhood. There had to be a way to fight. Somehow, he would find it."

Chapter Eighteen

Konigsberg, East Prussia
1941

The long train ride from Clermont-Ferrand to Konigsberg under the watchful eye of a young Nazi officer had passed uneventfully thus far, but had given Rainer pause to think about all that he held dear. Faces of his family, of Josef and all the Taffels, and of his idyllic vineyard life in Colmar slipped by as quietly as the pastoral villages, now dotted with German military placements. An occasional swastika transformed the countryside from its former state of tranquil warmth to a cold and colorless land like black and white photographs of sadness. How he might have treasured the opportunity to study with the likes of the experts with whom he would work if only the circumstances were different.

"Where is your home?"

Rainer's musings were interrupted by the officer who accompanied him to the dreaded assignment. The young soldier stared at him, speaking in his native German tongue. Rainer supposed him to be somewhere close to his own age. Defiantly, he resolved to provide as little information as possible and chose to speak French, knowing the officer would likely understand both his words and the intended defiance behind them.

"Colmar, originally. And you?"

"Rothenburg. My family is still there."

Rainer returned the gaze of the youthful officer. What was it about him? His eyes seemed to reveal a loneliness that belied the intense gaze from underneath the menacing SS hat. "Rothenburg, a beautiful German town, that one. I have been there with my grandparents many years ago. It reminds me somewhat of Colmar in the quality of its quaint village appeal. As a child I was fascinated by the surrounding medieval wall."

"The wall," the German repeated softly, now staring out the window, "Yes, I miss it, too. In my childhood, it offered protection from many demons."

There was only a vague hint of kindness, but Rainer sensed an unmistakable regret. Was he truly sincere, or was this a ruse? Deciding to err on the side of safety, Rainer proceeded with caution. "Childhood afforded much protection for us all from the harsh realities of adulthood, it would seem."

Now the German smiled more intentionally and extended an introduction. "Forgive me. I am Friedrich Volk. I already know your name, Rainer von Bauchelle."

"And what do you know of me, Friedrich?"

For a moment, the officer sat without looking at Rainer. Then, in flawless French, the young German faced him and replied, almost apologetically. "I know that you are miles from home in a place that you did not choose to be, doing what you did not choose to do. It is a most difficult burden to bear, I know."

Rainer understood that this officer knew he was now one of the French malgre nous, those being recruited against their will to serve in the Nazi military and civil service. Was Friedrich Volk also conscripted against his will, even as a German? He remembered the admonishment of his father to beware of shared information. In equally perfect German, Rainer replied. "Then let us aspire to see our childhood homelands once again."

Both settled in their seats with a measure of extended comfort and silence that overtook them as the train continued on, each lost in remembrance. For the remainder of the journey through Prussia to the Baltic coastal town of Konigsberg, they exchanged pleasantries and meandered through conversation laced with requisite platitudes, but perhaps more as each seemed to test the bounds of confidence with every exchange. As passengers waited to disembark at the Konigsberg station, the young officer leaned forward to speak in hushed tones.

"Another officer will be meeting you momentarily, Rainer." Friedrich paused only briefly. "By the way, you might be interested to know that Konigsberg Castle has a rather intricate system of underground tunnels. Dark and dank they are, with rats and such, but interesting former escape routes to the Baltic Sea. It is rumored, also, that Albert Goering, brother of Hermann Goering, might be an occasional guest at the castle, particularly if there is an occasion that is art-related. As a lover of art, you might appreciate knowing about him. It is whispered that he might be sympathetic to an anti-Nazi cause. I, myself, would not know the truth of these things, of course."

"Of course."

"Rainer." The German hesitated momentarily. "Good luck."

"And to you, also, Friedrich." Rainer's mind raced ahead as he considered what Friedrich had told him. He had never heard of Albert Goering, but the name of Hermann Goering evoked more fear and anger than he was wont to entertain. A World War I fighter pilot ace, Hermann Goering founded the Gestapo, the secret state police, and had been appointed commander-in-chief of the German Air Force, the Luftwaffe. Currently, he served Hitler as commander of the Wehrmacht, or entire German Armed Forces, and was as ruthless toward any non-Aryan as he was passionate in his appreciation of art and culture. It seemed a strange juxtaposition to Rainer, being able to love the transcendent beauty of art yet embracing hate for selected artists and peoples who had done nothing to deserve such. He reveled in a fleeting moment, a glimmer of camaraderie, perhaps even a kindred spirit in Friedrich Volk. But it was quickly replaced by apprehension and loneliness when he faced the new SS officer who lacked any semblance of kindness or accommodation. As he was commandeered to an awaiting vehicle and onward to his destination, Rainer felt the dread seeping into his body like the cold rain that had begun to permeate the city of Konigsberg. Once again, he faced the mounting despair of separation from the home he might never see again.

Chapter Nineteen

Rastenburg, East Prussia
The Wolf's Lair
1942

Sonne

Sonne could not sleep. After months of confinement in this wretched prison, she found a semblance of peace in the early hours of daylight. The morning was still a dark purplish hue, as dawn was slowly winding its way into view and the women had not yet been awakened. She stood by the door, expecting it would be locked until the guards felt so inclined to allow them outside for the fresh morning air. Surprisingly, the steel door swung open when she gently turned the handle. She smoothed the dowdy gray uniform that had been issued to them all and peeked into the large open area that would soon be well traversed by the boots of their captors. Small fortune was in her favor, she mused, as the guard most benevolent to all of the women, but to her especially, was standing duty nearby.

"Pssst, Officer Dietrich!" She motioned for the armed guard to approach, and he was more than willing to accommodate her as he noted the chestnut hair that cascaded about her shoulders and highlighted her youthful face. In the time that she had spent in the secret headquarters, she had come to believe that he was one of the German conscripted recruits who perhaps did not share in all of the Nazi ideology.

"Sonne," he breathed her name softly, "what are you doing about so early? And you know you can call me by my first name when no other soldiers are about."

"Please, Conrad. I have been awake for hours. I only want to walk about for a moment. Please? I feel sick and stifled in here. Please, can you help me?" Sonne motioned with her head toward the still slumbering women and pleaded with her eyes. She had long reckoned with the forced assignment as an official food tester, and the meals no longer frightened her. That reality was now merely a disrupting thought. The fear that she might never see her mother again, and the likelihood that her father was dead already were the thoughts that could reduce her to tears if she allowed the intrusion. Conrad had become somewhat of a superficial confidante and source of information about the progress of the war. Sonne wanted to trust him but was reluctant to allow herself to be too close.

"Make it look real, then. Do not converse at all with me and no sudden movements, as there are eyes all around," he whispered. "Do not take offense if I must be gruff with you." Conrad Dietrich smiled at her from underneath his dark helmet and motioned with the barrel of an Stg 44 German rifle for her to walk a short distance in front of him. Occasionally he barked out an order to stop or go. Sonne obeyed the instructions given and moved with caution about the open area that was surrounded by the bunkers, quarters of resident officers, and meeting rooms. She was aware of the passing eyes that followed her from a sprinkling of SS soldiers gathered near one of the concrete bunkers. But she was oblivious to the identity of one in particular, who watched with interest from a window with reinforced steel shutters as he rubbed his chin and then the small, dark mustache that underscored his notoriety for all time. Adolf Hitler studied her and his SS officer with only mild interest until she motioned toward the kennel where his pet German Shephard was being groomed and fed. The young soldier kept her from moving too close and positioned himself strategically between her and the animal as she squatted on the ground, calling with affection to the dog from outside the fenced area. The German leader pondered the scene as he donned a jacket and made his way outside. Perhaps an earlier-than-usual morning visit with his beloved canine would prove to be beneficial.

"Aufstehen!" Conrad commanded Sonne to stand with such suddenness that she knew something was amiss. Recognizing the urgency in his voice and seeing his eyes, now open wide and pleading with her to exercise great care, she stood still and faced him. The approaching figure became recognizable as he came into sharp focus, and she felt the knot in her stomach grow as did the fear and contempt. He was out and about much earlier than his usual time with his dog, based on information Conrad had shared. Even though Sonne knew he could not possibly remember her childish indiscretion from the Olympic games, she trembled at the thought.

"Good morning, my Fuhrer." Conrad dipped his head in slight deference to the one before them while keeping his hands on his weapon.

"What is your interest in my dog?" Adolf Hitler commanded an immediate answer, speaking directly to Sonne while not acknowledging the officer at all. Sonne gaped at him, clothed in a casual morning jacket and shoes. He appeared like any other man, of modest height and normalcy, were it not for what she knew of his character and limitless cruel ideology. Neither his hair nor mustache was as dark as the black and white newsreel photographs made them look. His eyes, however, were a surprise, as she had never been this close to the man. Instead of being cold, dark, and emotionless as a shark, they were large and of the clearest pale blue. Yet they were frightening in their intensity and hypnotic capacity. No wonder people froze when he fixed his gaze upon them. Sonne steadied her voice and prepared to address the Fuhrer of the Third Reich. She spoke over her fear with a calmness that conveyed as much clarity and strength as possible.

"Please forgive me. I felt sick this morning and did not want to disturb the other women. I just needed a bit of air, and this guard was accommodating enough to grant me a small measure of help. I appreciate the kind gesture. Please permit me to say that your dog is most beautiful." Visions of her house and family began to intrude on her ability to remain stoic. She heard her own voice waver, as intrusive homesickness invaded her thoughts. Try as she might, the waver in her words betrayed the yearning for home. "I could not help but think of my old spaniel, Klara. I named her after a cousin who died young whom I loved very much. She was my favorite pet, and the loveliest of creatures. It is evident that this dog is similarly cherished, Sir. Please forgive me. I truly did not mean to intrude."

For what seemed several minutes, no one spoke. The Fuhrer stared off into the pine and spruce trees surrounding the Wolf's Lair. When he finally looked back at Sonne, she was stunned to see tears in the corners of the formidable blue eyes. Beneath the mystique and the strange and powerful charisma that incentivized others to mete out unspeakable brutality was a flawed man, with some semblance of feeling hidden beneath the ugly layers of superficial superiority. She wondered how he had transformed from mortal to monster. How had he been allowed to come to power, to turn men against one another, causing so much death, destruction, and hate?

"Klara was my mother's name," he said, at last. "She was a most special woman and I loved her dearly. The name of my dog is Blondi. You have leave to pet her briefly, as long as a guard or her trainer is present. What is your name, Fraulein?"

Sonne hesitated before replying. She did not think Hitler had ever known her father, though he might remember hearing his name, if prompted. She hoped she was not asked for his name, not knowing if he was considered loyal to Nazis or no, or if he was even still alive. "I am Cotterena Becker, Sir."

"Becker. That is a good German name. You are not a Jew, are you, Cotterena Becker?" He asked it with sharp insistence with only a hint of condescension, but it was unmistakable in his tone. Sonne knew her life depended upon the answer and decided not to tell him about her family or that her father was once a part of the Reichstag staff, now relegated to service in the Wehrmacht.

"No, I am not a Jewess. My mother is descended from Vikings and my father is of Germanic descent. We are from Rastenburg, Sir." She hesitated before bluntly adding, "I test your food."

The Fuhrer now seemed to regard her with an unexpected bit of compassion. She glanced swiftly at Conrad. Beads of sweat had gathered in the cleft of his chin, and he stood motionless and silent. The German leader finally spoke, resuming a more characteristic tone of nihilation. "Your service to your Fuhrer and the regime is noted, Fraulein Cotterena Becker. Perhaps there are greater contributions in your future." With that cryptic declaration, Adolf Hitler turned and strode back to his bunker as swiftly as he had appeared. Conrad remained silent, still gripping the Stg 44 with such force as rendered his knuckles white. Closing his eyes, he drew a long, deep breath.

"Damn, why did I let you talk me into that?" His voice was fraught with relief as he whispered to Sonne, who now walked obediently in front of him toward the bunker where the women were held. She was amused at his discomfort, which fed her returning confidence as well as her growing trust in Conrad.

"I thought we would be all right if I appealed to his human side," she offered, "though I doubt he has one. He truly believes in his hatred and power over others. What a horrible existence. I find him empty and loathsome. I wish I could kill him and drag him through every street in the Nazi regime." Sonne pondered the secret desire just revealed to her sympathizer, thankful that the morning had not ended in disaster of any kind.

"Do not say that out loud, Sonne. You will be the death of me," he whispered back.

"I am going to find a way out of this nightmare, Conrad, if it's the last thing I do."

"It may well be the last thing, Sonne." He uttered the words with care but without a smile, before giving loud instructions to open the door of the women's residence. With great fanfare, Conrad put on a display of power, shoving her inside with the butt of his rifle that he covered with a hand so as not to harm her. Sonne would marvel throughout the day at her newfound supervised freedom to pet Blondi and her secret association with an SS officer. She would also wonder about the last words Adolf Hitler had spoken. What did he mean about 'greater contributions'? This delusional man recognized her humanity, yet seemed to gloat in knowing that the women in the block faced potential death daily for him. He appeared oblivious to their imprisonment, their unwelcome station in his regime as they consumed his food, mere test subjects in his installation of Hell on Earth.

Chapter Twenty

During a break from morning briefings with high-ranking officials of the Third Reich, Adolf Hitler requested Professor Dr. Carl Clauberg, one of the guest German physicians, sympathetic to and heavily immersed in Nazi ideology, to join him on the conference room portico. A chief physician and professor of gynecology at The University in Konigsberg, he was working at Auschwitz to implement techniques for genocide. Dr. Clauberg, a short heavy-set man with equally round dark glasses that accentuated his rotundity, was involved in x-ray sterilization procedures as well as in research on female fertility hormones such as progesterone in the treatment of infertility.

"Heinrich Himmler informs me of your continued productive work at Auschwitz, Doctor. I trust that the experimentation, sterilization, and necessary extermination will continue as scheduled?" Dr. Carl Clauberg nodded in the affirmative as he sipped on strong coffee, the aroma of which wafted through the compound and lent an air of false serenity to the otherwise morbid discussion. Wiping the corners of his mouth with a small napkin, he responded with enthusiasm to the inquiry from the Fuhrer.

"Yes, we are quite pleased with the timeliness of our effort in Block 10. Dr. Schumann and I have made ample progress in the areas of both sterilization and insemination, and even a method of producing ejaculation by stimulating the prostate. Science will help to promote a superior Germany."

Adolf Hitler was pleased, nodding and tapping his fingers together, as he perused the grounds below. He caught sight of the girl, Cotterena Becker, as she and the other women were allowed outside for a brief respite. The women talked aimlessly together in low, unanimated speech and kept close to one another. The young woman was quite exceptional with her soft chestnut hair and lithe but feminine figure, visible even beneath the ample uniform dresses the women wore. "I believe I have found a most suitable specimen right here among us for the special extension of the Lebensborn Project, when you are ready to proceed to the next step. She is young, appears to be of good morals, and a pure, racially perfect blend of Nordic and German ancestry. A rare beauty and readily available for this endeavor should the project be successful. At that time, of course, her status would be temporarily elevated, as she is currently one of the testers. If she proves useful we can utilize her in other endeavors. Once her Aryan background has been confirmed, I wish to see her selected. We can discuss more details of this project after dinner. We will be joined by Heinrich Himmler, whom I am certain will agree that we should proceed as soon as you are ready to do so. You will conduct this project in secrecy at Wolfsschaunze, if that is amenable to you. This aspect of Lebensborn will never be discussed outside of this compound. I will have a suitable facility prepared in the interim with your specifications for all of your work with her or any other of our chosen subjects for other experimentation."

"Excellent, excellent. I am most pleased to hear this news. It is my opinion that we are quite close to seeing this particular project come to fruition. How glorious it will be for all of Germany to have such an inheritance as this. I must offer a hearty, 'Heil, Hitler'!"

The German officers gathered once more in the meeting room to review war strategy. Down below, Sonne had no way of knowing that her deepest fears were only just beginning, and her strength would be tested as never before.

Chapter Twenty-One

Konigsberg Castle, East Prussia
1942

Rainer

"The opening private gala should be a reflection of the wonder of the Amber Room in its magnificently divine recreation, would you not agree, Rainer?" Thankfully, the renowned Dr. Alfred Rohde did not await a response from his most valued assistant as he perused the finished grandeur of amber, gold, and precious jewels that seemed to glow with their own light. "I will see to it that the staff are in place prior to the opening. Your sole responsibilities, Rainer, will be to insure that all of the encased candles remain lit and are contained appropriately as we have already reviewed, and that our guests are attended to at all times. You may recruit help, of course, as the number of candles is great, and we will have many distinguished guests. The Blutgericht tavern wait staff is at your disposal for the evening. If our guests solicit information, you may provide accurate educational facts about the Amber Room as well as for any other art pieces that are now housed within the castle confines. They will be available for visitor viewing, also. You will dress appropriately of course. A tuxedo has already been sent to your room. You will also maintain the highest level of professionalism, along with visual contact with me, in the event your assistance is needed on matters of smooth operation and attendance to the pleasures of our guests. All German dignitaries, of course."

"Ah, good morning, Dr. Rohde. I see you are already about the business of executing a most glorious affair in honor of the restoration of the eighth wonder of the world. It is indeed breathtaking. My sincere congratulations on all of your efforts." Dr. Rohde hesitated momentarily before acknowledging the diminutive looking man who had somehow entered the room that was temporarily closed to all but a select few. There was a hint of irritation as he acquiesced to the greeting from this visitor who seemed to Rainer to be someone of relative importance, simply by virtue of his presence.

"Welcome to Konigsberg Castle, Herr Goering. I am most happy that you have made the journey to help with the celebration of the return of The Amber Room to its rightful place in German ownership. However, the room is currently off limits while preparations are underway. Please forgive the inconvenience. The elements of mystery and surprise are essential to a successful opening. I hope you understand?"

"But, of course, Dr. Rohde. We would not want to diminish such an occasion. You have my utmost compliance in maintaining silence until the gala." The man turned to face Rainer, studying him unabashedly as he might a work of questionable art. "I do not believe I have made your acquaintance. I am Albert Goering, the younger, albeit less accomplished, brother of Hermann Goering." Albert Goering bowed ever so slightly to Rainer, not smiling at all but maintaining eye contact. This was the brother of the feared Nazi leader, the one Friedrich Volk had mentioned that day on the train.

"Good morning, Herr Goering. I am Rainer von Bauchelle." Rainer had learned, early in his forced tenure with The Third Reich, to speak only when asked for a response and to err on the side of brevity and courtesy.

"Von Bauchelle. That is a French name, no?" Albert Goering continued to talk, while Dr. Rohde appeared to grow more impatient with the interruption of preparation for the evening event.

"You are correct, Sir. I am from the Alsace region. Colmar, to be exact."

"Then that explains both the French and German influences in your name. Colmar, an exquisite place. Most excellent wines there between the Vosges, the Rhine Valley, and the Black Forest. I should like to visit again. Not to mention the abundance of museums and culture, particularly, the Bartholdi and Unterlinden."

Rainer smiled at the mention of his boyhood haunts, and the memories of visits to the cultural icons with Josef, as well as with his mother. Albert Goering did not wait for a response from him but turned quickly toward Dr. Rohde, as if in afterthought.

"By the way, before I leave, Dr. Rohde, I am reminded of something I heard just today, speaking of Alsace. You have likely heard that there was an attempt on the life of Gauleiter Robert Wagner? Apparently the work of the wretched La Main Noire and the Resistance. Several of them were captured, including young Marcel Weinum, himself. Another German putsch."

Rainer felt brief waves of apprehension, at the possible mention of those closely connected to Josef and lowered his gaze to the floor before realizing both men were looking at him. Steadying himself and attempting a calm demeanor, he remained outwardly detached though his thoughts were reeling like a tempest. Dr. Rohde spoke with resolute firmness and disdain.

"Indeed, Weinum will be beheaded, as fitting for a vile untermensch. He is being removed to Stuttgart, I believe. The others will be extensively questioned, no doubt, and likely executed, or perhaps be added to the planned collection, if they are deemed noteworthy, if Jews can be considered so." Rainer felt his own sharp intake of breath as deeply and covertly as he could manage upon hearing the words of Dr. Rohde, who appeared oblivious to the inner turmoil in his head and the nausea that gripped his body. *A collection? Of Jews? What could he possibly mean?*

"Well, do forgive me again for the intrusion." Albert Goering stared at Rainer. "I look forward to the evening festivities. I think I will have a libation in the tavern, if I can find my way there. Perhaps you would accompany me on the way and join me for a drink, Dr. Rohde?"

"I'm afraid I still have business to attend. But I believe you will find the Blutgericht enjoyable for refreshment. Follow the main archways and ask if you are not certain of the way. Any of the staff can assist you. Until this evening, I must take leave and bid you farewell." Dr. Rohde motioned for Rainer to follow, as he began to walk about the gilded room, making note of details to be addressed prior to the opening celebration.

"Very well, Dr. Rohde." Albert Goering smiled and called out. "I will await the gala this evening with great anticipation. It promises to be an evening of surprises, I am certain. Many surprises. Good day, Gentlemen."

Chapter Twenty-Two

Konigsberg Castle, East Prussia
The Amber Room Gala
1942

Rainer stared at his tuxedoed reflection in the small oval mirror that hung in his sparse quarters. Every nerve felt as if on fire, each muscle threatened to burst with tension. Thoughts of home and of Josef, vivid in detail, flashed in rapid succession, and he fought mightily to push them away. He briefly wondered if being among the upper guard of the Nazi party would change him, touch him with their poison. He felt a simmering hatred oozing like pus from the deep infection inside. Rainer whispered to assure himself, as he felt for the Star of David beneath the starched white shirt. *You are not like them. Remember, you were forced to be here.* He felt guilty, yet simultaneously excited at being able to view the re-created Amber Room in all its ambient glory. Brushing his dark hair in place one more time, he made his way through the cavernous stone hallways of the castle admiring its gothic arches and windows. For a fleeting moment, he saw himself and Josef as mischievous youths, running through the massive castle, a fortress fit for curious exploration and hiding. Of a certainty, they would have spent endless hours among the rooms and courtyard, chasing boyhood fantasies and fun.

Inside the priceless chamber, as workers scurried about to address the remaining details of a perfect gala setting, Rainer stood motionless as the gilded room came to life in the light of hundreds of candles. Even the ceiling glowed with a reflection of golden fire, as did the candelabras, vases, powder boxes, and even the sprinkling of chairs and tables strategically placed throughout the room.

"A magnificent kunstkammer, would you not agree?" Dr. Rohde, meticulous in attire and groomed to perfection, came to stand beside Rainer, raising his eyebrows to await approval.

"An invaluable art chamber, yes. It is breathtakingly stunning, Sir." Rainer continued, "The guests should be arriving momentarily. Is there anything else you wish me to take care of, Dr. Rohde?"

But the architect of this recreation was admiring the outcome of the gargantuan project, eyes scanning every detail. He seemed lost in the quiet nobility of the now completed room and continued as if he had not heard the request. "Did you know that most of Europe's precious amber comes from a vein deep in the Baltic Sea? Konigsberg was, in fact, a major port of amber trade during the days of the Teutonic Knights. Frederick I discovered the vast amounts of raw amber stored in his palace."

"Yes, Sir." Rainer was, in fact, relieved to talk about that which felt comfortable, safe, and normal, as he gazed about the finished room and responded eagerly to Dr. Rohde. "The craftsmen of that era, Schluter and Wolfram, perfected the techniques of softening the amber pieces with the exact amount of heat and pressure to render them more malleable. Once they were flattened and smoothed into pieces that could be fashioned together to create the mosaics, they implemented honey, linseed oil, and cognac to enhance the color and lustre of the newly built walls. With the thin silver and gold leaf used to back the wooden panels and skirting board, the room was impeccable in its original glory, no doubt. If I may offer my observance and congratulations, Dr. Rohde, it is difficult to imagine any setting more splendid than this, recreated in a more modern but true to the original state."

Dr. Alfred Rohde turned to face Rainer, taking off the dark round spectacles that he wore and wiping them with a linen cloth. He smiled with appreciation. This young intern had been of great service to him. Not only was he knowledgeable for one so young, he was adept at executing proper protocol for when to speak and when to remain silent. "Thank you, Rainer. You have been of great assistance to me and indeed to the Third Reich. Your eagerness to learn and your hard work will not go unrewarded."

Rainer rubbed his hands together, trying to conceal nervous energy and latent guilt at any association with Nazi Germany. He could not shake the image, nor the guilt, of a captured Josef as he responded the best way he could. "I hardly know what to say, Sir."

"I see our guests are arriving. Would you be so kind as to check on the readiness of champagne before you begin assisting our patrons?" Dr. Rohde was already greeting German officers, dignitaries, and their wives before Rainer could respond. While retrieving the champagne, much to his chagrin, he noted that the bottles were all from the Moet region of his beloved France. Like most everything that now decorated the great hall, they, too, had been looted. He oversaw the delivery of champagne to Dr. Rohde and the newly arrived guests and noted that one was the infamous Hermann Goering, who looked nothing like his brother, Alfred. The Nazi Goering was a large man, heavy set, with a round and full face. He also recognized the newly appointed Reich Minister of Armaments and War Production, Albert Speer, and vowed to avoid being in proximity of him if possible. Seeking a less obvious station in the room and fixing his gaze primarily on Dr. Rohde, Rainer remained as invisible as possible, while offering a random glass of champagne or an explanation of an art piece's background. Immersing discussion in the work of art, specific techniques used in its creation, or the history of the artist kept him in the realm of beauty and normalcy and served as a means of isolating himself from those he loathed. Such a sad paradox, this gathering of elites, all of whom celebrate beauty, culture, and gentility, yet mete out unspeakable indignity and cruelty to other human beings.

"Ah, Rainer, I believe, if my memory is correct? Dr. Rohde's intern?" Albert Goering appeared, smiling alongside a stately German officer with closely cropped hair combed into submission and garbed in full dress uniform. There was an abundance of military insignia fitting to one designated with supreme importance. His eyes, ice blue orbs of cold steel, were set close together under the short blond hair, accentuating the long nose that sat above his pursed lips. Rainer found him disturbing, almost frightening to be near.

"Yes I am, Sir. How may I be of assistance, gentlemen?"

"Rainer, may I present the SS Obergruppenfuhrer, Herr Reinhard Heydrich."

Rainer stared at the emotionless man before him who neither acknowledged his presence nor spoke, but appeared to wait for a response from one deemed beneath him. Rainer did not recognize the face, but from both title and presentation, knew he was one of Hitler's top henchmen.

"Welcome to Konigsberg Castle and the Amber Room, Herr Heydrich. May I get you both some champagne?"

"Rainer, before you bring libations, could you lend us a bit of your exceptional expertise and tell us something of the process used to bring this room to such life and grandeur?"

Albert Goering smiled at Rainer as he clasped both hands behind his back. Reinhard Heydrich interrupted with an abrupt and harsh tone, speaking in a surprisingly high-pitched voice that betrayed his otherwise masculine and disarming presence.

"I must attend to my wife. Excuse me."

Rainer watched as the ranking official turned his back from them and meandered through the gathering to find Frau Heydrich. His thoughts were interrupted by Albert Goering, who spoke in a voice designed to appear normal but was hushed and urgent.

"I knew the details of the restoration work here would not interest him and he would take leave quickly. Herr Heydrich is a much-feared man. He has an assortment of nicknames, you know. The Blonde Beast. The Butcher of Prague. The Hangman. Young Evil God of Death. Hitler refers to him as, 'The Man With the Iron Heart.' He also chaired the recent Wannsee Conference in which the Final Solution to the Jewish Question was formalized. Do you know what I am saying, Rainer?"

Rainer stared at Albert Goering, recalling Friedrich Volk's mention of his rumored affinity for an anti-Nazi cause. He wanted to respond with a thousand questions but was unsure of what to say to this man of questionable allegiance, who now seemed more than willing to confide in him. Could Friedrich have placed them in contact with one another? Did this Goering truly despise the Nazis, as he did? He watched in confusion, as Albert Goering pointed toward one of the candelabras mounted high on an amber wall panel and leaned closer to Rainer.

"You must trust me, Rainer. We only have a moment before others notice any excessive association. Behave as if we are discussing the room and listen carefully. The Final Solution is in reference to the deportation and extermination of all Jews. Your friend is in grave danger. He was captured along with others in the Resistance and is being taken to Auschwitz for strenuous interrogation. I don't know about any of his remaining family members, but your family could all be in imminent danger, I'm afraid, if Nazis know of any affiliation. I will place you in contact with someone here in Konigsberg Castle, Klaus Ludwig, who will help you procure safe information about your family. He will contact you in due time. Otherwise, never mention this conversation and treat me with the same formality in which you address all Nazis. Never mention my name except to this Resistance contact. Do you understand what I am saying?"

Rainer steadied his breathing as much as he could at the reference to Josef and their families and attempted to appear calm. Inside he was a mass of confusion and panic. Albert Goering was talking about Nazi-sponsored eradication of the Jewish race and culture from all of Europe. Albert Taffel and his own Pepere had been right, all those years ago. But not even they could have known of horror of this magnitude. Rainer stared at the Goering who was secretly sympathetic, helping the Jews and others to safety, while his brother, across the room, was a minister of terror. He thought about the admonishment from his father regarding the wisdom to know when to act with conviction.

"Yes, Herr Goering, I understand. I know Klaus Ludwig in the tavern, and I will await his contact. Thank you for all that you have shared, hard as it is to hear. Please _I have to know _ can you tell me about the Jewish collection? What did Dr. Rohde mean when he mentioned it earlier today?" Albert Goering studied an amber panel for what seemed several minutes as he waved his arm side to side in front of it. He motioned for Rainer to also face the wall, with his back turned toward the celebratory gathering.

"My apologies for being blunt my young friend. You cannot react at all to what I am about to tell you. The skeleton collection is intended to be an authentic anthropological display of the "subhuman" Jewish race. Regrettably, when completed, it will be housed at The Reich University of Strasbourg."

"My God," Rainer whispered, barely able to breathe.

Albert Goering paused as he observed the blood drain from the face of the fledgling art professor. Watching him fight for control that threatened to go awry was both awkward and painful. Goering pointed once again, animatedly, at an emblazoned amber panel and spoke with authoritative firmness that was tempered with concern. "Pray for your friend. And hold on to what little truth and beauty seem left in this wretched world. Those are glimpses of the only heaven we might see for quite some time. I will do as much as I can. I must be on my way. I trust that you, Rainer, will find your way, as well."

Left in the wake of a tidal wave of information and emotion, Rainer felt his jaw grinding, a stress response he had recently developed. He stared at the amber covered wall while attempting to let the intensity of the moment pass. What manner of men were these who could even imagine such acts of horror, much less see them to fruition? Not men. These were the most hideous of monsters, housed in human bodies. They were beasts that had ceased to have any measure of conscience or compassion, that could murder even children as easily as they might kill a bug. What would happen to the remaining Taffels, perhaps to his own family, if any of them were caught helping Jews or anyone else the Nazis deemed as untermensch? Was there any truth and beauty really left amid this insanity? Rainer could barely find the wherewithal to remain in the room among the people who would inflict such barbarity to those he loved, much less serve them with enthusiasm. He grasped for faith, for hope as he remembered his loved ones, praying as hard as he knew how. Where was the way to end this reign of madness? How could all of this be happening?

Chapter Twenty-Three

Rastenburg, East Prussia
The Wolf's Lair
Late 1943

After the midday meal, the women huddled together in the courtyard. The brisk air had induced involuntary shivering, and conversation was limited to sparse words between them. As fresh air breaks were limited, they never complained about the weather but had learned to savor the climate of the Masurian Woods even in the grip of winter, and to enjoy the small tastes of freedom afforded them. Without warning four guards approached the captives. Two of the men placed themselves on either side of Sonne, while the other two, brandishing weapons in menacing fashion, maintained an aggressive stance toward the remaining women.

"You, come with us." One of the officers nudged her in the direction of the main bunkers.

"Why, where are we going?" Sonne resisted, sensing immediate danger and looking wildly around for Conrad, but he was not visible anywhere on the grounds that she could see. Even if he were present, she knew he could not betray his allegiance by helping her.

"Move, now! Mach schnell!" The Nazi officer shoved her forcefully away from the women, glaring at her and enjoying the authority he commanded. When they had moved out of sight, the guards pointed Sonne toward a small but equally fortified cement bunker with the same metal shutters, netting, and appearance of the other buildings. Once inside, they stood waiting for whatever was going to happen next. A strong medicinal smell seemed to emanate from every corner, and Sonne could feel the nausea rise, along with growing fear, as she saw a man in white scrubs, an apron tied about his waist, making his way down the bare hall to them. The man stopped in front of her and pushed the dark circular spectacles up on his nose. His face was round as the glasses he wore, and his smile was an undisguised show of insincerity and infatuation with the power he wielded. He attempted to take her hand, but Sonne withheld it by crossing her arms tightly. The man was unfazed by her resistance.

"Good afternoon, Fraulein. You have been selected to help your country by contributing to the Lebensborn Project in a very special way. I am most happy that you are here. I am Dr. Carl Clauberg, and I will be performing this delicate procedure."

"Wait, what are you talking about. What procedure? I don't know anything about a Lebensborn Project." Sonne began to feel a sickening fear in her belly growing with each spoken word. Dr. Clauberg smiled.

"Lebensborn. Living birth, the spring of life, the breeding of Aryan children by the union of those that are racially pure and healthy. The highest honor a woman can bestow upon her country. Gebe Dein Fuhrer Ein Kind. Give Your Fuhrer a Child." He paused before continuing with emphasis on each word, while watching her emotional turmoil grow and gloating in the authority he wielded. "Hopefully, in your case our crowning glory, a product of experimental insemination with the sperm of a chosen Nazi officer."

"A child? No! No, it's not possible. I am not married, and I damn sure don't want a child right now. I did not ask to do this, please! I am a food tester, I test the food for poison, do you not know that? I cannot have a child! There must be a mistake!"

"Fraulein, perhaps you do not understand. The Fuhrer himself has personally selected you to contribute to this undertaking. This is your duty. It should be your privilege, as well." As the guards pressed closer, Sonne tried to take calming breaths, remembering the strange words of Adolf Hitler and what she must do to survive, but the horror of the moment was too overwhelming to bear. Dr. Clauberg continued. "I believe we have perfected our work with insemination. Your menstrual cycle has been carefully monitored by close calculation and timely inspection of the sanitary materials discarded by you. If you are successfully impregnated, you will no longer be a food tester but will continue to be fed the best food. However, if you insist on resistance I can also inseminate you with animal sperm and allow you to birth a monster."

The soldiers laughed, showing appreciative amusement at the lack of compassion from Dr. Clauberg, and stared at her with lascivious intention. Sonne bolted for the door, unable to contain the instinct for survival only to be blocked by the officers who had escorted her to this nightmare. Terror beyond reason had taken over as guards now restrained her arms. One feigned tenderness, though the wicked whisper had volume enough for all to hear. "My, what a wild tigress you are! We would make beautiful, perfect German children. What do you say, Fraulein? If this does not work, want to give me a try?" More laughter from the guards ensued.

"No, no, no! How could you do such a terrible thing?" Sonne fought harder, but a cold, stinging sensation began to spread through her neck, back, and arms. Dr. Clauberg never displayed emotion, even as the drug took effect on his combative patient. The room grew gray, then black, and all sound disappeared before she was rendered unconscious. Soldiers lifted her now motionless body onto a gurney, and attendants rolled the stretcher to the makeshift operating room. The work of the Nazi Lebensborn Secret Extension Project was ready to begin. Two nurses raised the bottom of the gray uniform dress, removed an undergarment, secured restraints, and placed the legs of the patient in stirrups. Dr. Clauberg moved closer, issuing instructions for adjusting the light in the room and at the operating table, as all were prepped for the experimental insemination procedure. He would take his time throughout this procedure, doing what must be done to promote the best chances at pregnancy for this young woman.

When piercing light began to return, Sonne tried to rub her aching head but could not. She attempted to get up but to no avail. Stiff leather straps engulfed her body and ensured immobility on the cold examining gurney. Her legs, no longer in the stirrups, were also secured. There was a hum of activity in the sterile room and the two female nurses stood close by as Dr. Clauberg issued instructions. She tried to scream but her body was still under the effects of the anesthesia and she could only mumble soft, barely intelligible words.

"No! No, no child. I don't want a Nazi baby. No! Please, no!" One of the nurses, an older woman, leaned close to her ear, patted her head, and spoke in a voice intended to soothe but only incited more disbelief and terror.

"Dear, we are done. You don't have to keep a baby. The Third Reich will raise it for you, of course, to be part of a super race, to accomplish amazing feats for Germany. We will keep trying this process, until you prove to be with child. You are one of the chosen now. You should be happy for yourself and this baby."

Sonne became hysterical as consciousness increased. She began to cry, straining and thrashing against her bindings, as terror, shame, and fear overtook her once more. Dr. Clauberg stood at the head of the operating table, looking down at his patient, still no emotion evident in the pitiless eyes. Placing fingers on either side of her face, he stroked her cheeks. The action was devoid of compassion, but rather done with mechanical and icy precision as he brushed away wayward tears. Sonne felt as if thousands of ants were crawling on her skin. Closing her eyes, she tried to shake her head back and forth, but felt the fingers press more tightly against her jaw and forehead. She felt herself losing clarity once more as Dr. Clauberg offered parting words.

"This child will be a culmination of all we are trying to accomplish, Fraulein. It is done, for now. No more food testing for you. Your quarters have been relocated, as well. You may socialize with the other women when time allows, outside. I understand you are quite fond of Blondi, as well, and may continue to see her under the supervision of a guard or Herr Turnow, her trainer and handler. In time, I am certain you will come to appreciate your newly appointed role in the creation of a racially superior Germany." Dr. Clauberg turned to his assistants, wiping his hands clean and removing the white apron from around his waist as he issued final instructions. "A guard will return to carry this woman to new quarters when she is more awake, and he can see that she eats as needed. We will examine her again at the proper time. Please return the room to pre-operative status while our patient recovers. Lock the doors before exiting. That is all. Thank you for the excellent work today."

Sonne shut her eyes once more, consciousness ebbing and flowing like tides, and let the last of the tears roll silently down her face and onto the new gray gown she now wore. Praying mightily for strength to endure the days ahead and recalling Lida's prudent instructions to remain strong, she focused on all she cherished: the safety of her bedroom at home, her family, and the other women in the Wolf's Lair. She had come to love each of them, her adopted sisters, and longed to be with them once more. More than anything, she wanted to be far away in another place and time.

Chapter Twenty-Four

Rastenburg, East Prussia
The Wolf's Lair
Late 1943

The sound of a door creaking open, softly at first but then louder as it thudded against a cement wall made her more alert to the presence of someone entering, or perhaps leaving, the room. A female voice belonging to the nurse who had spoken to her sounded commanding and impatient. "There you are. Please take this one to the new quarters. I'm sure you are already aware that she has had a surgical procedure and is to be observed for a few hours, in case of any ill effects. Call for us, if needed. When she is able, be sure she has water and food, but do not leave utensils or other items in her room. Carry her gently. Stay with her while she eats. Keep her room locked, of course, and she is to be supervised, especially around the other testers outside."

With tender care, Conrad Dietrich lifted Sonne off the metal table, spiriting her out of the room before she could speak once more. His arms were reassuring and strong, and she felt an intuitive measure of comfort despite knowing that she would no longer be allowed to live with the other women. Twilight was mercifully beginning to invade the compound as Conrad whisked her away from earshot of others, his long boots making gentle impressions in the dark ground. Few were outside, as the evening meal was being served and most seemed oblivious to the pair.

"Sonne," he finally whispered into the soft mass of hair that hung across her face, "I'm so sorry, Sonne. Can you hear me?"

"Conrad," she breathed heavily, "I was praying you would be the one to come."

"Sonne, I didn't know. God, I'm so damn sorry. I'm so sorry. Don't speak any more. Don't say a word until we are completely alone, and then you can tell me what happened. I will stay with you as long as I can and we will find a way to get you out of here. I promise, I will do everything possible. I need some time to think of the safest way. You're going to have to trust me."

Sonne leaned into the dark warmth of Conrad's uniform, tears finding their way down her cheeks yet again. She wondered if it were possible to survive the unthinkable. If it were true, that these Nazis could impregnate a woman with donated sperm, what other atrocities must they be doing in the name of the Third Reich? How could one human being do such evil to another? Closing her eyes momentarily, she drew the deepest of breaths and anticipated the time alone with Conrad. It felt comforting and safe to be held close to his body. Trusting him would be necessary to survive, perhaps even to achieve a miraculous escape. Did he really intend to help her? Even so, Sonne knew she could never return home as long as these Germans were in power. Of a certainty, punishment for her escape would be inevitable and would put her mother in great peril, also, if Alsa were even still alive. As she sensed Conrad's footsteps slowing and saw the familiar, odious cement walls of yet another bunker building, she held fast to his jacket with her left hand and pressed her head deeper into his chest. He squeezed her back, and addressed the soldier at the door by name with an air of formality that Sonne knew was feigned. She kept her eyes closed.

"Rolf, open the door here and at her room so I can get this experimental one inside. I am to remain with her and see that she eats and is recovered completely before I leave. Will you bring the prepared meal? She gets the already tested stuff now, same as the

Fuhrer." The guard grinned knowingly at Conrad, reaching out to place a hand over Sonne's breasts.

"This is the prettiest and perhaps the youngest one of the bunch. May not be too bad an evening, my friend, with her still out of it." Conrad turned his body away from the officer and took a measured step back, as Sonne winced at the intrusive and obscene touch from a Nazi stranger.

"Nah, this one here is off limits, at least for now. But I want first go at her, if that order is removed. She's a sweet piece." Sonne listened, as intently as her body would allow, to the brief bout of explicit male banter and laughter that ensued and waited until Rolf was well away. Conrad placed her with the gentlest of care on the single bed in the stark room and pulled a blanket to her shoulders. He whispered with urgency, his eyes conveying deepest despair and regret.

"Speak softly, Sonne. The door is locked, but it is not sound proof. Should someone knock, stop talking and act as if you detest me. Maybe you hate me already. I don't blame you. Damn it, I am so sorry. I wish I could have stopped this."

Sonne nodded, wondering how it was that one could be so compassionate, while others embraced the hateful rhetoric toward anyone they chose. Gazing at the small rectangular windows atop the room, Conrad removed his hat and placed it on the small chest. Sonne surmised that his close-cropped head of hair might have one time been full of subtle waves. He struggled to look into her eyes. Fear of emotion that threatened to escape from the place deep inside where he kept feelings he dare not display bubbled at the surface and threatened to boil over. Staring out the slim row of high windows, he knew he had to be in command of himself at all times. A careless mistake might cost them both the ultimate price. Conrad whispered with conviction, clinching his fists, as he tried to erase intrusive thoughts of Sonne in peril.

"I want to kill these Nazi bastards myself. But I know that whether I came to be a part of them voluntarily or no, I will be considered just as guilty as these purveyors of terror. Anyone captured in the Wolf's Lair by the Allied Forces will most assuredly be shot or hanged with those who gave the orders to do harm. I promise you, Sonne. I will find a way to get you out. Perhaps both of us will make it. But you will get out."

Conrad stopped talking and came to sit beside her in the lone metal chair next to the bed. Resting elbows on knees spread wide apart, he massaged his aching temples with a vigorous motion as if doing so would generate the near impossible escape plan from the three security zones in the fortress. The momentary lapse into quietness was a brief respite from the inherent evil that seemed to be everywhere. Sonne felt both safe and fearful, though she knew the latter was likely the more realistic state. She found herself reaching for Conrad's hand as the need for reassurance and connection became overpowering. In the midst of the silence, she chose to tell him about the clandestine project and her horrific ordeal, though barely able to speak the words aloud. Somehow his validation of her, despite the shame she felt, mattered in a way that she could not explain.

"They held me down and gave me a shot of some kind. Dr. Clauberg said that I was selected for part of the extension of the Lebensborn project. I tried to fight, but I just couldn't. I don't remember anything he did to me, but he told me what he was going to do. They want to impregnate me with a Nazi baby. Dr. Clauberg said he could inseminate me with animal sperm instead, if I chose to resist. How could this be happening, Conrad? Testing food doesn't even bother me anymore. I hope to God it really is poisoned and you can get me some. That would be salvation now. I don't want to have one of their monster Nazi babies! How could they do this? How? What are they doing to those they really hate, if they could do this to me? They think they are the only ones of any semblance of worth. They've taken my humanity. I'm nothing now. A lab rat. A baby vessel to be used, then trashed." Sonne began to tremble, then sob, as her grief rushed in, a tidal wave of despair. Grabbing her shoulders, Conrad embraced her tightly as he dared, stroking her hair and whispering, his anger mounting.

"No, Sonne, no, you are so much more! Please trust me. I am going to help you. I will find a way. I can't stand seeing you hurt. I have come to care for you very much. Surely you must know that by now. I may die trying, but I will get you out of this place. I promise you, we will find a way." He held her to his chest, both his tears and hers dampening the dark SS uniform until her breathing slowed and she finally found the temporary haven of sleep. Conrad held her as long as his arms would allow, rocking her with intentional gentleness and wishing this moment could last.

When Sonne awoke the following morning, a military issue blanket had been added to her bedcovers and pulled over her shoulders where it brushed under her chin. A white handkerchief was folded around hidden contents and left on the set of drawers beside the bed, alongside a metal cup of water. Conrad was gone. With swollen eyes and a throbbing head, she reached first for the water and then for the handkerchief, unwrapping the tiny cargo inside. Two pieces of dark lakritzen, or salt licorice, had been left for her. They were Conrad's favorite candies that were rationed to the SS officers. Sonne bit slowly into the chewy goodness, savoring the feeling of warmth it rendered and decided to rewrap the other for Conrad. He loved her, though she had never heard him speak those words. They were not necessary. His actions conveyed the deepest affection, and Sonne knew now that he would risk his own safety for hers. While she cared for him greatly, she wondered if she could love him. So intense were her daydreams that she never heard the door creak open.

"Ah, you are awake, Sonne. I see you have found the lakritzen, as well. I hope you will also feel like eating? I have brought you some fresh fruit and toast."

Her face turned a light crimson at the interruption of intimate thoughts involving him. Sonne smiled while chewing more deliberately on the salt candy and motioned for Conrad to sit beside her. He smiled back, a genuine display of emotion and relief, as she combed through her long hair with her fingers and secured it into a bun atop her head, with loose pieces falling gracefully around her face.

"I can take you outside in awhile, although it is quite cold. I thought you might want to visit with the other women, or perhaps see Blondi, who shares your affection, also. By the way, I have managed to pull duty as the guard assigned to you, for now. I convinced them that I could persuade you to trust me about Lebensborn and participate with more willingness. I think it will buy us a day or two." Conrad lowered his voice before continuing. "I have an idea to get you out of here, to get us both out of here. But I need you to fully understand that we will likely be executed if we are not successful. I won't proceed further until I know you truly want to do it and understand the great risk involved. We don't have much time to prepare. With some smart and careful thinking, we just might be able to pull the damn thing off. But, Sonne, above all else, you cannot mention a word of this to anyone if we agree to do it. Not even to the women. No one."

Sonne nodded as she reached out to touch Conrad's hand. He blushed and leaned close enough to breathe in her softness, and smiled at her genuine expression of affection.

"So, how do you feel about a train ride with me?"

Chapter Twenty-Five

Natzweiler-Struthof Internment Camp
30 miles SW of Strasbourg; Alsace, France
1943

Dr. August Hirt, former SS medical chief at the time of the battle for France, now director of the new Institute of Anatomy at the Reich University in Strasbourg, closely examined the list of transfers from Auschwitz for the Jewish skeleton collection that were due to arrive this day. Although the original conception for the project included seventy-nine Jewish men, largely commissars in the Red Army who had been captured by the Wehrmacht, as well as thirty Jewish women, two Poles, and four of Asian descent, a typhus epidemic had reduced the final number of selections. Overall, Dr. Hirt was quite pleased with the reports of the physical measurements and general condition of the procured specimens. These candidates would be kept in Block Thirteen for approximately two weeks, where they would be moderately well fed to improve their appearance for the body casts of their corpses. Wishing to examine each one personally as they disembarked from the cargo vehicle, Dr. Hirt rose from behind the sturdy wooden desk and scanned the entrance area to the grounds of Natzweiler-Struthof from the picture window in his office, as he barked out instructions to the assisting commandant.

"Please confirm the remaining body count and procedure for this undertaking."

"Yes, Dr. Hirt. There are eighty-seven inmates present and accounted for: fifty-eight men and twenty-nine women. Photographs and anthropological measurements will be made and background personal data noted. Upon the induced gassing of each prisoner, anatomical casts of the bodies will be made before they are de-fleshed. The heads shall be separated from the bodies and properly formalin-preserved in a hermetically sealed tin can. Once all are received at the Anatomical Institute laboratory in Strasbourg, research on the skulls, with all noted pathological racial features, will be meticulously recorded for the display. Incidentally, Doctor, one of the inmates was a ranking member of the French Resistance, a close operative of Marcel Weinum. Clearly more intelligent than most but without the wherewithal to mount a successful uprising, it would seem. Typical Jew. However, he was deemed an appropriate physical specimen for this collection and thus was not executed at the time with the others in Stuttgart."

"Point him out to me upon arrival, Commandant, so that I might see this piece of untermensch."

In the receiving area of Natzweiler-Struthof, the officers unloaded the human freight in the bright sunlight, illuminating the frailty of the captured and the cruelty of the captors, against the backdrop of the rugged Vosges Mountains. They lined up in defeated obedience as each was inspected like cattle before their leg iron containments were removed. Though not malnourished as were most detainees, all had suffered the physical and mental effects of imprisonment. To the most casual observer the eyes of the imprisoned were destitute and empty, with all hope of salvation gone.

"You, step forward." The Commandant motioned for an officer to assist a male prisoner in separating himself from the line of Jewish captives. "You are the one captured with the Resistance?"

The prisoner stared past the guards into the beauty of the distant mountains, fixing his gaze on memories that only he could see and remained still and silent. His head, once graced with thick curls of dark brown hair, had been shaved close to the scalp but was held high. He stood in proud defiance, having reconciled with both fate and faith. The slow, deep breaths to steady his resolve were infused with the rancid smell of death. The horror of this place only served to enrage him further. He would never go without a fight.

"You will state your name and prisoner number," the guard commanded, as he pressed the barrel of a rifle into the abdomen of the Jewish man. "And you will do so now." But the vanquished one remained silent, as did the entire line of captive bodies, now devoid of spirit. The officer, sensing a brewing conflict he was determined to win, pressed the captured man further. "It seems that this one has nothing more to say, Commandant. Not so important, now. Not that he ever was." The guard, only slightly taller than the prisoner, inched closer to the resolute man, and whispered, trying to intimidate, to goad a response from this Jew. Their noses almost touched, and the barrel of the rifle now pointed at the expressionless face of the man. The guard glared at the determined captive he could not break. "I smell you, you stinking Jew. You vermin."

For a moment, the eyes of both men locked and held each other with contempt. Without warning but with lethal precision, the prisoner grabbed the barrel of the gun with his left hand, shoving it under the chin of the stunned guard while grabbing the butt of the weapon and pushing down hard on the now inverted trigger. In a violent explosion of blood and bone, the body of the officer, head barely attached and eyes still opened wide in disbelief, fell to the ground along with the rifle. Smiling with crazed eyes that embraced both victory and what would surely happen next, the prisoner turned toward his captors, arms and open palms raised. His entire body blood-soaked and reeling from the blast, he shook with the laughter born of release from captivity. In one last act of resistance, he lifted his eyes to the majestic mountains he had loved since childhood and saw the faces of those who had also loved him and shouted to the heavens.

"Josef Taffel, a Jew, you Nazi bastards!" And in a hail of gunfire, he was free.

Chapter Twenty-Six

Konigsberg Castle, East Prussia
1943

Rainer sat at a wrought iron table with benches, waiting in the cold noon air and sunshine of the sprawling castle courtyard for the contact provided by Albert Goering. Though the city of Konigsberg had been periodically hit by Soviet Air Force bombings, the massive castle with its genteel courtyard had remained intact. He often wondered if outside forces had any idea of the treasures still contained within. How ironic that fine art such as the Amber Room and other valuable pieces might be his saving grace, for now. If only he could know what was happening with his family, perhaps his mind could be more at peace. Simply thinking of home resurrected the sights and smells of the vineyard and of the Alsatian spice breads that Maman and Memere prepared. What he would give to be carefree once more, to run through the quaint streets of Colmar with Josef, looking for boyish adventures among the cultural beauty of its buildings, streets, and museums, and picking grapes at harvest time. Rumors of the cruel German-appointed gauleiter, Robert Wagner, abounded, and he feared for how his loved ones might be faring. The man was now known as "The Butcher of Alsace," and was as vicious toward those who sympathized with Jews as he was toward the Jewish race. Thousands had already been sent to internment camps and impending death.

"Good day, Rainer."

Rainer looked up from his musings and greeted the friend who offered him a freshly made hot pot of weisse bohnensuppe and a small loaf of pumpernickel bread. "Ah, Klaus, bartender and cook extraordinaire of the Blutgericht, I see you have brought some amazing cuisine. I feel guilty eating as wonderfully as we do compared to the rest of Europe during this godforsaken war. I've actually grown quite fond of this white bean soup. My mother would love it, as well. How goes it today?"

Klaus Ludwig laid the metal kitchen tray on the table beside Rainer and swung long legs over an iron bench. He had opted to work in the castle restaurant and tavern while attending school, and eventually made the transition to full time work there to assist his own family during wartime. His father had managed the establishment before him, and upon his death from sudden illness, Klaus had felt it his duty to continue the family culinary and libations enterprise. German heritage ensured his safety as well as a livelihood, instead of relegation to Nazi military service. He had cultivated a secret partnership with Alfred Goering, thanks to local underground resistance workers, and had volunteered to assist Rainer into the fold as another covert operative. Typically, he would share any news of the Alsace area and the war in general, or news that might impact Konigsberg and the castle. Today would be much more difficult.

"Rainer," Klaus paused, removing his gloves and knitted scarf, "I hardly know how to tell you. I am afraid that the news today is very bad." He looked away for a brief moment, giving Rainer time to reflect while he chose his words as carefully as possible. Observing the deep pain and compassion in the eyes of his friend, Rainer set the food on the iron table and leaned forward with his forearms, fingers locked together in a tight grip, and waited for the inevitable.

"My family?" he whispered, watching Klaus for clues.

"No." Klaus said softly, shaking his head. "Not your family."

Rainer looked down, then upward across the courtyard walls into the sky and trees beyond the castle confines as understanding dawned, though he fought to push it aside. But the inevitable came at him like a bullet he could not stop and exploded full force.

"Josef?" It was a statement, more than a question, as he and Josef both had considered this horrific moment, but now Rainer could not escape the juggernaut of sudden grief, the merciless tears creeping in, uninvited. His whole body ached as if he had been beaten until the breath left his chest.

"I'm so sorry to be the one to bear this news. He was transported to Natzweiler-Struthof from Auschwitz, where he had been interrogated prior to selection for the skeleton collection. Josef understood what was going to happen to him there, I'm sure of it. He made an unbelievably courageous decision to act, though I doubt it will surprise you. Rather than obey with meek compliance he managed to overpower a Nazi officer, which was quite a daring feat. Josef killed him in front of prisoners and officers alike. He knew full well the guards would shoot him instantly, which they did. He chose this, Rainer, on his own terms, not theirs. What a brave and honorable man, your best friend." Klaus paused, placing a reassuring hand on Rainer's shoulder for a brief moment before removing it and taking a seat across the table. "It may give you some comfort to know that before he died, Josef shouted his name and allegiance to Judaism," Klaus smiled. "Then he called them the Nazi bastards that they are."

Rainer smiled at the thought of Josef's brave defiance. His own body began to shake with loss so heavy it seemed he would suffocate under the weight. He wept with abandon for his friend, as the scene played out in his imagination. Cradling his head in both hands, he knew he would never be able to rid himself of the images. Josef, imprisoned and tortured, screaming, and wild-eyed. Josef, bloodied and ripped open, those brown eyes forever frozen in time. Josef, being the most stubborn, brave, and valiant man he would ever know. Defiant to the end, just as he said he would be. Josef's smiling face the day they tumbled out of Eglise St. Martin, in their youth. Josef, dead, never to roam with him again. Josef and the damned judensaues. Wiping eyes that were now swollen and red, Rainer looked at Klaus, trying to smile.

"*Memento Mori*, my friend. You did it." Rainer tried to find composure and solace as Klaus raised his eyebrows, his lips twisted into a questioning gesture. "*Memento Mori*. It is a significant reference from our childhood. Even in death, Josef made his life mean something more. So damned stubborn. He would never fully concede to Nazi atrocity." Rainer instinctively reached for the Star of David underneath his shirt. "Neither will I."

Chapter Twenty-Seven

Rastenberg, East Prussia
The Wolf's Lair
Late 1943

The day had been monumentally sad for Sonne, despite the prospect of escape that would take place this night. She tried to quiet the hypervigilance, as every nerve pulsated with anticipation and fear. The risk of leaving brought the possibility of freedom, and of death, which she had decided would be a welcome fate if the only other option were life in the Wolf's Lair. Yet, leaving the women who had become her family for more than a year, without being able to tell them goodbye or how much she had grown to love them, had proved challenging and more heart wrenching than Sonne could imagine. She made note of their faces and names, writing the history of each in her memory as best she could. Conrad had assured her more than once of the need for complete confidentiality about their plans, and while she knew he was right, her heart ached to tell them goodbye, to promise that she would find salvation for them all. Each time she was allowed an outside visit, she had found herself overcome with emotion. The women never suspected anything other than perhaps that she missed them. They cried with her, unaware of the dangerous plan. Blondi, too, had responded with unbridled affection, wanting to jump in a greeting of joy despite the training designed to negate the canine habit. If dogs could intuit the unspoken, as Oma had always told her, then Blondi too would carry her secret.

After the evening meal Sonne tried to nap, but to no avail. Now she sat on the edge of the metal frame bed, waiting patiently in the dark for Conrad. He had been painstakingly thorough in his instructions to leave behind what few possessions she had. With the exception of a photograph of her mother and father which had been removed from the frame and hidden in the pocket of the drab gray uniform she still wore, she was careful to leave her temporary quarters appearing as if nothing were amiss. It was an easy task, as she wanted nothing from this hell to remind her of the horror that had happened here. Sonne placed a hand on her belly, praying that she did not carry a child with her but quickly pushed the thought aside. This night she must not dwell on that possibility, but only on the here and now and making a successful escape.

Once more she nervously removed the combs holding her hair at the nape of her neck and twisted the soft chestnut waves into yet another bun, securing it more tightly this time. The escape plan had been made quickly, born of both necessity and availability. Joseph Goebbels, Nazi Minister of Propaganda, had been meeting with all high-ranking officials for most of the afternoon, with dinner and a rambling routine lecture by Hitler being the culmination of the day's military strategizing. As the administrative schedule was fairly rigid and therefore predictable, Conrad had remained confident that the train returning Goebbels to Berlin, where he also served as gauleiter, would leave some time after midnight and travel the approximately three hundred fifty miles with few stops, if any. The Wolf's Lair was entrenched in landmines to assure no entrance into the fortress by intruders. Unless the location of each mine was known, escape could only happen via the road into the complex, which was unlikely given the extensive security. The rail system ran the length of the compound and directly through the middle and was the only other possible route of escape. It was also the least guarded area, being under the assumed total control of the Nazis at all times. An extra munitions and supplies car usually served double duty as the rear lookout of the train, occasionally holding additional baggage for the occupants. A guard was routinely assigned to boxcar duty, though most of the SS officers detested the assignment, as it meant extended time in Berlin in the company of the demanding Goebbels as well as the uncomfortable train accommodations. Conrad had easily secured the assignment for this trip.

At night there were few signs of life emanating from the Wolf's Lair, as metal shutters were closed to ensure heightened secrecy and security from air visibility and attacks. Most were asleep at this late hour, with only a minimal number of guards focusing on the outside perimeter of the compound rather than the center. Though the moon was an eerily glowing sliver of an orb, thick clouds hid most of the light and provided a fortuitous measure of added cover as a uniformed Conrad Dietrich made his way to Sonne's room and rapped softly on the metal door. Two quick taps followed by a pause and two more taps. Recognizing the agreed upon safety code, Sonne opened the door and closed it behind him. She looked radiant. Her face, freshly scrubbed, reflected eager anticipation. She brushed away the soft wisps of hair that had abandoned the rearranged bun. Her wool gabardine overcoat was buttoned across the dull gray dress that inched out from underneath.

"Remember the plan, Sonne," he admonished, Say nothing until I tell you to speak. If we are stopped, follow my lead."

Sonne nodded in compliance, eliciting a brief smile from Conrad. She squeezed his hand, looking into his eyes with a focus and calmness that belied the odds they faced. Neither spoke as they stepped into the quiet hallway and made their way to the farthest side of the building, closest to the Masurian Woods that surrounded the entire headquarters. Once outside the cold air was gripping, as if a stark reminder of the limitless danger of their undertaking. All was quiet and black. Sonne was grateful for the bleak darkness that masked her growing apprehension. Together they had agreed the risk was worth the chance of freedom, and now there was no turning back. If they had remained, even in the event of liberation, the likely consequences would be execution, as they would be aligned with the Third Reich either way. The Allied Forces would have no way of knowing their true allegiance. To Sonne, there had only been one clear choice.

"Slow down, Sonne. Careful steps." Conrad reminded her gently, as she had begun making rapid strides in front of him. "We will be there shortly."

When they caught sight of the train, they crept along the edge of an adjoining building on the woods side until they reached the tracks next to the loading area where the train was awaiting the signal for departure. Conrad held her arm tightly, guiding each step with his left hand while holding his rifle with his right. A Luger pistol with an extra magazine was tucked securely in the rucksack on his shoulder, along with a small canteen of water, a goodly sum of money, a handful of lakritzen, and instructions for Sonne, if dire circumstances should necessitate such once they departed the train. She had been reluctant to master the mechanics of shooting the pistol, but had learned as much as she could without actually being able to fire the weapon inside of the compound.

"Stop!" he whispered suddenly, his voice beginning to reflect the urgency of the moment as he lunged forward again to place a firm hand on her shoulder. "Do you see the back of the train? When I say, you walk quickly to that spot with me. I will get you inside. Then I need to be sure that all in the Goebbels party are loaded and boarded. After that I will let the main guard know that I am ready, as well. Remember, do not speak until I tell you. Follow my lead if we are discovered."

Sonne breathed in the cold air and tried to quiet her fears. Conrad had thought of everything. He took a last look at the surrounding landscape. It helped that the Wolf's Lair was kept as dark and quiet as possible at night, with few outside, to foster lack of detection by enemies. He gently nudged Sonne forward. Together, they walked at a pace just short of an all out run to the back of the modified boxcar. Conrad placed an arm around her waist and hoisted her to the first step of the platform, which was elevated a fair distance from the ground. Opening the door, he motioned for her to lie on the floor in a far left corner of the car, away from the small door window, and covered her completely with a military issue blanket.

"I will be right back, I promise. Remain completely covered, just in case. Stay here and don't make a sound. So far, all is according to plan." Conrad whispered, patting her shoulder.

Sonne lay quietly in the dark, thankful to be on the train at last and yet terrified at the prospect of capture. Holding tightly to the warm blanket she closed her eyes, awaiting Conrad's return and praying for safe travel. The quiet of night in the Wolf's Lair seemed more magnified than usual. Her heart beat wildly with anticipation. She could almost hear it in the silence, pounding inside her chest like a church bell. Sonne wondered what would happen in the morning, when an attending SS guard came for breakfast and found her missing. Would her friends be happy, or even know, that she had escaped? Perhaps they would be hopeful that they, too, would make it out. Would they understand why she did not confide in them? Would they be questioned about the escape, or punished? Unwelcome panic gripped her throat, and she found herself struggling to breathe normally, as visions of Dr. Clauberg and the makeshift surgery room clouded her mind once more. Closing her eyes tightly, she tried to imagine her family, including Oma, together once more all around the warmth of a glowing fire. Her thoughts were interrupted by footsteps on the steel platform of the train. Two soft taps, followed by two more. Conrad slowly opened the door.

"Don't speak yet. Stay quiet and still." He spoke barely above a whisper. More footsteps could be heard crackling across the hard ground down the length of the boxcar toward the door. Sonne held her breath. Another German voice, deep and commanding, issued a muffled check call as he knocked on the wooden door. "Alles gut!" Conrad replied quickly, rapping on the door in return as he set the lock bar and assured the guard that he was ready for departure. The footsteps moved once again beside the car, loudly at first, then retreating into the stillness. Finally, the great steam engine began to grind forward. "It's safe now, Sonne," Conrad said under his breath. "You can come out now."

Sonne pushed the blanket from around her head and felt the anxiety began to subside. A folding military issue cot and pillows, with extra blankets, had been placed nearby, along with a lidded bucket to be used as a toilet at the far end of the compartment. Conrad perched on his knees beside her, bathed in the eerie light of a dimly lit lantern, removed his SS hat and coat, and grinned a broad, deep expression of happiness as he bowed his head in her direction. She was taken aback by the newfound normalcy in both his appearance and demeanor.

"Your carriage to freedom, as promised, Milady. My sincere apologies for the meager accommodations, however." Sonne tried to speak, but the words drifted somewhere far away between relief that flooded her thoughts and an irrepressible sense of apprehension for what the future might yet bring. Even when danger was done, would she ever be able to escape the irreparable damage that haunted her every thought? She tried to look away, but this time there was no hesitation as Conrad rushed to embrace her tightly as he dared, stroking the hair he had longed to touch and whispering reassurance.

With his promise of a new beginning, she released a fraction of the anguish and terror of the past year to one who was more than willing to take it from her and collapsed in his arms.

""Shhh, it's okay. Sonne, by breakfast time in the morning when they discover you missing, and then put the pieces together to know that neither you nor I are where we should be, we will be hidden away and on the next step of this journey. They will be on the lookout, of course, but I am confident we will prevail with our plan. Oh, I almost forgot!" Reaching into the rucksack, Conrad retrieved a light green dress with three-quarter sleeves and a cloth covered belt. "I bought this for you in Rastenburg. I hope it fits. You will have to forgive me, if it is too big. I figured that would be better than too small. At least the belt will make it work until we can get you something more suitable."

Sonne held back more tears as she felt the softness of the dress against her face and breathed in the newness of the garment. She was finally free of the prison garb and a step closer to the life she once owned. Conrad turned his back to her as she donned the dress and took the pins from her hair, releasing the soft curls into cascades around her face.

"What do you think?" Sonne smiled, placing her hands on her hips and raising her chin. "Do I look like a fashionable lady?"

"You look the height of fashion, Miss Becker," Conrad stated, pleased with his choice, then added, "but you have always been a lady to me, no matter what you wore."

"It is beautiful, Conrad, and you didn't need to buy it. Thank you for such a generous gift."

"My pleasure. Oh, if you are hungry, I have some rations and plenty of lakritzen, of course. If you'd rather sleep a bit, the cot is yours. Or, if you want to talk, I'm not going anywhere for a few hours." Conrad smiled, his eyes warm with a sincerity that was intoxicating. Sonne sat beside him, pulling a blanket over their legs and reaching for his hand.

"Really, thank you, Conrad. I'm deeply grateful to you and forever in your debt. You have risked everything to help me and I will never forget that. Right now, I'm too wide-awake to sleep, and I'm not hungry. Well, perhaps a piece of the lakritzen. You have me hooked on that treat." Sonne returned his smile warmly and kissed his cheek. Despite the low light, she could see the blush on his face and was amused at his newly displayed vulnerability to her. "But now," she hesitated, squeezing his hand, "please, I want you to tell me the whole story about you, all of it. Tell me how it was that you came to be an SS officer. Tell me about your family. I want to know about who you are."

Conrad shed the blanket and stood slowly, stretching to his full height of over six feet as he spread his hands wide. "I'm just above a hundred and eighty two centimeters. An SS soldier had to be at least as tall as Heinrich Himmler himself since he is the commanding officer. He is much shorter than I, so as you can see, I mastered that requirement fairly easily. The only time in my life that I did not wish to do so." He paused briefly, reaching for the pillows and another blanket from the cot, and handed one of each to Sonne before settling back on the hard floor next to her. Reclining on one elbow he began to relax. He had been reluctant to tell her much before this moment. Now, he wanted to tell her everything, to allow her deeper entry to a part of the past he held with regret. Somehow, it would make a difference.

"I am the oldest of five siblings, and was usually required to set the example as we were growing up. I was an exemplary eldest, very compliant when it came to matters of family, even when I disagreed. That happened with more frequency with each year of age, which I suppose is not so unusual. My father became disillusioned with the government when I was approaching adolescence. After a cut in his pay and tougher times set in, we moved and I spent the remainder of my formative years in Munich, where he met Adolf Hitler at a rally. My father became enamored with the National Socialist German Worker's Party and eventually could talk of nothing but his firstborn son being a part of the new movement that he thought would help so many. Then, he saw it all as dedication to the common good, to a strong Germany. I think he let his anger and frustration convince him that Hitler was going to bring about needed progressive change. As far as many were concerned at the time, he was just another political aspiree, although a very charismatic one. He made people believe in a better, more prosperous Germany. We did not have any close friends who were Jewish, so I suppose it was easier to choose to be neutral about their status and to pretend that it didn't matter. The talk of them and of others being less than human did not happen immediately, but came about rather insidiously. I am sure that my father did not see the horror at first, though I wonder now what he would think if he were here. He has since died, but not before seeing two of his sons become Nazis."

Conrad glanced up at Sonne, pain evident in his face, as she sat hugging her knees to her chest and listening to details of the family saga, of his fall into the Nazi nightmare. Her sea green eyes softened in the pale light of the lantern as the train hummed over tracks to a new life, and he found himself secretly wishing to preserve this time with her forever. Though he wanted to tell her just how much he had come to love her, he knew, perhaps more than she, of the necessary time needed to deal with the horrific experiences she had been forced to endure. Instead he smiled, enjoying the moment he wished would never end.

"Where was I? Sorry, I was lost in a daydream, I guess. But anyway, since I had always been taught to respect and obey those presumably older and wiser, I only minimally attempted to dissuade my parents at the time, particularly my father, from the idea of my becoming a German soldier. By that time he had managed to convince most of the family to believe the party rhetoric, though I'm fairly certain my mother was not happy when I was actually conscripted into service. A few of my siblings were active as Hitler youth, so you can imagine the excitement when the family was told I had been selected for Waffen-SS recruitment. Then, the soldiers were considered even more elite like the ancient Roman Praetorian Guard, I suppose. I was very athletic, hardworking, fit, educated, of sound character, and considered racially pure. A perfect candidate, in the eyes of the government at least. All I knew was that I should please my family and make them proud. I'm not sure I can ever erase the guilt I feel now."

Sonne heard every voice inflection, observed each movement of his body, as Conrad described his youth and indoctrination to her. She felt his need to share the shame of it all. It seemed they both had a terrible burden to bear.

"Conrad, listen to me. You were, and still are, a good son, and an even better human being. I will never forget all you did for me. The women there in the Wolf's Lair, they knew it. They all said you were kinder to them, especially when other guards were not around. All of the horror that these monsters are doing happened gradually. No one could have known for sure what was going to happen. Evil often initially masquerades as gray, not black and white. Please continue. What happened when you were selected?"

Conrad bowed his head and ran tired fingers through his hair and across his eyes before raising his gaze to Sonne once again. "Since then, qualifications have been eased as the need for more Nazi soldiers continues to grow. When I was selected for Waffen-SS duty, I was highly trained, then sent to the secret Wolf's Lair. At first, I was more isolated from the happenings outside, though we all became more familiar with the Fuhrer's wild rants and growing evil intentions as the Nazi march for power continued. He also was becoming more unhinged, and we were made aware of work camps that were in fact death camps, too. By then it was indeed too late, and those of us who secretly abhorred what Nazis embraced – and there were more than one would think - had to consider our own safety and survival, as well as that of our families, so we were somewhat forced to blend into the madness and sell our very souls. So, yes, there are definitely soldiers who are unwilling to divulge their true feelings and loyalties, for fear of repercussion. I wonder if we will ever be able to be rid of the guilt. As for my family, my mother is now dead, my sisters were in Switzerland, and I don't know about where my brothers are, or even if they are alive. I pray they will remain safe until this war is over, and that we can be reunited."

"Conrad, wait." Sonne could almost feel the ache inside him, like a malignant tumor that attached itself to his every thought, fed on the guilt he bore, and now created more fear for what might happen to his family. "Conrad, what you are doing for me, for both of us, is the bravest, most courageous, most noble thing I know. You have chosen to act in the name of all that is good and decent and sane, despite the risk of your own death. I'm terrified at what may yet come. But, because of you, I have a chance and I want to do what I can to help, too! You are very special to me, Conrad."

As if drawn by forces unknown, Sonne reached a hand to cup the curve of his face. Conrad put a hand over hers, felt the softness of her, and leaned close enough to feel the warm, sweet breath on his face. He traced the full lips with his fingers before pressing the gentlest of kisses there and wrapping her as close to his heart as he could.

"I adore you, Sonne," he whispered. "I've got you and will do all I can to keep you safe." She closed her eyes and reveled in the warmth and security that was Conrad Dietrich. Resting an arm around his strong shoulder and the other across her belly, she thought about what could be and pushed the intrusive thought away. For now, fear of the unknown would have to wait.

Chapter Twenty-Eight

Berlin, Germany
Late 1943

"Sonne, wake up. We're almost there." Conrad nuzzled her with one hand while unwrapping the blanket from around her shoulders with the other. He had been over the escape plan hundreds of times in his head, but staring out the small window in the boxcar door at the familiar land sliding by, with each framed scene putting them closer to a chance at freedom, he wondered if all the attention to detail would pay off. The endgame, the risk of both death and a new life was upon them, as the final piece of a daring plan was about to happen. Sonne shook off the remnants of sleep and stared at Conrad. While she slept, he had replaced the Waffen-SS uniform with casual dark pants and a light blue work shirt with leather bound suspenders. He had shed any evidence of association with Nazi Germany. He looked completely different and more handsome than she had thought possible. *Like a caterpillar to a butterfly,* she mused.

Conrad missed her appreciation of his changed appearance, as he was now hypervigilant of the task at hand and fully engaged in activating their escape plan with the precision of battle strategy. "Remember Sonne, whatever happens, keep moving and act as if you are supposed to be there. Blend into the crowd as best you can. I transferred the contents from the rucksack, which I will keep, into the bag I brought for you, along with a hat. This bag is more suitable for travel for a lady and the hat will also make it harder for you to be identified. With these, along with your coat, you will look more like one who lives here rather than an escapee in that old gray uniform you were made to wear. Besides, and no disrespect intended here, but soldiers will be much more interested in finding me than you. But if you were to be discovered with me, you would be killed or taken back for more of the same at the Wolf's Lair. Otherwise, they will likely not look for you any longer."

Unless they thought I might be pregnant with a Nazi officer's baby, perhaps. Sonne squashed the intrusive thought, but she knew the possibility would remain an albatross for some time to come. Conrad motioned to a fashionable looking Swiss Army bag sitting on the cot. There was a shoulder strap along with two buckled straps on the front, and the leather was of the highest quality. An Alpine hat sat next to the satchel. Sonne slipped on her overcoat, twisting her hair back into a pinned mass underneath the new hat and attempted to smile through growing apprehension. "They are beautiful, Conrad. I can't believe the pains you've taken to make this all possible."

"Everything you need is in that bag, just in case. Emergency instructions and plenty of money. Lakritzen, too." The faintest hint of a smile flashed and disappeared as he lifted the strap of the bag and placed it over one shoulder and across her body. "I'm leaving a bit of intentional evidence on the floor, with a few other items for them to find. The crumpled up note there will indicate train departure and arrival times. The impression will be that we are headed possibly to Bremen, or more likely to the port city of Hamburg, which would allow water routes to escape to Sweden. There is a train leaving for Hamburg shortly after our arrival in Berlin, but of course we will not be on it. Hopefully, they will spend their time looking in that direction while we continue on our way. When I tell you to go, do not hesitate at all but hop off the platform and then keep walking at a normal pace through the terminal. Go out the closest exit away from this train, then down the street to the Gasthaus. Get some café, look over the instructions in the bag, and wait for me there. Say as little as possible to others, but if anyone asks, remember you are just passing through enroute to family in Hamburg."

"I wish we did not have to leave separately, Conrad. I feel much more secure with you." Conrad's eyes danced and appeared to brighten, though he remained focused on what was about to happen. Sonne wondered how long it would take him to reconcile the part of his life that had been spent as a Nazi. Perhaps helping her to safety would chase some of those demons away.

"This is the safest way, Sonne. I will be right behind you, once I get you off the train. But we cannot acknowledge one another until we are well away from the station. Are you ready?" Conrad motioned her to join him by the door. Stepping into the cold, pre-dawn Berlin air and onto the platform, Sonne felt as if every nerve were on fire. As cloudy fingers of gray light began to creep across the sky, Conrad studied the front of the train like a hawk looking for prey. With one of his hands gripping her shoulder, Sonne could also feel the mounting tension as she clutched the satchel strap across her body. When the steam engine slowed almost to a stop, she could feel Conrad's grip become more intense, then release. She knew it was time and vowed not to disappoint him as she readied herself to make the leap toward freedom.

"Now, Sonne, go!" She never hesitated, making the jump off the platform with both feet, as Conrad gave her the gentlest of nudges. The landing was solid, even though the grass was still damp with a crisp wintergreen fragrance. With a cursory adjustment of her bag and coat, she walked with purpose toward the closest entrance to the station. As she knew, there was literally no turning back now, though there was a sense of desperation in wanting to know that Conrad was close behind. Inside the dim light of the terminal, she scanned the layout for the closest exit that led to the side of the station away from the train tracks and began walking in that direction. A small crowd of people migrated through the early bustle, with just enough motion that Sonne could easily blend in with the rhythm of their movement. But as she approached the first intersection, each heartbeat pounding as she made the right turn toward the intended exit, a commanding voice pierced the early morning, blaring out each word from the entrance to the terminal.

"You, Dietrich! Stop!"

Sonne froze, as did other onlookers, and watched in disbelief. A defiant Conrad, eyes and lips pursed and arms and legs churning, began racing for the intersection moving in an intentional leftward motion, away from her. He mouthed only one word, as their eyes met. *"Go!"* Sonne's shoulders sank as she turned her back to the horrific scene, knowing she could not help him. Damming the flood of tears threatening to escape, she wound her way out of the station. Surely her heart would break in two before she could get out. She could hear his voice in her head as she tried to think. *No matter what happens, Sonne, keep moving. Survive. Remember the plan.* Scanning the passersby, she approached an elderly couple in front of her. Though their backs were to her, they exuded an aura of kindness and protection by the tender manner in which they held onto one another while walking away from the station. "Excuse me, please. I am new to Berlin. By any chance, are you headed into town? If you don't mind the imposition, might I walk in that direction with you, or could you help me be sure I am headed the right way?" She tried to force a smile but could feel the tears, merciless and brutal, an unstoppable tidal wave now cresting and threatening to break. "I am headed to the funeral for a relative, and I am just so overcome and tired."

"But of course, dear. We have a daughter about your age. How sad for you to make such a trip. We have a car and would be honored to give you a ride."

"Thank you so much," Sonne whispered, wondering if Conrad made it to safety. "I am very grateful for your assistance." Her voice trailed off into nothingness. She slid into the backseat of the Kdf wagon. As the man cranked the engine to a warm hum, a single gunshot blasted from the other side of the station. No one moved. The three looked at one another in stunned silence. Sonne felt her whole body buckle under the weight of now unfathomable grief.

"We need to leave here immediately," the man swore under his breath. "It's no longer safe anywhere, damn them all."

Sonne closed her eyes, clasping her hands together and pressing them hard against her forehead. The sound of the shot fired and vivid images of Conrad running for his life were now ingrained forever in the deepest recesses of her mind. He had been her last hope, and she had yet to tell him she loved him. For a moment consumed in regret, she found herself entertaining the dangerous idea to join him, to jump out of the car and run toward the officers and shout her allegiance to him. Perhaps death would be the best solution now. Somehow her fingers, as if guided by Conrad himself, unfastened the satchel and found the folded instructions he had left. Sonne read each word, finding strength and solace in them as if he were sitting beside her. Conrad had known this might happen and had made her safety a priority, even above his own life.

"My Dearest Sonne, it is my hope that you and I are reading this note together, and that you will keep it always as a reminder of how much we overcame to find freedom. If I am not with you in body, then know that I will most assuredly be with you always in spirit and in faith – and that I am rejoicing in the knowledge that you will be spared from more indignity and cruelty. Your safety and happiness are my greatest desires. Live well, Sonne! I love you. Forever yours, Conrad."

"Dear, you are crying!" The woman reached for Sonne's hand. "Let's get you out of this place, away from all this madness." *I may escape, but how can I ever be rid of the madness?* The thought stung like a violent slap across her face. Sonne gave a best attempt at a smile and nodded in agreement. As the car eased into growing Berlin traffic, she glanced at the last part of Conrad's instructions. Konigsberg.

Chapter Twenty-Nine

Konigsberg, East Prussia
Early 1944

Konigsberg Castle was breathtaking, even in wartime. The massive bell tower rose into view like a great Poseidon from the nearby Baltic Sea. Sonne shivered underneath the overcoat and Alpine hat and clutched the treasured satchel to her chest as she made her way to the front gate of the castle. The long train ride from Berlin had allowed the intensity of all that had happened to soak in like the coastal winter air that blanketed the city. Upon trying to contact home she discovered, according to an old neighbor, that her mother had recently died after a brief illness, and the Nazis had seized the family home and its contents. Though she had never received word, Sonne knew her father was likely dead, perhaps even executed by his own government. She now embraced her status as an orphan and vowed in the memory of Conrad and her family to pursue the journey to freedom, wherever that path might lie. She maintained a firm stance at the entrance gate as guards scrutinized every detail of her youthful beauty.

"I am here to see Herr Ludwig, in the Blutgericht. He is expecting me."

"Excuse me, my apologies, Miss. I am Rainer von Bauchelle. Klaus Ludwig is occupied with unforeseen stocking and purchasing issues at the moment, I am afraid. I also work here in the castle. If you will come with me, I will be most happy to escort you directly to the Blutgericht." Ignoring the guards, Rainer motioned for the young woman to follow him along the outside path to the castle wine tavern. "May I carry that satchel for you?"

"No, thank you, I can manage." Her fingers held the straps on the bag in a vise grip against her side. She stared ahead of him as they walked without speaking. Even if he had not known something of her plight, he could almost see the immensity of sadness that was evident in the way she carried herself with slow and painful movement. Her green eyes were pools of untold sorrow. But in her, he also sensed the reserves of strength and compassion that defined a rare beauty and character. When they were out of range of the sentry guards, he stole a glimpse of the wisps of chestnut hair that had fallen from beneath her hat and brushed against her cheeks.

"What is your name?"

"Sonne Becker," she said, still without looking at him.

"Miss Becker, I have become a close friend of Klaus Ludwig, through our professional association here in the castle. I don't know much about you, but I do know that you have been through a most difficult and painful ordeal in getting to Konigsberg. For whatever that may be I am so sorry. I do understand at least a small measure of your loss." Rainer took a deep breath and lowered his voice, unsure of whether to share his vulnerabilities with this stranger or not. But he felt compelled to reach her in whatever way he could. "I just lost my most cherished friend. His name was Josef Taffel. He was a Jew, shot at Auschwitz while committing a most daring act of bravery. I'm very sorry for whatever you have endured, and for the loss of any who were dear to you. Klaus has arranged for your housing and has a position for you in the tavern here. We will help you as best we can, I promise."

At the show of heartfelt kindness by one who had experienced a similar loss at the hands of Nazis, Sonne felt her composure weaken. Tears of relief and sadness gathered in the corners of her eyes. She was so tired of crying, so tired of living in fear. She blinked hard and raised her eyebrows skyward to force the tears away. It was an old trick her mother had once taught her, to keep from being emotional in public. It worked more often than not. But this pain was too intense and the tears trickled out, merciless and hot, as she tried to wipe them away before this man could see them.

"My friend, his name was Conrad, and he was a man who became a Nazi soldier to appease his family. He never wanted to be a part of such a brutal regime and shouldered tremendous guilt for having been any part of it." Sonne spoke as painfully as she moved, her words only reinforcing the agony that Rainer could see. "The two of us were going to make a new beginning, far from all of the hatred. But I think it is everywhere now. I have no more family left and nowhere to call home anymore. I'm pretty sure I will never truly be able to escape the enormity of this loss."

Rainer hesitated before responding. This Conrad had been much more than a friend to her. She had lost family, as well as the person with whom it seemed she might have planned to spend the rest of her life. No wonder the devastation was so deep. He stopped walking and pointed to a nearby bench underneath a patch of trees. "I know it's very cold, but perhaps you would like to sit a moment before we go inside? I am so sorry. I did not know what Conrad meant to you. Please forgive me if I have been intrusive. We can just sit without talking before I take you to the Blutgericht, if you like. I know you've had a hard journey, Miss Becker."

Sonne nodded and sat, removing her hat and smiling at him for the first time as the frigid air seemed to be a refreshing balm. His breath caught somewhere in the back of his throat and Rainer understood, in an instant, how easy it had been for Conrad to love her. Light auburn hair tumbled beneath her shoulders. Her childlike innocence, despite what she had experienced, only heightened her beauty. Rainer had never felt an attraction such as this. He sat waiting for her to speak, wanting to know how she and a Nazi soldier had come to care for one another enough to attempt a perilous escape, and all that had happened in the past that made her the woman before him now.

"Please forgive me, I don't mean to be rude. Call me 'Sonne'. And thank you for your kindness. Yes, it has been most difficult, and I am grateful to Conrad and all of you in this network who have risked helping me to get this far. If I can just find a place to settle until the war is over, I can find my way. I'm actually a dedicated worker, a quick study. Who knows, perhaps when my head is more together it will only take a dozen repetitions, as opposed to a hundred, for me to learn a task or two in the castle."

"We won't hang you from the bell tower if it takes awhile to adjust, Sonne. That's a beautiful and unusual name, by the way."

"A nickname from my grandmother. Short for 'Sonnenschein' because she always said that I was her sunshine. I hope I can live up to that name now."

Despite the tragedies that had marred her life and left her with no one for support, she was persevering. Sunshine indeed. Such was a mark of true integrity, and he found himself drawn to her even more. He imagined what Josef would think of his instant infatuation and could almost hear the teasing whisper. *Damn, she just lost the man she loved! Besides, she's way out of your league. I think you better call in some reinforcements, my friend. But not to worry, your wingman is here! 'Jew need all the help you can get in the arena of love!*

How he wished his best friend were here to chide him. One day, perhaps the world would know of all those such as Josef, Conrad, and now Sonne. Rainer wondered if he could ever be free of the guilt that plagued him and live up to the honor and bravery that defined the friend he loved and missed, and now the courage demonstrated by this woman. If he were lucky, she would allow him the pleasure of her company in the days to come.

Chapter Thirty

Konigsberg, East Prussia
1944

Since her arrival in Konigsberg, Sonne had been a source of joy and hope to Rainer despite the bleakness of war. She was becoming knowledgeable in every aspect of tavern operation and shared in his love of wine and winemaking. They often took their noontime and evening meals together, along with Klaus and other staff. When good fortune prevailed for Rainer, meal breaks were spent with only the two of them, talking in a quiet corner of the castle or walking about the courtyard, unless either was summoned away for additional duty. On occasion, they were invited to the home of Klaus and his family to share in a meager meal.

This afternoon, Sonne had accompanied him to the Prussia Museum, housed within Konigsberg Castle, to see the extensive library collection. Now they stood in the center of the Amber Room, past closing time for the general public, and experienced its majestic splendor. Rainer watched in satisfaction as Sonne perused every detail of the fiery amber and the gold and jewels ensconced about the room.

"It is magnificent, Rainer. This place seems to have a radiant glow of its own," Sonne whispered, as she turned to face him. "Though I am honored to be here, it saddens me that it was stolen, as were so many pieces that we have seen today."

"Perhaps one day, all will be restored to their rightful places of exhibition, and the world will be as was intended." Rainer mused. "There will be nothing Nazi left."

Without warning, Sonne turned from him, covering her eyes with a hand. Soft sobs crept from the painful place where she hid her deepest fears. How could she tell him?

"Sonne, what is wrong? Did I say something to hurt you? Please, I am sorry. Talk to me." Rainer rushed to her side, pulling her to face him, as he searched her eyes for clues.

"It's not you, Rainer. It's me. I can't keep this inside much longer. I don't know what to do, I'm so scared."

Rainer studied her face, watching every move as she struggled to reveal her secret. "Sonne," he spoke in a hushed tone, "Whatever it is that is hurting you so, I am here. I am your friend, no matter what it is."

She stared into the golden panels of amber and up into the ceiling, wishing for some kind of healing to wash over it all and end the nightmare she had hoped would never happen. "You are wrong, Rainer. There will be something Nazi left." She stepped back, placing a hand on her belly as her eyes pleaded with him. Unwanted tears made their way down her cheeks, making tiny droplets on her blouse.

Rainer paused feeling his heart shatter, as understanding sunk into his bones. He had to choose the next words with care. "Sonne, having Conrad's child is nothing for which you should be ashamed. It will be all right."

To his surprise she laughed through the tears, looking upward once again and wringing her hands before finally meeting his gaze. "If this child were Conrad's, that might be true. I'm afraid it is of a more sinister nature."

Rainer could do nothing except stare in silence as he imagined the worst possible violation against her. Appropriate words were nowhere to be found. He went to her, wrapping her body as close as possible and stroking the softest of hair. Placing both her hands and head on his chest, Sonne sobbed in uncontrollable sorrow, her tears soaking his shirt. The revelation of her secret had been simultaneously cathartic and painful, like an infected wound that had just been lanced.

"Tell me what happened." Rainer offered. "I've never asked you. It was your information to share, and I did not want to intrude. But you know I want to help you."

"Do you know of the Wolf's Lair?" Sonne whispered.

"I have heard mention of it by Dr. Rohde and knew it had something to do with Hitler, but I never knew for sure. What is it?"

"It is Hitler's secret eastern headquarters, just outside of my hometown of Rastenburg. It was built in 1941 and is still being fortified. The Nazis used Jews and other prisoners of war to build the facility, keeping them for six-month periods and then sending them to the death camps. By constantly rotating, isolating and even killing their workers, the Nazis kept an added layer of secrecy and security. I was kept there as a food tester." She stopped momentarily, looking at Rainer for both absolution and strength. She had tried to fight the growing feelings she held for him, but could not. In him, she saw the same depth of character that Conrad had possessed. He continued to hold her, his brows furrowed in question as his fingers tightened about her shoulders.

"A food tester?"

"For him, for Hitler." She hesitated before continuing, her voice barely audible. "There were fifteen women. Fifteen incredible women who all became my friends, my sisters. We had to eat the food before he did to be sure it was not poisoned."

"My God. Sonne, I had no idea. I'm so sorry."

This time Rainer held her with unbridled affection as he felt her tears dampen his chest. She began to reveal the horror with which she had lived for the past two years. The nightmare tumbled out like an unstoppable flood.

"The SS guards watched us eat his meals before they were served to him. Some laughed at the women who cried or vomited with fear. We became a family, never knowing when any of us might die. Conrad was a guard there, but he was not always with us and of course could not control what happened to us. We became friends, though we could not communicate much with one another right up until we made the decision to risk an escape. No one else knew how we felt about one another, though I know that some of the women suspected as much. I guess I would not even admit it to myself. One day, SS guards took me to a bunker there, a makeshift medical room of sorts. A doctor there said that they had been doing experiments with insemination. He said I was chosen to help perpetuate the Nazi regime as part of a special extension of the Lebensborn project by having the child of a high-ranking Nazi. I tried to get away, but of course could not. There was no way to escape the three security rings or the landmines, even if I had miraculously managed to get out of that torture chamber. The doctor said he would inseminate me with animal sperm and I would birth a monster, if I were unwilling to help them."

Sonne stopped long enough to wipe her eyes and breathed as deeply as she could. Finally, someone could know her secret. Rainer waited, sensing the need for patience, as she shared the rest of her ordeal. "Once I was inseminated, I was isolated from the others and fed the very food they were forced to test. Sometimes I still feel sick to my stomach when I try to eat, just thinking about them. They are still there, and I could not even risk telling them I was leaving. But Conrad found a way for us to try to escape before the doctor could further examine me or try the procedure again. Train tracks run through the middle of the compound, so rail presented the best

178

possible means of getting out. Joseph Goebbels, the Reich Minister of Propaganda and a horrible man, had his own personal train. Late one night after all day meetings of the members of the Third Reich elite, Conrad managed to sneak us both into the back boxcar of Goebbels' train, minutes before it left the Wolf's Lair. But in Berlin, they caught Conrad after I had exited the train and was inside the station. I escaped. He did not. I saw him run and heard the shot after he was out of sight. He ran deliberately away from me, so that I would not be discovered. He knew we both had a better chance of escaping if we were not seen together in the train station. I will never forget what he did for me, never."

"He sacrificed himself for you," Rainer said aloud, as he silently paid homage to Conrad's bravery and affection for the woman he had also grown to love.

"Yes." Sonne smiled, as the tears welled in her eyes once more. "As best as I can figure, I will have a Nazi baby between September and October. May God forgive me, I wish this were not so. This poor innocent has a horrible Third Reich monster for a father and a mother that feels beyond guilty for wishing that it would never be born. Does that make me an evil person, too? What will I tell this child? I can't let anyone else know I'm pregnant, I can't! If the Nazis here found out who and what I was, they would send me somewhere to have this baby. They might even kill me for escaping the Wolf's Lair with one of their SS guards. I'm not showing now, but it won't be long before I do. What do you think I should do, Rainer? I've made it this far, but what now?"

"I don't know, Sonne." It was the most forthright answer he could give. "At least I don't know right now. But together we will find a way. Conrad got you here. I will help you with whatever comes next, somehow. Do you trust me to do whatever I must to make that happen? You and I can figure it out together. Klaus can help us."

Nodding her head, she glanced upward at Rainer and planted a gentle kiss on his cheek. He took her in his arms again, this time as more than a friend, and kissed the softest of lips, feeling his body and soul aching to belong to her. "I care for you very much, Sonne. I think I have done so from the moment you arrived here. We will figure all of it out. For now, just take care of yourself. This is not the child's fault, you know. Answers will come, in due time."

Sonne gave a weak smile. *So will this baby.* She kept the thought to herself as Conrad held her in the serenity of the quiet museum, quietly searching for an answer. There was one person who could execute this much of a miracle. He wondered how long it would take Klaus to contact Albert Goering and if the good Goering would agree to help them, even if a way out were possible. He remembered something Friedrich Volk had said about the tunnels underneath the castle and smiled. Perhaps Friedrich had knowingly given him a way. Tomorrow he would seek them out when time allowed.

Chapter Thirty-One

Konigsberg, East Prussia
June, 1944

In the dim candle light of Klaus Ludwig's sitting room, Albert Goering crossed his legs, shifted left in his chair to face Rainer, and pondered the observation made with regard to the vast differences between him and his Nazi commander brother.

"It is an odd relationship, mine and Hermann's. As brothers, we are close. We are also different in almost every conceivable way. He is stocky and heavy, with blue eyes. He loves politics and power and embraces loud, bombastic behavior. I am tall and slender, with brown eyes. Musical. Hopefully, a bit more cultured, a lover of the ladies, perhaps even charming." The younger Goering smiled broadly beneath his moustache, and reached for a cigarette and lighter. Klaus set glasses of port on the hassock tray and went to pull the thickly woven curtains across the picture window. "Hermann knows full well what I do. He does not make any attempt to stop me, as long as I don't get caught doing anything to get him in trouble with the Nazi elite. It is our odd way of expressing loyalty as brothers, all of the scholarly psychologists might say. So, in addition to excellent contacts in Moscow, London, and the United States, I have what one might refer to as a bit of protective immunity, I suppose. In the past, I have been most fortunate to use it judiciously to assist Resistance efforts in a number of places. As export manager for the Czech factory Skoda in Brno, I asked for workers from the Theresienstadt concentration camp. They filled a truck up with them, all those wretched damned poor souls. I drove it into the woods and released them. It is perhaps the most wonderful feeling I've ever experienced."

"I don't understand," Klaus frowned. "So despite your differences, people just give you whatever you ask?"

"Because I am a Goering, they tolerate me, though I am certainly a source of annoyance to some." Albert Goering smiled, dragging off his cigarette.

"So you think it may be possible to get Sonne and me safely out of Konigsberg?" Rainer ventured.

"Yes, I believe it can be done if we exercise great caution and plan with prudence. I believe I can get you to Sweden via a merchant ship, and then to the States with your young lady."

"How long will it take to make these arrangements?"

"I can procure the necessary paperwork and credentials that you will need in due time. If I may inquire, what is the urgency with getting out of Konigsberg now?"

Rainer and Klaus exchanged glances. For a moment, no one spoke. Albert Goering poured another glass of port.

"Sonne is pregnant. Of course, she does not want to deliver the baby here in this place, in the middle of war."

"I see. If I may be so bold – is this child yours?"

Rainer hesitated before responding, looking directly into the eyes of the brother of one of the most cruel and powerful Nazis. "No, not mine. But I have asked Sonne to marry me, and we will raise the baby as ours. I love her very much and accept an early start to our family. We have plans to be married next week, in the cathedral tower. Klaus has arranged for a priest to do the nuptials."

Albert Goering tapped the ashes from his cigarette and puffed several times before speaking. "Please forgive my bluntness. You have said that she was held at the Wolf's Lair prior to coming to Konigsberg Castle. Is this baby a Lebensborn child? Was it consensual sex with an officer, or was she raped? Or was there someone before you?"

Rainer stared, momentarily caught off guard by a subject he had not been prepared to broach. "Yes. The whole ordeal was a part of the Lebensborn project, Sonne says. It was rape. But, more complicated, I'm afraid. She does not know who the father is. She escaped the Wolf's Lair, where she was forcibly made to be a food tester for Hitler, then used as part of an experiment with insemination. All they told her was that she would have the baby of a high-ranking Nazi or be inseminated with animal sperm. She fought with everything she had."

Albert Goering crushed the remains of his cigarette in a nearby ashtray, and lit another, as the smell of fresh tobacco permeated the sitting room. "There is apparently no limit to the barbarity and inhumanity with which they will act if it serves their purpose, my brother included."

"Herr Goering, what exactly is their purpose, besides creating a racially pure Germany or European Empire?" Klaus asked, as he reached for the bottle of port.

"Why that is simple, really. World domination. Certainly, you don't think they intend to stop with this side of the Atlantic, do you? Hell, Adolf Hitler has broken every treaty, every promise he's ever made. He becomes more delusional with each passing day. What confounds me is how he enticed men and women, German citizenry, and legions of young people, with much more capacity for reason, to become pawns in his insidious game. He is as charismatic as he is demonic. But the Allies will prevail in the end, as they have now invaded Normandy en masse with Americans and are closing in on victory and an end to this living hell. The Axis powers are losing, though they will never acknowledge that until the bitter end. It won't be long before Konigsberg is attacked yet again by either the Royal

Air Force or the Red Army. This time, I believe it will be decimated. And when liberation is impending, all of the precious cultural collections will be moved by the Germans, or else they will be destroyed in the attack."

Albert Goering studied both men through the smoky glaze, watching the serious expressions on their faces. "Rainer, you will soon be assisting in the dismantling of the Amber Room and Castle Museum and in preparing other works of art for secret transportation to Berlin, or perhaps the salt mines and caves throughout Germany. Konigsberg Castle will be all but abandoned, if not completely destroyed. The Nazis have no intention of returning any of the paintings, jewelry, books, manuscripts, money, or any other of the countless items they have stolen. Many thousands of expensive collections and other pieces will be out there somewhere after this war is over, with little to no way to adequately trace the provenance gap for them. Art repatriation, if you will, will be a massive effort that will extend far past my time, or perhaps even yours. Some may never be found. Most importantly, there will be those who will stop at nothing to protect or retrieve these valuable items. They would even kill for them. While it will take decades to find and return stolen goods to the rightful owners or their remaining families, thieves will be relentless in tracking down where they are and stealing them, yet again. Then there are the countless forgotten children who have been saved from the death camps who no longer have parents, and those whose parents have been killed because of their allegiance to an Allied cause. The consequences of this holocaust and war will be felt like waves from an earthquake, throughout the continents. So, yes, I can help you."

Rainer beamed at Klaus, who nodded his head in agreement, as they offered their appreciation. Albert Goering, brother of one of the most brutal purveyors of Nazi terror, smiled in return as he made a request of his own.

"There is something, Rainer von Bauchelle, that you must do for me, and for many who have been unfortunate casualties in this tragedy of worldwide proportions. It will be no small endeavor and will come with great risk and impact to your life. You have said that you stand ready to act, even if it means sacrifice. I will hold you to that promise in return for your chance at safe passage. I will also find out about your family and try to get word to you as to their whereabouts and safety. If they are still alive, you will not be able to communicate directly with them for a very long time, I am afraid. Let me be direct. I need you to transport as many valuable pieces of art as we can manage to secure, as well as take some of the aforementioned children to safety in the United States. This endeavor will also carry risk of your being associated with theft of Nazi stolen goods or being labeled a collaborator. We can discuss the details of a plan once they are finalized. Will you agree to these terms?"

Finally, absolution for him might be possible. Rainer imagined Josef's face and those of the judensaues staring at him from the past. Now was his chance. Perhaps the demons would not haunt him forever.

"Yes, I will do whatever you need."

Albert Goering leaned forward, balancing forearms on his knees, and studied Rainer's face.

"Do you know of the tunnels that run beneath the castle to the Pregolya River and the Baltic Sea?"

"I have heard of them, and think I know where at least one entrance is."

"I will make you a map and give it to Klaus. You must memorize everything and keep it hidden. From this point on, I will no longer be in Konigsberg. Klaus will help you finalize the details."

Rainer thought of all those he loved, of his beloved France, and of his father's insistence that he would know when to act when the time came. Finally, he might make a difference.

Chapter Thirty-Two

Konigsberg, East Prussia
July, 1944

Rainer held his pocket watch inside a tight fist as the hour hand approached midnight. He had been awake for over an hour watching Sonne as she slept, her gently bulging belly rising up and down and barely noticeable underneath the layers of clothing. He had smuggled her into his room after the evening shift in the tavern so that they would be prepared to escape in the most efficient manner. They both thought it best to keep their marriage and the impending birth of a child a secret for as long as possible. He wondered how this all would impact Sonne, having to endure yet another life-threatening attempt at freedom. She was a strong woman, but this, along with her pregnancy, would most certainly affect her for years to come. Now she rubbed the sleep out of her eyes and used her fingers to comb the thick hair into submission. As soon as the bell in the massive tower began to sound, he motioned for her to follow. The great sound of the booming bell would camouflage any noise they might make as they slipped into the dark hall and made their way through the cavernous corridors to the closest tunnel entrance. Glancing at their surroundings, Rainer pulled the door of the turret open, guiding Sonne within and closing it behind them. Once inside, he whispered a reminder of the plan to reach the docks.

"We will feel our way to the bottom because we can't use a lantern as long as there are windows. At least we will have a small bit of light from the outside. It will only be for a handful of floors. Once down to the sub level, I've left a lantern, so we can find our way through to the exit. When we get to the docks, we assume our

187

new identities. Rainer von Bauchelle and Cotterena 'Sonne' Becker will be relegated to history, for now at least. Are you sure you are ready for that?"

Sonne squeezed Rainer's hand and smiled as she pulled her hat further down her forehead.

"As long as it is with you, I will manage. I know who and what I am. I meant to ask you earlier. 'Catherine and Ray' are appropriate American names for us and shouldn't take long to get adjusted to, but how on earth did you come up with the last name of 'Easter'?"

Rainer grinned, pulling out the Star of David underneath his shirt, now with a silver cross that had been added to the chain.

"You know, Easter. Resurrection. New life. A new beginning, though we will never forget the old. Maybe one day, we can be a part of whoever remains in the von Bauchelle and Becker families, when the search for lost treasures of art is no longer a priority. For now, you and I are enough. Sonne gave a weak smile and found solace in Rainer's embrace of their future with this baby, and any other children they might raise. She was happier than she had ever been, and yet there was a visceral sadness that clung to her heart like frost. Surely it would disappear along with her buried secrets when they were safely out of Europe. As they made their way through the damp and lantern-lit sub tunnels toward the docks and the Swedish merchant ship ramp, Sonne clung to that hope as tightly as she held Rainer's arm. Fear had become an ever-present mainstay in her life, though she fought mightily to keep from being consumed by it.

"Guten abend. Aren't you the girl from the tavern? It is a late night for a stroll, don't you think? What are you both doing out at this hour?"

The German sentry stepped in front of the couple and brandished his weapon as he questioned their presence outside the castle gates. Rainer put an arm around Sonne's shoulder and responded with precision and confidence brought about by days of painstaking anticipation.

"Yes sir. Please allow me to introduce my new wife. I work in the castle, as well, with Dr. Rohde in the museum and Amber Room. We are on our honeymoon, and of course we cannot leave the city. But we wanted to pretend we were strolling the moonlit streets of midnight in old Paris, instead. A fantasy, of course, but we beg you to allow us that small courtesy, please?" Rainer motioned to his side, unbuttoning his overcoat and pulled the left flap open enough to retrieve a bottle of wine provided by Klaus in the Blugtgericht. An inscribed note was secured to the tag on the bottle. "This was intended to be the bribe for whichever guard was at the gate when we returned from our quiet evening out, with our own wine by the waters. We just wanted our special day to last a little longer before returning to our lives inside the castle and the rigors of war."

The guard read the inscription aloud: "We appreciate your helping us to enjoy a brief reprieve while we celebrate our marriage. Many thanks. Enjoy."

"Please, we just want a little more time to ourselves," Sonne offered. "You understand, don't you? I bet you have a loving wife or special girl?"

The guard perused her from head to toe as she smiled at him with unabashed flirtation, and clung tighter to Ranier's arm, taking a cue to utilize her femininity.

"Please," her eyelids fluttered up and down, "we just want a little while longer to enjoy what we can of a honeymoon until Germany wins this war, and we can celebrate in a more fitting way. You can keep the wine. It is a superb red. Please say you will help us?"

The foot sentry hesitated before returning the bottle to Rainer and bestowing a faint smile upon Sonne.

"Perhaps you will allow me a drink in the tavern sometime, then?"

"But, of course," she replied, returning his smile. "I will be there tomorrow and the remainder of the week."

"Have a good evening. Don't be out much longer. Congratulations on your marriage."

The soldier called over his shoulder as he made his way down the boardwalk toward the main castle entrance. They held their breath until the guard was out of sight, finally sighing with relief as their bodies leaned against one another in the chill of the night air.

"When hell freezes over, you can have that drink!" Sonne spat the words out with a sarcastic bite when the sentry was out of earshot.

"Sonne, my love, it appears that your beauty ensnares the strongest of men," Rainer teased as he hugged her close. "You have triumphed and I am so proud of you."

"Well, some men are also quite gullible," she quipped, placing a light kiss on his cheek. "Ignorant bastard! Not like my husband!"

Carefully glancing around the perimeter of the docks in case other sentries were lurking about, they made their way up the ramp to the docked vessel as rapidly as they dared. The Swedish merchant ship was emblazoned with the large blue and yellow field and the word "Sverige" was painted on the sides and deck, to indicate the ship status as a neutral Swedish vessel. Most of the cargo to be delivered in Konigsberg had been iron ore, wood, tungsten, and sardines. The smell of fish and salt added an inescapable thickness to the air already pungent with the scent of ore and coal. On this return voyage, the ship would carry payment of Nazi gold and quantities of coal back to Sweden. Sonne hoped the conditions would not sicken her. Now seven months pregnant, she was still well hidden in her overcoat but had experienced bouts of morning sickness. She knew that the sea route they would travel would be safer than most since Sweden had trade arrangements with both the Allies and the Nazis, all in an effort to keep Sweden insulated from participation in the war. Sonne thought it fascinating that Sweden could remain untouched amidst all the atrocities and wondered how long it might be before the Nazis decided they wanted to capture the neutral haven. Regardless, she knew that this was the best possible way to make a safe and rapid departure, and that Sweden had agreed to allow them safe but anonymous passage. With the assistance of Albert Goering, whose connections she surmised were as vast as the Baltic, they had managed to find a window of escape. The grizzled sea captain glanced at the passports with only mild interest as he motioned them forward.

"Welcome aboard, Mr. and Mrs. Easter." His speech was hushed, but clear. "I'm sorry that your sleep accommodations are of the steerage variety, as this is not a passenger vessel. We should be putting out to sea as soon as the remainder of the shipment is ready. You may make yourselves comfortable and walk about the ship as you choose, once out to sea. However, I suggest that you remain below deck, out of sight in your designated holding area until we are safely out to sea. Even though generous compensation has been made for you on this voyage and the smallest of protective details have been made, we are still under the auspices of Germany until we set sail and are well out of port. You might want to check on your cargo that has been stored below. The rest will await you in Stockholm, I am told. Try to get as much sleep as possible. You will be in need of it for the second leg of your journey to wherever it is that you are going. Breakfast, meager as it will be, and strong coffee, will be served in the morning. I trust that the remainder of the trip will not be too demanding for you. So far, conditions are favorable for optimal travel. Good night to you both."

In the haze of lantern light at the bottom of a steep and narrow stairwell, two cots with pillows and heavy blankets appeared etched in the center of the darkened cargo hold. Sonne swallowed hard as her eyes adjusted to the scant light. Rainer squinted as the windowless perimeter of the room came into focus and went to examine the wooden crates stacked floor to ceiling among the built-in shelves.

"How much of this is ours? What in the world will we do with all of it?" Sonne asked.

Rainer ran an outstretched hand down the length of a second tier crate marked with a designated red circle and found the large secured metal box that had been tucked behind. It was where Albert Goering said he would find it. Without hesitation, Rainer placed the box on one of the cots and opened the lock with the key he had received. Inside, a note lay atop a mass of coins and paper money. He grabbed Sonne by her shoulders and his voice shook with excitement as he read the words penned within:

"Safe travels and best wishes for a happy life. *Memento Mori*."

"By God, he did it! A damn genius! He stole the mother lode from those Nazi pigs! Their own money! I can't even count how much!" Rainer fought to contain emotion. "Not just the money. Art, Sonne! Books, jewels, more! Saved! Priceless, historic stolen art! I had no idea it would be this much! It's part of what Albert Goering meant when he said we have to return the favor. It will take years and secret work with those who can help us, but we can right a piece of the wrong. Think of it! One day it will happen, my love!"

Tears rose in his eyes as he pulled her close and whispered.

"We will do this for Josef, for the women in the Wolf's Lair! For our families and all of Europe that faced the atrocity of the Third Reich!"

Sonne began to weep with him at the thought of the women still in captivity. Try as she might, the sadness never went away. Sometimes it lurked, as an ominous shadow, rather than dominated her thoughts. But it never left her. She prayed their efforts would alleviate the pain she could not shake.

"What is SC? Is it a code of some sort?"

"South Carolina. The tiny southern state where we will live that borders the eastern side of the Atlantic. I'm told we are going to be on the outskirts of Charleston, South Carolina, which is where I hope to find work at a college there. Our home will be in the beautiful and pristine little outlying town of Summerlea. The people are supposed to be hospitable and less concerned with the prim and proper trappings of the more cultured Charleston, or so I'm told. They will be less concerned about the details of our background, and it will be easier to assimilate into small town life. A church there will help us get settled. I know we have talked about our story, but let's review again. They think we have been living and working in Finland and believe that we have collected funds from generous benefactors to help the orphaned children we will bring with us from Stockholm. Of course, we know that part is technically true. A generous and brave benefactor, indeed."

"About them," Sonne gave a slight tilt of her head and smiled, as she rubbed her eyes, then her belly, in an unconscious maternal gesture. "About the children saved from the death camps. How old are they, do you know? You never said how many there might be. Do we know anything about them?"

"Albert Goering didn't say, exactly, so we don't know much at all. Fifteen. Maybe more. We will take all that we can and the church and community has pledged to help us. A plane will transport us all to the Army Airfield in Atlanta in the American state of Georgia, and a bus will take us to Summerlea, South Carolina. Arrangements have all been made."

"My God. I can't even imagine being a child and facing life without my family. Do you think Europe will ever be free from the Third Reich? Will we ever be able to go back there? I hope the women were able to escape somehow. I pray it every day."

"I don't have those answers, my love. But one day, Mrs. Catherine Easter, we will find out."

Sonne smiled. They were almost home, even though it was to a place they had never been.

"Well, Ray Easter," she whispered to her husband, "do you know anything about your von Bauchelle family?"

"No, not yet," he whispered back, stroking her hair as he held her close. "Albert can hopefully get news of them all perhaps. I pray they too are safe." Silently he wondered if they were still alive, or how long it might be before he would ever know anything about them.

Chapter Thirty-Three

Colmar, France
von Bauchelle Winery
1944

"Your effort to hide Jews and other undesirables to Germany was daring and rather ingenious, I must say." The German officer, tall and commanding, motioned to the spider web-enhanced wall that had been opened to reveal a hiding room, as other officers went about the task of gathering bottles of cremant that would be confiscated for Nazi consumption. "It is regrettable that one with such skill and passion for the winemaking craft decided to make a most unfortunate, and shall I say, stupid and traitorous decision to harbor the undesirables. You could have been a part of the most glorious country this world has ever seen. I will ask you one more time. Where is Rainer von Bauchelle?"

Albert von Bauchelle, restrained on each side by soldiers, stared into the cold eyes that regarded him with disdain. He raised his chin in proud defiance.

"I was a part of the best, before the Nazi vermin arrived. I don't know where my son is. But if I knew I'd never tell you. Vive la France!"

In one sweeping motion, the officer drew back a gloved hand and struck the elderly man across the face with enough force to buckle his knees. Blood gushed from his mouth. Albert hung motionless, suspended between the arms that held him, as drops of crimson dotted his shoes and the ground below. Alain struggled against the officers that also subdued him, and pleaded for the life of the remaining von Bauchelle patriarch.

"No! Please don't hurt him! He's an old man! Surely you can understand that? You have his oldest son, who fights in the Wehrmacht, and his youngest assisted with your art procurements. Doesn't that mean anything? This winery can still produce the very best cremant for you. Take what you want but please, I beg you, please don't hurt him!"

The boots of the commanding officer made the solitary sound of ominous steps across the floor. After considering the pleading of the distraught son, the officer struck him with the same unabashed force. Alain rocked with the blow, standing as upright as could be managed. The officer moved to within inches of his face.

"Regrettably, it simply means your brothers were infinitely smarter than you. We have our orders to dispense with all traitors, especially those who help Jews. We will rid the Third Reich of all those who are not loyal. Perhaps I should shoot you first, then him. Unless you can tell me where Rainer is?"

Alain felt cold metal placed firmly against his forehead, as the officer pressed harder while taking a step backward. He glanced at Albert, unconscious and still hanging precariously in the middle of the two soldiers. At least the old man would not witness what was about to happen. He fixed his own eyes on the soldier that held the gun to his head.

"The Allies are now here. France and my brother will be saved! Vive la liberte," he whispered. "Rot in hell."

The explosion and splatter was instantaneous, causing the surrounding officers to be sprayed with blood and tissue. The soldier turned to the men securing Albert and spoke with casual and detached indifference, as he wiped Alain's blood from his cheek.

"Stand him up. Wake him, if possible. I want him fully aware of what is happening and to be reminded that it is by his own doing. I want him to know his worthless son is dead before we shoot him, as well. Once we are done dealing with these traitors, take the bodies out back and throw them on the heap with his wife and the other useless Jews they were hiding and burn them all. See if any other von Bauchelle family members are still in the area. Someone in the community will know. Kill them all. There won't be another one left in this world, long after this war is over."

Chapter Thirty-Four

Summerlea, South Carolina
St. Jude's Home
1950

The South Carolina day was clear, cooler than most for this time of the year, and seemed a precursor to the arriving autumn days with leaves that were just beginning to blush in light shades of red, yellow, and orange. As the white-robed minister made his way to the front of the gathering of staff, parishioners, town dignitaries, and children of varying ages, a local TV reporter was overheard commenting about the unusually seasonal temperature.

"In these parts it's often said that, if one doesn't like the weather on a particular day, just wait 'til tomorrow. We South Carolina natives certainly know that there could be a fifteen degree temperature change within a day, and that would not be out of the ordinary for us. Today, however, could not be more perfect for such a heartwarming occasion as this. It looks like they are ready to begin, so let's join in now."

The venerable priest adjusted the stole around his neck and motioned onlookers to move in closer to the podium, where a yellow ribbon hung in front of massive wooden doors. "As Rector of St. Jude's Episcopal Church, I welcome you all to this celebration as we finally open the doors of St. Jude's Home for Children. Our congregation and parish staff, along with the wonderful community of Summerlea, have embraced this undertaking of the past several years with utmost care and love. Until we could design and build an appropriate facility, the children have stayed in our old, but well-renovated Sunday school building. With the assistance of some of our skilled and talented parishioners, we turned a part of that facility into a makeshift lodge, and now, a school. Today we have something truly special."

The priest swept an open hand toward the young family on his immediate left and paused. The man, in dress pants, brown and grey sweater vest and tie and a dark grey tweed overcoat, held the hand of a little girl, who twisted and turned in place as she brushed dark curls away from playful eyes and fussed with a barrette that matched her red dress. The woman, beautiful but thinner than normal for one who had just given birth a second time, wore her light chestnut hair gathered at the nape of her neck, and was clad in a fashionable brown skirt and buttoned up green cardigan that matched her sea-green eyes. Wrapped in a yellow blanket trimmed with dancing teddy bears was a newborn baby girl whom the woman held close to her chest.

"I want to take a moment to introduce and recognize Dr. Ray Easter, his lovely wife, Catherine, six-year-old daughter Josie, and brand new baby girl, Rennie. As many of you know, Ray was in Europe teaching and working on his doctorate when he met and married Catherine, who was originally from Finland. They had both been living and working there for quite some time when the war broke out. When they became aware of the many orphans in that country, Jewish children whose parents had perished in the death camps, as well as those of families that were unsympathetic to the Nazi cause, they began a quest to help. Many of the children were from neighboring Norway, Denmark, and of course, Finland, and were hidden in Sweden because of its position of neutrality. Thanks to their selfless kindness and courage in working to get these children out of war- torn Europe, we now have the privilege of a permanent ministry for our church, this community, and beyond. In a moment we will cut the ribbon, hear more from Ray and Catherine inside, and enjoy a hearty reception prepared by the amazing women in our parish. We ask you all to join us in asking God's blessing for our work and for all who will reside within. Welcome to St. Jude's Home."

As clapping and cheers grew, then subsided, the crowd began to meander into the new facility that had been carefully crafted in stone and wood to match the rest of the lowcountry coastal church campus. A rabbi, whose appearance was orthodox in a requisite black jacket and hat with trimmed beard to match, caught up to the Easter family.

"Well done, Ray and Catherine. I must also extend thanks from our local Jewish community for allowing the refugee children to continue receiving instruction in their faith and in Hebrew, as they learn to become citizens here. I dare say, the partnership has been a boon to both faith communities and good for Summerlea, as well."

"Thank you, Rabbi. We love all of these children as our own." Catherine nodded toward Josie, who was at the end of her ability to be patient while adults spoke. She grabbed her hand with a gentle motherly tug.

"Please excuse me while I take this active little scamp in for some refreshments. I'll see you both inside." Catherine kissed the cheek of her husband Ray, who wiped his brow, but could not erase the flash of images that rolled through his head, like scenes from an old movie. All from childhood, mostly of Josef, his family, Colmar before the war, and those damned judensaues. Wondering if they would haunt him until he drew his last breath, he smiled at the holy man.

"We are honored to help, Rabbi. I know the parents of these children would have wanted them to continue in their own tradition. I would want my kids to be brought up in their Christian faith, as well. Of course, we have local children here now from different cultures and backgrounds, and they are learning to embrace their

200

differences, as well as their shared humanity. It has been a bit of a challenge for the rector here, but he has also grown and come a long way in his understanding of the issues our orphans face. When he retires in a couple of years, I look forward to being able to assist in the interviews for a new priest, as well as perhaps an assistant youth minister who might also connect with these children, especially our teenagers."

"I'm certain the quality of ministry will continue to be excellent, Ray. We stand ready to help as needed. If you don't mind my asking, how is Catherine these days? The past few times I've been around her she seems distracted, more anxious. Was this pregnancy and delivery more difficult for her, perhaps?"

Ray shifted uneasily, thrusting hands deep inside pants pockets and shaking his head. There was no longer any denying, since the rabbi had taken note of increasing changes in Catherine's demeanor and behavior.

"Rabbi, I'd like this to remain between us for awhile. Yes, she had a tough time delivering Rennie and it has caught up with her. She's lost her appetite and a little of her usual zest, it seems. She eats mostly meat, and not much of that. The doctor thinks that it could be a touch of postpartum depression. We're keeping a close watch. Hopefully it's only a temporary setback. I appreciate your being comfortable enough to ask."

"Of course, Ray. If there is anything we can do, just let us know. My wife, adhering to our warm southern tradition, seems to think cooking solves many ills, and she's happy to bring over a kosher dish or two. By the way, she is also making something for both your girls and wanted to know their given names. If you could call or write them down, maybe?"

"Yes, Josefine Alsa and Catherine Marthe. I will write them down for you and leave them in your box in the new office. It will be your first official mail here."

The rabbi clapped Ray on the shoulder with one hand, and gave him a vigorous handshake with the other. "Again, my friend, St. Jude's Home is an amazing accomplishment and legacy. Mazel tov."

"A sheynem dank, Rabbi." It was both an instinctive and immediate response, one in which the rabbi could intuit a lingering personal connection.

"Your Yiddish is commendable, Ray. Impressive."

"I have had the most excellent teachers, Rabbi _ poor Christian sinner that I am."

The rabbi did not attempt to return the humor, but studied Ray Easter as if mining for clues to an ancient mystery. "Perhaps you will tell me about those teachers, Ray, when the time is right and you are free to do so?" Visions of Abner Taffel and Josef sipping cremant and toasting his acceptance to the University of Strasbourg loomed inside Rainer's head, a painful reminder of the past he still concealed. More than anything today, he hoped they would be proud of him.

"Perhaps, Rabbi. One day."

Chapter Thirty-Five

Summerlea, South Carolina
Easter residence
1958

The pristine beach that graced the front of the dunes by the Easter home was perfect on this day. Glistening with the remnants of a waning high tide, the sand was firm beneath a cloudless southern sky that boasted of soft summer breezes. Scattered beachcombers searching for shark's teeth, sand dollars, and whatever treasures the sea chose to offer meandered by, smiling and waving as visitors tended to do in these parts.

Rennie Easter watched with eight-year-old glee as her father scooped her mother out of a folding chaise lounger and carried her, flailing and protesting, into the frothy surf. Rare days like this were magic, when her mother transformed from the sad, diminished woman that she had become into the playful and happy woman that Rennie kept in her memories. As Ray and Catherine frolicked in the crashing waves she glanced at Josie, who was lying on her stomach, with toes dug into a mound of sand and reading another of J.R.R. Tolkien's Lord of the Rings trilogy. Josie loved immersing herself into a fantasy world where wizards ruled and hobbits abounded. She often referred to herself as one of those halflings, not quite human. At fourteen, she was also becoming a woman, beginning to transform with an undeniable beauty. Her hair, darker than any in the family but with a familiar tinge of auburn, was piled high on her head and rested in an unceremonious whirl atop her visor. Aquamarine eyes, hidden now by aviator sunglasses, could be dark with the moodiness of adolescence, or clear and insightful with the glimpses of approaching maturity. Josie was intense, like her mother had become, but devoid of the routine melancholy that sometimes held Catherine Easter captive.

Rennie had no doubt her mother loved her children with fierce devotion. She frequently replayed the fondest of memories in her head. Closing her eyes, she could see the family game nights, camping trips to the mountains and at their own beachfront, and events at St. Jude's with the orphans and parishioners, who all adored Catherine's tender ways and magnetic smile. Somewhere along the road to the present, the essence of Catherine Easter had withered and all but died. On occasion she slept late, drank a bit too much, and locked herself in the bathroom after meals, complaining of nausea and stomach upsets. While her physical beauty was still evident, something evil was eating her soul. Josie had become especially resentful of their mother's strange behavior, and displayed occasional defiance by making angry comments about the dysfunction. Rennie winced recalling the time her mother had begged out of eating toasted marshmallows on the beach with the family, which had prompted the worst of explosive teenage angst from Josie.

"You care about other people, but you keep letting yourself go! Why? What's wrong with you, that you don't want to participate with us, and you have to sneak off the way you do after we eat? Don't you want to be normal? I'm sick of it! Why don't you just flush yourself down the toilet next time you're in there throwing your guts up? I hate you!"

Rennie, somehow knowing that Josie reacted out of her own sadness, remained more compassionate toward the mother she needed to be strong. She vacillated between the same frustration with the odd behavior and a sad longing, even a twinge of unwarranted guilt, for the continued disappearance of the exceptional mother that used to be Catherine Easter. After the verbal eruption from Josie, along with the accompanying slam of her bedroom door, Rennie remembered running to her mother, gripping her waist as if she might lose her forever and crying with overwhelming grief. She knew even then, though she did not fully comprehend it all, that her father was trying in desperation to hold them together. He repeatedly spent individual time encouraging each to focus on their love for one another, and to remember that Catherine struggled with her memories of the orphan children as they first appeared. Both Josie and Rennie knew that there was a sickness inside her, that it was connected to her past, but felt frustration that it held her captive today. They prayed daily for her to shake the illness that ate away at her body and crushed her spirit. Some days were better than others. But the unspeakable demons that were known only to her mother dwelled inside and still screamed to get out.

And buried deep inside was the secret that Catherine still kept from them all.

Chapter Thirty-Six

Summerlea, South Carolina
St. Jude's Home
1958

"Fr. Geoffrey, we're so glad you are here. You've already met my wife, Catherine, so let me introduce our girls. Josie and Rennie, this is Fr. Geoffrey Radcliffe. He is the new assistant priest here at St. Jude's. He is going to work with our children in the Home, the church youth program, and even teach a class or two for some of the older students."

Ray gestured toward the girls with a proud fatherly smile. The new priest was younger than the one who had retired, and Rennie liked him immediately. He was muscular, good looking, with thick brown hair that almost touched against the requisite clerical collar. It was a bit longer than was the current style but seemed to fit his casual personality. He moved with an easy youthful gait, and his smile conveyed an affable mix of cultured polish and country charm. Josie blushed and stood taller when he looked her way. She ran a hand across the hair band that matched her plaid clam diggers, and fluffed the curls that had been created overnight with a combination of pinned orange juice cans and bobby socks. Rennie could not help but grin at Josie's reaction to the new priest. It would provide fodder for sisterly teasing that would begin as soon as the adults were out of earshot.

"I'm so excited to be here," Fr. Geoffrey offered. "This is one of the most beautiful areas I've ever seen and the people here are welcoming and warm. I actually can't wait to get to work and to become better acquainted with you all. I hope you will be here on this campus often, and of course, I'll see you at church."

Rennie and Josie lagged behind their parents and the young priest. Rennie leaned closer to her sister and motioned for her to come nearer.

"What?"

"He's coolsville, isn't he?"

"How would you know about coolsville, Miss Eight Year Old Ankle-Biter?"

"Because I saw your face turn red when he spoke to you. Admit it, you're kookie about him. And Dad says he plays the guitar, too. Oooo, Fr. Geoffrey and Josie sitting in a tree. K-I-S-S-I-N-G!"

"Shut up, Rennie! Drop dead twice, you little creep!"

Rennie laughed, seeing that she had gotten beneath the skin of her sister, since she had been thrashed in teen slang. She responded in kind, sticking her tongue out at her older sibling.

"What, and look like you?"

Josie smiled, gently punching her shoulder, and stopped walking.

"He is pretty coolsville. I mean, for a priest. How old do you think he is?" "Dad said around twenty-four or twenty-five. He's ten years older than you, at least. Too old for you. Besides, he is a priest and all. Anyway, Donald Webb likes you. He stares at you in church with googly eyes." Rennie shook her head and rolled her own eyes at Josie, smiling.

"So?" Josie smiled, too. "Donald Webb is weird. Besides, priests in the Episcopal Church can marry, silly. The priest who left was married. Don't you remember? I don't think I will ever get married or have kids. I'm just going to hang out and see what happens. I want to be a teacher, anyway, so I will have lots of kids like these here."

Rennie punched Josie's elbow and ran toward her parents. "I know a secret!" She mouthed back at Josie, who brushed the hair out of her eyes, and regarded her little sister with disdain.

"Yeah. Like I said, cruising for a bruising, you little monster."

"Girls!" Catherine called out from the door of the Home cafeteria. "Hurry in, the luncheon is starting and Fr. Geoffrey is going to speak."

"Josie loves Fr. Cool Cat," Rennie teased.

"Uh, knuckle sandwich!" Josie narrowed her eyes and held up a clenched fist.

"Josie?" Rennie stopped on the sidewalk and waited for her older sister.

"Now, what?"

"I really like him, too. I wish I could come to the youth meeting when he meets all the teenagers. I want to hear what he has to say about our youth activities."

Josie smiled. "He's a halfling, too, I can feel it. I'll tell you all about the meetings, if you can be quiet."

"Hey, Josie?"

"Geez, Rennie! What?"

"You think Mom will eat the food here today?"

"Who knows, maybe? She usually tries, at least in front of other people, to eat a few bites of her meat. But, then she slinks off to hide in a bathroom and throws her guts up sometimes. I think Dad needs to make her go back to the doctor. Or see a shrink or something." She smiled down at Rennie, tugging on one of her braids. "Let's not think about it, right now. We have a priest to meet."

Rennie smiled up at her sister and winked as they walked up the steps to the back door of the cafeteria. "Later, gator."

Josie winked back. "After 'while, crocodile."

Sometimes the teasing solidified their sisterly bond and made their mother's strange behavior easier to bear, although both wondered if she would ever be all right again.

Chapter Thirty-Seven

Fr. Geoffrey Radcliffe studied the girl who had not said a word throughout the entire youth meeting, which was unusual given her usual thoughtful commentary. Though he was not sure what was on her mind, something had consumed her attention all evening.

"Josie, would you help grab a few of these prayer books and help me carry them back into the sanctuary? Your dad should be done with his meeting by the time we get them in there. Hey, good meeting tonight, everybody. All of you have rides home, right?" After a flurry of goodbyes, he faced the reticent teen. "Josie, you were awfully silent tonight. You usually have insightful comments to add to our lively discussions."

Josie turned away, embarrassed, as tears rolled down her cheeks. She could not let him see her cry. Sensing her need for space, Fr. Geoffrey made no attempt to approach her but offered words of encouragement instead.

"I could tell something was worrying you. You know, we all have those things in our lives that sometimes weigh us down. It's okay to cry. It's also okay to talk about it with your youth minister, if you want. Perhaps it would make you feel better." Josie faced the priest she secretly adored, wiping her reddened eyes and trying to take on a more adult demeanor.

"Fr. Geoffrey, can you promise not to tell my father that I talked to you, if I tell you?" The young priest rubbed his clerical collar in the thoughtful way he always did when being guarded but truthful in his responses.

"Yes, I can, provided it's not something illegal or dangerous to you or another person. Why do you think your dad doesn't need to know about whatever it is that is hurting you, may I ask?" Josie hesitated. She had never told anyone outside of the family about the bizarre behavior her mother exhibited, as well as her sad bouts of withdrawal. Tears welled to the brim and spilled over once more. She held a hand over her eyes, her voice shaking as she whispered.

"Because it's about my mom, and I don't want her or my dad to be mad at me for telling anyone."

"I see." Fr. Geoffrey sat in a folding chair, and motioned for the distraught teen to take a seat in another. He ran his fingers through the thatches of brown hair and leaned forward, resting forearms on his knees. "I might be able to guess, Josie. But, I've most often found that seeking help and being honest is rarely wrong. Perhaps you and I can figure out the best way to get the help needed, and you won't have to keep this hurt a secret much longer. My guess is that your dad may have concerns of his own." Josie softened under the careful ministration of comfort.

"I love my mom. But she has this problem and it's getting worse, I think. She doesn't eat a lot. Really, mostly just meat. Sometimes, she goes in the bathroom and throws up. She doesn't do stuff with us like she used to. Last night, I heard her and my dad arguing. They never fight, not like this. But my dad was so upset, and my mom kept crying and saying she was sorry."

"I'm wondering if you heard anything your mom and dad said, Josie?"

"Just some. That is until they went outside to go down by the beach to talk. Probably so we couldn't hear them. Rennie was already asleep anyway. My dad said things like, "You need help, the girls need you too" and 'You have a responsibility to yourself and us'! And Mom said something like, 'You know why this is so hard, and I'm trying to get better'. That was when they went to the beach. I don't know what it was all about, but it feels like it must be my and Rennie's fault, somehow. I mean, why else would she be so unhappy with us sometimes? She finally came back inside, but my dad stayed out on the beach for a long time."

Fr. Geoffrey spoke in a slow, even pace as he offered pastoral wisdom. "Josie, I've known your family for two years now. There is no finer family here at St. Judes. One thing I do know is that this is not your or your sister's fault. All families have difficult situations to face at one time or another, as do each of us personally. I do know a little about what you face." Fr. Geoffrey hesitated only for a moment before he decided to disclose a piece of what shaped his choice to be a priest. "My father, who is no longer living, had terrible bouts of anger_ rage even_ that we never understood until we found out some of the conditions in which he'd had to live. In some ways we all have tough obstacles to face as we live our lives the best we can. That's why our faith is so important in our lives. How about this? Could you and I talk about a way that you might help your family so that you don't have to worry and hurt like this? Perhaps you would also feel better if you didn't have to keep a secret from your dad or your mom."

"Okay. Yeah, okay that would be good. Hey, Fr. G?"

"Yes?"

"Did your dad ever get better?"

"No, sadly he did not. But he might have had we all been able to talk about it and face it head on, instead of trying to hide it all the time. At any rate, it would have been better than doing nothing." Fr. Geoffrey kept a watchful eye on the wall clock. Thankfully, the meeting Ray Easter chaired would last for another half an hour.

Chapter Thirty-Eight

Summerlea, South Carolina
St. Jude's Home
1962

Rennie could barely contain her twelve-year-old excitement as her father lifted the small suitcase out of the trunk of the old Chevy and tossed her stuffed teddy bear into waiting hands. Rembrandt, the family Labrador, bounded out of the car with Rennie, barking and circling her in exuberant canine fashion. As Josie Easter rose from the opposite side of the car, Fr. Geoffrey was struck by her appearance. Though she was most often dressed in appropriate teen garb, on this day she had metamorphosed, a girl into a young woman. From a distance, he thought she mirrored a young Audrey Hepburn, with dark hair pulled into a classic upsweep away from crystal eyes that still pierced with intensity when she was serious. Her dress was a sleeveless pale yellow, with a belted waist and skirt that brushed just below her knees. A string of pearls accented tiny pearl drop earrings, and a pair of pump heels added to her statuesque look. She was now eighteen, he reminded himself, as he quickly averted his gaze to Catherine, who leaned against the car as the girls gathered their belongings. Ray came to her side, kissing her cheek and waving her on to help Rennie and Josie as he took Fr. Geoffrey aside.

"Well, Father, I can't thank you enough for the offer for the girls to stay here while we attend the museum tour in Europe. When the Atlanta Art Association contacted me to go, I immediately thought about how good this might be for Catherine. It's a chance to reconcile a bit with what she left over there during the war. We have not been back since, and I'm hopeful that some healing will take place after these many years."

"Ray, you know your family belongs here, always. Rennie has looked forward to one of our flashlight crab hunts on the beach, followed by a world famous St. Jude's marshmallow roast. Having Josie here to assist with the younger children will be good for us, as well as her, I think. She has said that she will major in education come August, I hear tell?"

"Yes, her plans are to attend the College of Charleston, and her dream is to teach here. Of course, I've told her she will have to interview, like any other applicant. She loves this place immensely, though. Rennie, too, bless her heart. You know, she is turning into quite the accomplished little artist. Is my bragging father side beginning to show?"

Fr. Geoffrey smiled as he watched the girls playing with Rembrandt. Catherine patted the caramel colored fur. She seemed happy, but somewhat aloof. "Is Catherine looking forward to the trip?"

Ray shook his head, glancing upward, then down. "She says she is. We had begun to make some headway. She finally agreed to see the therapist you recommended and also a dietician to try to exorcise all the baggage she's been carrying around. She and the girls were so happy for a little while. But as the departure date got closer, the unhealthy behavior seemed to reappear some. Maybe it's just the idea of finally going back. That, and we've never really been away from the girls, both of us at the same time. Which reminds me, I need to give you these to keep secure for us." Ray pulled two envelopes from the inside of his suit and handed them to the priest. "If you would, please store these in the file cabinet in my bell tower room. They are for the girls. The information is specifically for when they are both well into adulthood, but we wanted to go ahead and write it all down for them before we left. Catherine and I thought this would be a good time to record some family history. Catherine also left something for Rennie that she's been keeping in a lock box there, as well, and I have left something there for Josie. Oh, would you please check on everything at the house for us while we're gone?"

"With pleasure, Ray. I'm certain all here will be fine, not to worry. You know, the kids here are thrilled when your girls come over, and even more so now that they and Rembrandt are staying for an extended visit. You and Catherine enjoy all that today's Europe has to offer. My prayers for peace and healing go with you both."

"Thank you, Padre. You have all of our contact and flight information. We'll call you before we get on the plane in Atlanta, and again when we get back and on the road home. The Atlanta Art Association office can reach us in the event of any emergency." Ray smiled as he took a proud glance around St. Jude's Home and Church. He had grown to love this place, his southern home, almost as much as he missed the Alsatian vineyard country that was his beloved Colmar. How Catherine would have adored his boisterous and loving family, especially his mother, Marthe. He often imagined all of the von Bauchelle family visiting South Carolina. What an asset they would have been to the children and staff here. Perhaps Catherine would find solace and healing in being able to witness, firsthand, a Europe devoid of Nazi atrocity. He hoped they could find a way to reconcile all that had happened there, and to one day be able to share their heritage with Josie and Rennie.

"Look after my girls, Father."

"That's a given, Ray. They are in good hands until you get back. Have a safe flight, and you and Catherine enjoy the trip."

Chapter Thirty-Nine

Despite it being a workday for him, Fr. Geoffrey loved Sunday mornings such as today at St. Jude's. Seeing the young residents sprinkled about the sanctuary alongside parishioners that had chosen to be mentors and friends only accentuated the vibe of family in this special place. This was the home that he too had longed for, and finally found. Ray and Catherine would be home late this evening or early tomorrow and no doubt would be thrilled to know how well Josie and Rennie had done in their absence. Josie had shone maturity beyond her years in working with the children there and he had no doubt that teaching was what she was meant to do. He had found himself thinking of her often, of the woman she was becoming, but had always forced the intrusive thought aside. She still had college, boyfriends, and many life experiences before her.

Checking the time, he had approximately twenty minutes to finish his cup of coffee and catch a glimpse of the news before walking over to the sacristy to vest for the morning service. As the picture on the antiquated black and white console came into focus, a more somber-than-usual morning anchor was in the middle of a breaking news report:

"Again, if you are just tuning in this morning, there is devastating news coming out of Paris where Air France Flight 007, a Boeing 707, has crashed upon takeoff at Orly Airport, killing all of the 130 passengers and most of the crew on board. Only two French flight attendants survived, remarkably unscathed, as they were seated in the tail section of the plane, which broke away from the fuselage before it crashed into a vacant cottage in Villaneuve-le-Roi."

Slamming his coffee cup on the console top, Fr. Geoffrey made a frantic motion to grab the flight information Ray Easter had left from the top of the dresser. There it was, just as the newscaster had said it. Dropping to his knees in front of the set, his shaking fingers reached for the volume as he fought the sick, helpless panic that rushed in waves through his body. He rubbed the white clerical collar that now felt tight enough to restrict his already frantic breathing and tried to gather composure as the news anchor continued.

"Air France had recently opened its new office in the downtown Atlanta area, and this flight aboard the aircraft, named the Chateau de Sully, was the inaugural flight. As such, it was filled with 106 of Atlanta's elite cultural and civic leaders, acclaimed art experts, and art patrons, who had gone to Paris as part of an Atlanta Art Association's month long excursion to see Europe's art treasures. We will have more information about exactly who was on that passenger manifest as details about this horrific crash come in. As a gesture of conciliation, Dr. Martin Luther King, Jr. and activist/entertainer Harry Belafonte have announced their plans to cancel the sit-in that was scheduled to protest racial segregation. For now, we concur with Atlanta Mayor Ivan Allen in noting that this will forever be the day that Atlanta stood still."

As soon as he turned the TV off, Fr. Geoffrey wished that he had not. At least the drone of the news kept him in that moment, absorbing information, being a receptor rather than having to act. Now, the silence of the room was unforgiving, a vacuum in which he had to look death and grief in the face. Cradling his head in his hands he cried as he prayed, rocking back and forth. His body shook with the weight of the catastrophic news. He knew he would have to be the one to tell Josie and Rennie. God Almighty, this could not be happening, not to Ray and Catherine, not to these girls.

Think. What is the best way to handle this horrific loss? People will need me to be strong as they grieve. Josie and Rennie, especially, have to hear this from me first. The parish and all of the children and staff will have to know, as well _ unless some of them already had seen the report, or heard it on the radio."

With one more prayer for strength and guidance, Fr. Geoffrey rose, making the call to the rector of the church who would handle the morning service and console a congregation that was sure to be in need of pastoral care. After splashing water on his face and taking as many deep breaths as he could muster, he began the difficult trek to meet the children as they made their way across the courtyard to the morning service. He would take the girls to the bench where Catherine loved to sit before services on cool summer mornings. Though he well knew death was a part of life, he had never been called upon, in his relatively brief tenure, to relay news such as this to the children of cherished friends, all of whom he had grown to love as family.

They looked so happy, these young folk meandering across the grounds, with little ones skipping about while motherly Sisters of St. Clare herded them toward the church. Josie, now the quintessential college girl, had learned to accentuate her striking dark beauty and attracted the attention of the older boys, who circled as close to her as they dared. Rennie had acquiesced, at least on Sundays, to Josie's sisterly attempts to make her tomboyish appearance more feminine. In her soft green dress and manicured curls of chestnut hair, she showed signs of becoming a beauty, as well, with a kind of wholesome radiance that beckoned to others. Fr. Geoffrey greeted the entourage with as much normalcy as he could muster, wishing he did not have to be the bearer of life- altering pain, but knowing he could not leave such a task to another.

"Good Sunday Morning, one and all. Sisters, would you please take these young sojourners on to church, while I have a moment with Josie and Rennie?"

A freckled six-year-old with a gaping hole where front teeth used to be grinned wide enough to swallow a watermelon in a single bite and tugged at the black pants of the beloved priest. Proud enthusiasm bubbled over as the young one sought approval. "Fr. Geoffrey, look, both my front teeth are gone now! The tooth fairy came last night and I'm going to put a nickel in the plate at church!"

Fr. Geoffrey patted the youngster on the head, ruffling the slicked back Sunday-combed hair. "Bradley, that's terrific, thank you. We will use that nickel wisely, my friend. Josie, Rennie, if you two would come with me please?"

"What's wrong?" Josie asked, cutting through the façade of pleasantry. She was intuitive almost to a fault. The nuns flashed expressions of confusion but said nothing as they guided the throng of children down the sidewalk. Fr. Geoffrey motioned for the girls to follow and turned his back to them in one simultaneous sweep as he pointed to the courtyard, fighting against yet another burst of emotion. He sat on the bench in Catherine's favorite spot and took one final deep breath of courage.

"What is it, Father Geoffrey?" Josie was insistent, stopping a few feet away in her stoic refusal to sit. Her clear eyes flashed beneath a furrowed brow. Rennie stood in the middle next to the bench, fear and confusion all over her as she looked back and forth between Fr. Geoffrey and her sister.

"Josie, Rennie. I hardly know how to tell you. I'm afraid there has been a horrific accident." Fr. Geoffrey sought to look into each of their eyes as his voice trailed into the moment of despair. Josie clenched both fists and took a step back shaking her head, as dark curls cascaded around her face.

"It's Mom and Dad," Josie said angrily, then louder. "Tell us now, isn't it? Tell us!"

"Fr. Geoffrey, where are they? Are my mom and dad coming home?" Rennie whispered.

The young priest looked at Rennie, grasping her hand. He would never forget the sheer hopelessness on that youthful face. He wondered what his own expression revealed to them. There was no withholding the inevitable pain any longer. "I'm so very sorry, girls." He took a needed breath of air, trying to reassure himself that he could deliver the pain as best as a priest and friend could. His voice quivered underneath the massive weight. "Something went wrong as their plane was taking off to come home."

"No! No, no, no!" Josie screamed, her back already turned as she ran across the courtyard and disappeared behind a huge water oak.

Rennie dissolved into an inconsolable heap in his arms, her tears bathing his shirt already damp from his own tears. Her body shook with the enormity of loss for one so young. Fr. Geoffrey held her close as his eyes wandered to find Josie, who was sitting on the far side of the tree. Though he could not see her face, he knew she was there, as her long legs lay crossed and exposed on the greenness underneath. He wondered, for a fleeting moment, if she would forever hate him for being the one to tell them of the untimely deaths of their parents.

"Fr. Geoffrey?"

"Yes, Rennie?"

"What will happen to me and my sister? Are we orphans now? Can we stay here with you? I don't want to be adopted, I just want to stay here with you."

The young priest continued to hold her as she clung to his waist, her head still resting on his chest.

"Of course, you can, Rennie. If you and Josie both want to be here, St. Jude's is your home, as well as your church family."

"Josie is going to college in two months. Will I be here by myself?"

"I'll be here, kiddo. I'm not leaving. Everyone will be here. And Josie won't be far away. She will come to visit and be here for holidays, I'm sure."

"Why did she run away from us?"

"Well, I guess because teenagers have lots of crazy emotions inside as they are becoming young adults. Losing your parents, especially like this, is something that will always be with you both. But I promise you, as I promised your father when he and your mom left for Europe, I will do my best to look after you. St. Jude's is your family, too, and we are all here for you for as long as you want."

"Rennie? Fr. Geoffrey?" Josie stood before them both, eyes now red and swollen. "I'm sorry. I shouldn't have run away like that. Rennie, you're my little sister and I shouldn't have left you to deal with losing Mom and Dad. I feel so overwhelmed, like I'm drowning in the hurt. I didn't stop to think of anyone but me. Please forgive me. I'm so sorry."

Tears streamed down her cheeks once more as she extended open arms to Rennie, who sobbed with her. They embraced with the fierceness of children left with unimaginable sorrow and no one but each other to absorb it all. Fr. Geoffrey stood to wrap an arm around each girl, trying to alleviate as much of their pain as possible as he held them close. "Do you think my mother is well now? That she's finally at peace?"Josie stared at him hard, her blue eyes burning, demanding a real answer. It wasn't a hysterical question coming from a distraught child, but rather one asked as one seeking healing for a loved one and reassurance of the hope that she had been taught about all her life. One day, she would indeed make an excellent teacher and mentor. Fr. Geoffrey smiled. She deserved a frank response.

"I do. And for that, I'm thankful, though sad as hell. Catherine was trying to shake whatever it was that consumed her. Never doubt that your parents loved you both beyond measure. I knew them well enough to know that it is the one thing they would say to you now if they could."

"Thank you, Fr. Geoffrey. Can Rennie and I have a few minutes to sit here?"

"Of course you can. How about if I run to my office for a moment? You can stay as long as you like. I can bring you both some lunch, if you are not ready to be part of the Sunday meal with the parish. Or you may want to eat with your friends. Either is okay, you know."

Josie smiled at him, this time with genuine relief as she sat with Rennie. He always knew what to do. She knew they would rely heavily on him and the parish here at St. Jude's. "We will be inside shortly and decide about lunch." As he walked away, Josie called out once more. They were a gut wrenching sight huddled together, hand in hand, facing life without their beloved mother and father. "Father G, will you help us with all of this? I mean, I know there are all kinds of important things we will have to do now."

"There will be plenty of time for that, Josie. I will be here for the two of you for anything you need. Always."

As he watched the girls from his office window, Fr. Geoffrey hoped that he and St. Jude's would be a presence in their lives for a very long time. Lord knows they would need all of the support they could get now and in the days to come. They all would.

Chapter Forty

Summerlea, South Carolina
St. Jude's Home
August, 1962

Fr. Geoffrey sat in the bustling cafeteria of St. Jude's Home,
trying to converse with one of the board members over the hum of
lunchtime activity while looking across the room at the girls seated
at Rennie Easter's table. He could not hear the conversation but kept
a watchful eye. The new girl, Bonita Drake, had creamy ebony skin
and large dark eyes. She isolated herself at the end of the table of
chattering girls, glaring at the ones sitting nearby and sulking
beneath an unkept afro hairdo. She had been abandoned by her drug-
addicted parents, according to the letter tucked into her knapsack
when she was found walking down King Street in the middle of
nearby Charleston. Now she picked at her spaghetti and salad,
deliberately chewing with her mouth open. She tried to antagonize
others into reinforcing her feelings of inadequacy and loneliness. Her
rage was a tour de force of its own.

"Ew, so nasty! Why do you eat like that? No wonder you don't
have any friends. Don't you have any manners at all?" One of the
girls stared, her face full of obvious disgust. The gaggle of pre-teens
around the new girl picked up their plates as they exited the table
and made their way to the trash area. Looking back, they shook their
heads and giggled behind hands that covered mouths as they
wandered outside into the nearby courtyard. Only Rennie remained
at the other end of the table, looking down at her food and eating
with forced effort. Today had been difficult, as Josie Easter had left
for college and now she felt the recent loss of her parents even more

deeply. She was oblivious to the machinations of Bonita Drake that were designed to create disruption.

"You the one whose parents died?" Rennie continued to stare at her plate as she swallowed another sip of chilled milk and wrestled with a tiny bite of spaghetti. "Hey, I'm talking to you!" Bonita pressed harder. "That sign in the office say that St. Jude is the saint that guards kids like us. You know, the ones no one wants. Even you and yo' fat ass college girl sister. You ain't nothing special. Nobody wants you, neither."

"Leave me alone." Rennie spoke without looking up.

"You ain't nothin' but a cheap white cracker. No wonder your damn parents died and left you."

"I told you to shut up, Bonita!"

"Ooooo, come on over here and make me, if you think you can, honky." Twirling a chunk of spaghetti with her fork, and flashing a wicked smile, Bonita shoved the entire bite in her mouth and smacked until the sauce began to drizzle from the corners of her mouth. Sensing that she was pushing her prey closer to the edge, the eyes of the young black girl narrowed to razor sharp slits as she went in for the kill. "Malcolm X, he say he glad all them white folks died in that plane crash. He say God must have wanted 'em all dead. He celebratin' they dying. Me, too. Especially yo' mama and daddy."

From where he sat observing the girls, Fr. Geoffrey was surprised when Rennie's plate of spaghetti and salad landed squarely against the chest of her tormentor. White noodles stuck to black cheeks and hair, as thick red sauce splattered and clung to what seemed every inch of Bonita's clothing.

"Shut your black mouth or I'll shut it for you!"

"White bitch, I'll cut your ass!"

"C'mon, then! Nobody likes you, Bonita! You're too busy trying to stir up trouble! You're so mean you don't even want to give people a chance to like you! Just leave me alone!"

Rennie was standing now and gave the table a violent shove as an exclamation point to her exploding anger. Bonita was upon her quicker than Fr. Geoffrey could motion the sexton for assistance and reach the two, who were now exchanging pummeling blows and throwing as much spaghetti and salad at each other as they could grab from the dining style bowls on the table. Fr. Geoffrey grabbed Rennie by the arm as she drew back to strike again and wrapped her as close to him as possible. She erupted in tears, struggling momentarily before collapsing into the security that wrapped her quivering body. Bonita kicked and twisted in a violent attempt to break free from the sexton who, although he was a big black man, had difficulty in trying to subdue the angry young girl. Fr. Geoffrey motioned for the custodian to allow the anger to ebb and flow.

"Let go of me! I said let go of me, damn it!" Bonita fought the big man hard for another few minutes before showing signs of emotional retreat. Her breathing, once fast and labored, slowed to a more even pace, and silent tears rolled down the cheeks still covered with food. Fr. Geoffrey kept his voice low and spoke slowly, smiling only with his eyes at the sexton who now held a passive Bonita.

"Girls, when you are calm and ready to help clean this mess up, we can let you go. I need your word that you are ready. Rennie?"

"I'm okay. You can let me go," she mumbled.

"Bonita?" The young girl sat in silence, holding on to one last vestige of anger before succumbing to the request from the priest. "Yeah. Yes, okay. I won't fight." Priest and sexton maintained eye contact as grips were loosened and calm restored amid a battlefield of dishes and food. "Girls, I need you to help carry these bowls and plates over to the cleaning area for the ladies in the back, and then help Mr. Harry wipe up all of this mess. Now, please."

Both girls complied, moving dishes and utensils without speaking, and squeezing sponges into a bucket of soapy water as they wiped the tabletop clean. The sexton cut his eyes toward Fr. Geoffrey, who showed only the shadow of a smile as he watched the girls now working together without speaking to each other.

"Can we go now, Fr. Geoffrey?" Rennie finally pleaded. She held a sponge, and Bonita a roll of paper towels as they asked for permission to leave. Both were covered in noodles and sauce, with decorations of lettuce and slivers of carrots hanging from their clothes. Bonita's thick afro looked like a Christmas tree, with noodle tinsels hanging in clumps about her face. Rennie, whose chestnut hair was braided, had noodles that appeared to be woven into her hair. With crisis now averted and the humor of the situation more evident, Fr. Geoffrey shook his head giving way to a visible smile.

"Not quite, ladies. Who knew that spaghetti and salad could make such a mess, right? Before you can go back to your rooms, we need you to clean up first. There is a hose out back here. You can take turns using it and then sit on the steps in the sun to dry up before going back to change clothes. I will walk back to your rooms with you, and then we can chat."

"Fr. Geoffrey," Rennie whispered, "Are you mad at us? We're in big trouble, aren't we?"

The young priest crossed his eyes and made the sign of the cross in the air. "No. God forgives. And so do I. Go, my children, quickly, before minds are changed and I feed you to the lions!"

Rennie smiled at the priest and sexton and breathed a meek word of thanks as she wiped sauce from her face. "Thank you, again, Father G. And we're sorry. At least I am. I guess I shouldn't speak for her."

226

Bonita looked up again, as all waited for her response. "Yeah. Okay, yeah, I guess. Me, too."

Fr. Geoffrey smiled and gestured toward the back door of the dining hall. "Apology accepted. So, since cleanliness is truly next to godliness, how about you two go on outside and see how many noodles you can count while you're cleaning up."

The girls complied with silent obedience, moving outside into the humid heat of a Carolina mid-summer. Rennie unwound the garden hose beside the back door and turned on the water at the spigot. Sliding out of her sneakers, she began to brush at the spaghetti that stubbornly clung to her clothing. A few limp strands fell to the grass at her feet. "Worms," she said, smiling at Bonita, who regarded her with curiosity, before fully comprehending the intended humor.

"You're a crazy ass white girl," Bonita said, shaking her head.

"And you're an insane black chick." Rennie shot back, still smiling.

From inside the screened porch behind the doorway to the kitchen, Fr. Geoffrey and the sexton observed the interaction of the girls.

"We need to go out there yet, Father G? Sounds like they fixin' to crank up." The sexton had whispered over the shoulder of the priest standing in front of him.

"Not yet, Harry." Fr. Geoffrey raised a hand and whispered back. "Let's see what happens." Both men waited and watched, prepared to move if necessary. Rennie held the end of the hose out to Bonita.

"Here, hose me off."

"Girl, I ain't your slave." Bonita growled. "Hose your own damn self off."

"No, seriously. You do me, and I'll do you. That way, we can be sure we got it all. All the worms and the blood and guts." Rennie smiled broadly, making a face at Bonita and motioning for the surprised girl to squirt her.

"Damn," Bonita mumbled, shaking her head. "I get to take a hose to a white girl. Maybe God does love me after all."

"Awww, it's so cold!" Rennie shrieked with delight as water hit her head and body while bits of food began to collect on the soft grass around her feet. When almost every trace of battle had been washed from clothes and skin, the girls collapsed, soaking wet, onto the back steps of the kitchen porch. Bonita dug in the ground with the back of her heel and gazed up at the shady pines and the burning summer sun.

"You miss them? Your folks?"

"Yeah, I do. A lot. I miss my sister, too. How about your family?"

"Not really. They loved drugs and liquor more than me. That's okay, I don't need 'em."

Rennie stared, searching for words of comfort. No wonder the girl was so angry and hateful. "Drugs can make people do terrible things, you know. But your parents gave you a name that means 'beautiful' in Spanish, so they must have loved you at least some."

"How you know what my name means?"

"My parents lived in Europe during World War II, before I was born. They spoke a few languages, and my dad told me that word. He loved art, like me. My sister, Josie, she likes language, too. She is studying to be a teacher. What do you like, Bonita?"

Bonita looked away from Rennie in the direction of the great oaks and Spanish moss as she pulled out a pick that had been stuffed in a pocket and fluffed her drying hair once again into a fashionable afro. "Me, I like to sing. Been singing since I was a baby. Well, almost. I heard Miss Leontyne Price on the radio one time. Then I heard Miss Ella Fitzgerald sing the same song just a little bit

228

different. I used to pretend I was singing it to my own baby, when I rocked my doll. I wish my mama had sung it to me. Wish she'd done a lot of things."

"Can you sing it to me now? Please? I want to hear you sing."

"You want me to sing it now? Ain't never sung nothing for nobody but my family and my dolls."

"So? Can't we be your family now? C'mon, Bonita, sing. I really want to hear it."

"Gotta stand up," Bonita smiled, puffing her chest out and stretching to full height. "You know, to get lots of air. Don't laugh or I'll put the damn hose on you again."

"Cross my heart." Rennie smiled, readjusting her seating on the steps to face Bonita, who folded her hands together at her waist, closed her eyes, and began to sing. The soft, lulling, pitch perfect melody of George Gershwin's "Summertime," from the opera *Porgy and Bess* was sung with such emotion that Rennie found herself brushing a tear from her eye. She clapped enthusiastically for her newfound friend. Bonita curtseyed low, enjoying the positive attention, perhaps for the first time in her young life. From the kitchen porch, the priest and sexton remained still, mesmerized by the surprising vocal performance from the streetwise youngster.

"Damn." Fr. Geoffrey whispered, as Harry chuckled. "Can't wait to see what she can do with Amazing Grace."

Bonita flopped back on the steps beside Rennie, who eyed her with new appreciation. "Wow, Bonita, you have a gift. The music teacher here is going to love you!"

"Not so sure I'm staying. Mostly lily-white people here. Hardly anyone like me."

"C'mon, Bonita. You will like it here, if you just give us a chance. Tonight we're going to the beach to catch crabs with flashlights and nets, and then make s'mores around the fire on the beach. And we will sing, I know you'll like that!"

"Catch crabs with a damn flashlight and a net? And what the hell is a s'more?" Rennie threw back her head and laughed harder than she had in days. It was catharsis and redemption all at once. Fr. Geoffrey watched as she explained the nuances of demobilizing the mostly smaller crabs by shining bright light in their eyes and quickly scooping them up in a net and dropping them in a bucket.

"After we catch enough, everyone stands in a circle and Fr. Geoffrey turns the bucket over and we all run away from them. Then we eat the s'mores, which is short for 'some more', as in 'I want some more'. You will, too, they are so good. Toasted marshmallows, squares of chocolate, and graham crackers made into a sandwich. So gooey and good!"

"Think they gonna be all right now, Father?" Harry asked.

The priest smiled, knowing how proud Ray and Catherine would have been to see their daughter reach out to another hurting soul, while she herself was still burdened with unimaginable grief. "Harry, I think our job here is done." He grinned again. "We can work on Bonita's language and music skills at a later date."

Fr. Geoffrey stopped one more time to watch the miracle of friendship begin. Josie would have made the 'kindred spirits' reference, no doubt. He wondered how she was doing, just down the road in Charleston at the college where Ray had been a much beloved professor. He found himself hoping that she would return to St. Jude's to teach when she had finished with college days. By that time, Rennie would no doubt be in college somewhere, pursuing her great love of art, like her father. In the meanwhile, he and the rest of St. Jude's would wrap them both in as much love and security as they could. He pulled out a notepad and scribbled furiously, smiling at Harry.

"Just a reminder to get Bonita a little private instruction with our choir director so she can get some formal training while participating in the music program. There's no telling how far that girl can go. I predict these two will be best friends, and they will make a big difference in this old crazy world. You watch and see."

Chapter Forty-One

Somewhere in the Appalachian Mountains
Wulfsreich Compound, Georgia
October, 1975

The rabbit ears on the Zenith Chromacolor TV helped with reception deep in the recesses of the mountain woods. The burly man in the corduroy recliner settled back into the worn chair after turning up the volume on the console and wiping pizza crumbs from his sweatshirt. He reached into the styrofoam cooler on the floor and listened intently as the pretty young girl on camera continued to answer questions in front of some museum in Atlanta.

"Yes, St. Jude's Home in Summerlea, South Carolina is celebrating twenty-five years of helping orphaned children grow up in a loving and nurturing environment. I'm very excited to be going back to such a special place."

The reporter adapted a conciliatory tone as he leaned close to the chestnut-haired beauty and placed a hand on her shoulder. "Rennie, you work here at the High Museum, where your father had last assisted before that fateful crash in Paris that killed both your parents and many from the Atlanta art community. I understand that you and your sister were actually raised at St. Jude's after their deaths, is that correct?"

"Yes, that is right," the young woman said. "My sister Josie was eighteen at the time of the crash, so she was mostly at the College of Charleston, where my father was an art professor when he and my mother founded St. Jude's. I was twelve years old at the time, so all of my teen years were spent there. Not many people knew about us then. Outside of my family home, St Jude's was the most loving environment I could have had. Today, my sister teaches there, alongside a wonderful staff, our wonderful priest, Fr. Geoffrey Radcliffe, and an amazing supportive community. We, like others, have been most fortunate to have St. Jude's and I can't wait to celebrate all of the good being done there."

"Rennie, you have followed in your father's footsteps, so to speak, in your chosen profession as an artist and as one who is currently working in the field of fine art. What can you tell us about your parents and their legacy?"

The young woman smiled, facing the camera and brushing hair out of her eyes as the gusty Atlanta breeze kept the late summer heat at bay. Burly Man leaned forward toward the console, stuffing another bite of sausage pizza deep into his throat and chewing with a vengeance.

"Ray and Catherine Easter were my parents. They met in Finland, where my mother grew up and my father moved there after his parents died. Both were still in school and working when they were trying to have a courtship. They had both lost their families, so the war of course changed everything for them. They were instrumental in helping to bring war orphans to the United States. They were able to obtain some land and work directly with the Episcopal Church in Summerlea to start the St. Jude's project. It has been immensely successful. We have about seventy-five children there today, and many will return for our anniversary celebration."

The reporter droned on about the charitable home, its residents, and the reputation of both its founders and benefactors. In closing, he complimented the young art intern on following in her father's chosen profession and wished St. Jude's Home much success in the future. She had smiled, all pretty and sweet looking, into the camera and said how much she hoped she could live up to the memory of both Ray and Catherine Easter. Burly Man hoped so, as well.

Turning off the television, he reached for the black rotary phone receiver and dialed a number. He swallowed yet another swig of beer while waiting for the voice on the other end.

"Hey, man. You catch the news just now? You remember the name Ray Easter? That art professor who lived on the coast down in South Carolina? You know, the one that came from Europe that started an orphanage for some of those Jew babies and all? Yeah, the one that died in the plane crash back in '62. General always had that guy on his radar for Nazi art, remember? Couldn't prove anything, and didn't pursue much after the dude died. Well, he has a grown kid. Two of 'em, actually. One who teaches there at the orphanage. Guess what the other one does? Yeah, she's a damn artist, just like daddy. Good news is they are having a twenty-fifth anniversary celebration of the orphanage. Bad news is, it's this coming weekend. Think she knows anything, or where he might have kept stuff or who might have helped him, if he's our guy?"

The voice on the other end ceased only momentarily before giving instructions. "We need to get someone down there to find out all she knows. If our shit is there or she knows something, then we plan the next step. You have her name, all the details?"

"Hell yeah. Rennie Easter. Young, maybe mid-twenties. Real pretty. Think we can get something together by then?

The voice on the other end crackled with static, but the words were clear. "Whatever it takes."

Chapter Forty-Two

Rennie Easter stood beside the doorway of Fr. Geoffrey's classroom as his students made their exit, laughing and romping about in the youthful manner that reminded her why she made this trip. The priest, still youthful in appearance, had fine streaks of gray that highlighted his otherwise brown hair that was cut shorter than she remembered, but still stylish. It had been a couple of years since she had been back to St. Judes. When she had been awarded the internship at the High Museum in Atlanta, the need to immerse herself in the profession that had been her father's became her clarion call. Every day spent in the creative world in which her father had worked brought her closer to knowing him, as well as her mother in a strange sort of way. Even though Catherine had fought hard to beat whatever it was that had plagued her soul, she never fully recovered from the strange eating phenomenon. Rennie never doubted that her mother had loved her family more than anything. She still felt pangs of guilt for not being able to understand, or to help. Josie had been angry at both parents for not being able to fully stop whatever it was that had captured Catherine's spirit and virtually killed her before her body died.

Now a teacher here, perhaps Josie could feel the same connection with her parents that Rennie did in the art world. Coming back to this place, her home, to celebrate the twenty-fifth anniversary of her parents' work would be both special and painful. She had experienced another level of pain six months prior, with the breakup of what had been a tumultuous relationship in which her art friends had said they worried about her "Van Gogh state of mind". She had been reluctant to submit herself to more emotional baggage from the past but knew her presence here was needed and expected.

"Rennie! There's our esteemed fine art professional! I'm so glad you came early!" Fr. Geoffrey rushed to embrace one of his special ones, smiling and laughing as he now held her at arm's length, paying tribute to the beauty that she had also become. "You look wonderful. I have to say, Atlanta must agree with you, although we miss you terribly, of course. Have you seen Josie yet?"

"Yes and no. I peeked in her classroom, but she did not see me. She looks like quite the teacher in there. I can't wait to catch up with her. We've talked by phone, of course, about once every two weeks or so for a few minutes. Long distance is so expensive. We haven't seen each other in a year, since she was here and I was in Atlanta. I really wanted to be here, but being the low guy on the totem pole at work, I guess I felt like I had to go over and beyond, you know?"

"Yes, we were all disappointed that you weren't here for the holidays. Perhaps this year we will see you, I hope?"

"Yes, you will, I promise. I had some soul searching to do. I was more angry and sad about Mama and Daddy than I ever wanted to admit. It impacted my life in ways I had not acknowledged. But I exorcised a few demons and a crazy relationship or two." She glanced at the beloved priest wistfully. "The purging is all done, and Rennie Easter is back on the rise."

Fr. Geoffrey smiled, nodding affirmatively and hugging her shoulders once more. "Thanks be to God. More details about that later, perhaps? Oh, by the way, Josie and I would like to take you to dinner this evening on the Isle of Palms. All the oysters and shrimp we can handle with a few cold brews, of course. Before we go, though, she wanted to visit with you for a minute or two, if that's all right." He rubbed his clerical collar.

"I would love to do that and see the Isle of Palms! Driving over the Ben Sawyer Bridge and across Breach Inlet where the ocean comes into view has always been one of the most comforting experiences for me. Not to mention I've really missed walking on the beach. Bonita is coming in from New York City this evening, too, but I'm not sure when. I offered to pick her up from the airport in Columbia, but schedules got crazy and she said she wanted to rent a car, go by the music department at USC to visit, and take her time driving. I don't want to miss her, though."

Fr. Geoffrey smiled once again, pulling out a scrap of paper from the black shirt pocket beneath his clerical collar.

"You're in luck. Bonita called and caught an earlier flight out of the Big Apple and is coming on to Charleston. She should be here in time to go with us, as well. It will be wonderful to hear about all of her accomplishments and to see you two together again. Unfortunately, I've got to take care of a few things for tomorrow before we can leave for dinner. Let me go attend to these pressing affairs first and change clothes. Why don't you find Josie and you two can take that sister walk on the beach. Unpack, freshen up, and I will see you all at six o'clock. Oh, and I almost forgot. Ethan will be here tomorrow and wants to catch up with you and Bonita. Sean is also coming with his wife and two children. Many faces that you will remember from those years."

In an instant, she saw them all, eager and lively, just as they had been that day in Fr. Geoffrey's class, when Ethan got caught chewing gum, engaging in his usual antics. "I can't wait," she grinned, as the memories swirled about. "So, is Josie bringing whoever it is that she's been seeing? She finally told me there was someone special, but I don't have a name yet. It's about time, I must say. What do you know?"

Father Geoffrey grinned broadly but shook his head. "I think I need to let her tell you all about him. A lucky guy."

"Darn it, I thought I could get at least a name from you! Come on, Padre! Guess I'll have to be in suspense awhile longer. Is he coming tonight?"

"Yes, I think he's going to show up. Oh, one more thing, Rennie. I know you did a regionally televised news interview at the High Museum in Atlanta about this anniversary event in honor of Ray and Catherine. I read the nice article in the paper, as well. We would love for you to do a similar local television interview tomorrow, if you are up for it. Would that be a problem?"

"Not at all, I would love to help. Thank you for asking me. It's going to be an eventful weekend, I think."

"Indeed it is, Rennie. In many ways, I hope."

Chapter Forty-Three

Summerlea, South Carolina
The Easter Home
October, 1975

Rennie stood on the deck of her childhood home and let the past flow in like the waves that rushed the pristine beach and playfully ran back to the sea. They were still here, all the memories, safely tucked into every crevice of wood and gentle sway of sea oats that brushed against the salt air. The essence of Ray and Catherine, of family, was everywhere and never more prominently than on a crisp sunny day as this. There was a variety of fresh seashells spaced methodically on a deck rail to dry, just as they used to be when she and Josie were childhood collectors, proudly displaying each to their parents. Catherine's ceramic pots had been recovered from the storage area underneath the house and now contained lush greenery, fiery croton and coleus, goldenrod, and pansies. In a corner were three large pumpkins of varying sizes and buckets of seasonal mums, just as her mother lovingly arranged them at the first glimmer of her beloved season of autumn.

"I thought you and I might paint some of those shells like we used to do with Mom and Dad." Josie smiled as she stood by the deck stairs.

"Josie! I wasn't expecting you for another thirty minutes or so! Wow, everything looks wonderful!" Rennie rushed to embrace her sister, then stepped back momentarily. Josie was more alive, more beautiful than she had ever seen her. Her eyes shone like blue diamonds set against thick dark hair and peach fresh cheeks, and her smile was big as the Atlantic high tide. She exuded a happiness and confidence that Rennie had not witnessed in years.

"OK, cough it up. What's going on? I mean, you've always been gorgeous, but I've never seen you like this. For someone pushing thirty-one years of age, you look stunning! It must be the new mystery man you've been so cryptic about! I think I've waited long enough already to become the favorite sister-in-law and coolest aunt I'm one day destined to be! So, when am I going to meet Mr. Wonderful?" Rennie motioned for her sister to let the awaited news spill forth. Josie hesitated only for a moment before the big reveal and smiled again.

"We've been seeing each other romantically for the better part of a year. But we wanted to be absolutely certain before we announced anything. Rennie?" Josie reached for her hand, and held on tightly. "It's important to me that you are as happy about this as I am. I think you've kind of suspected for a little while, though. You've known him for years, and love him like a brother. As for me, I think I've always loved him, even before I really knew it for sure."

Instinctively, Rennie's hands migrated to her mouth as comprehension slowly dawned. She grabbed both of Josie's hands in hers and shouted. "Wait a minute! Stop! What? You mean Fr. Geoffrey? Our Fr. Geoffrey? Oh my God, oh my God, Josie! Of course, I'm happy! I'm ecstatic! Fr. Geoffrey is going to be my brother! Wait. You two are going to keep St. Jude's going, right? You're not leaving, are you?"

"Yes," Josie breathed, excited that her younger sister was on board with her future. "I mean, yes, we are staying here. Geoffrey and I plan for this area to be our home. Rennie, are you all right with him and me living here in this house, I hope? Of course, it is always yours, too. Mama and Daddy wouldn't have wanted it any other way."

Rennie took in the surrounding view once more. The plants, the deck just as her parents would have maintained it, the house looking better kept than it had in years. "I wouldn't have it any other way, either, Sis. Just keep me a spare bedroom open for when Atlanta gets to be too much. I only have one question for now. How long have you two had feelings for each other, and how in the world did you eventually decide to act on them? Does the rest of St. Jude's know?"

"Ok, that's three questions, but I'll answer. I've always loved him, deep down, but wasn't sure how he felt about me. When I realized that ten years difference isn't so big when both of us are way into adulthood, I just kind of let it evolve. We've been romantically involved for a year. The nuns know, as well as the bishop of our lower diocese of South Carolina, of course. As you might also have suspected by now, the oyster roast this evening is actually an impromptu engagement party. Geoffrey assisted with some pastoral care and events at The Citadel and became friends with General Seignious, the president there. General Seignious has graciously given us the use of the Citadel Beach House for the evening and is sending some of the cadets to help with the preparation and cleanup, maybe to spin a few tunes on a jukebox."

"Oh, lord," Rennie rolled her eyes, wincing with the memory. "I went to a Citadel homecoming weekend once and we all ended up at the beach house that night for a major party. Not my best look. My first _and maybe last_ experience with tequila, I think. My date said I told an arrogant upperclassman that his momma swims out to meet troop ships, or something crude like that. I haven't been back there since then. But I'll behave tonight, just for you."

"Rennie, you were always so spirited. I've always admired that about you. Hey, before we go any further, I'm going to grab us a glass of wine. Let's enjoy a few more minutes before we need to get ready for tonight." Josie disappeared through the screened porch,

241

kicking her tan pumps off inside the door and returning, barefoot, with a bottle of cabernet and two glasses, as the porch door slammed shut behind her. "Hey, Ren, there is a car parked out front across the street, an older model puke green chevy van. Not yours, I hope? It was sitting there when I got home."

"No, not mine, although I thought about trying to sneak off to Woodstock in something like that with Ethan Werner and a few of his buddies from USC, remember? Probably just some lost tourist trying to find his way back to the mainland." Rennie slid into one of the Adirondack chairs on the deck and pushed another over for Josie.

"See, that's what I mean," Josie offered, "You'd have gone to Woodstock with them in a minute if you hadn't been the only girl and didn't have a part-time job at the museum while you were in college in Columbia. You were such an adventurer. You still are, I think."

"And to think I've always secretly admired your quiet, more reserved side!" Rennie squeezed her sister's hand. "Josie, Mom and Dad would be so happy right now. You know they loved Fr. Geoffrey _ Geoffrey, I guess it is, now _as if he were their son."

"I know," Josie mused, in quiet contemplation. "They will be here in spirit all weekend. I've been missing them a lot lately. Tonight, there will be a few other priests there, any of our staff not on duty at the Home, as well as a few friends. Geoffrey hired some additional weekend security for the anniversary homecoming and is feeding them tonight at this event, too, as part of their payment."

"Security?" Rennie raised her eyebrows. "You mean for parking and such?"

"Yes, that too," Josie said. "With many from Charleston, the art community, and surrounding areas coming into Summerlea, and with all of our kids running around, Geoffrey thought some additional security might not be a bad idea. Anyway, he has invited the off duty officers that have been hired for the event to attend this evening. We plan to announce our news to the rest of St. Jude's tomorrow, so it will be done before Saturday. We wanted to keep that day all about St. Jude's and Mamma and Daddy, and not about us."

Another hour rolled effortlessly by, as more wine was consumed, memories jogged, and the bonds of sisterhood strengthened. Only the incessant ring of the telephone inside stopped the reunion, as Josie retrieved the call. In a few minutes she came running back outside, her bare legs and tanned feet peeking out from beneath the gauze skirt that billowed around her in the afternoon coastal breeze.

"We gotta go get ready!" Josie announced. "Bonita has arrived and she and Geoffrey are going to just drive over right now, so we will have a few extra minutes to pull ourselves together and ride with them to the beach house."

"Yikes," Rennie said, eyeing her watch. "I had no idea it was this late. Oh my gosh, I can't wait to see Bonita. It's been two years. She will go crazy with this news! Hey, dress code for tonight, Sis?"

Josie stuck her head around the corner as she adjusted her silver hoop earrings. "Oh, very casual. Oysters to shuck and beer to drink. Your bell bottoms and warm boots, if you have them. Don't forget a jacket. It's going to be pretty cool here tonight with the breeze, remember."

Rennie rifled through her suitcase, tossing items on the old white wrought iron double bed and settled on a pair of flare-leg jeans to go with her cowboy boots and a winter white cable knit sweater with a cowl neckline. With no time for electric curlers, she fluffed her chestnut hair with a light spritz of hairspray underneath and touched up her makeup and cologne. Grabbing a leather-collared denim jacket and a red print scarf, she tucked a small hairbrush and a tube of strawberry lip gloss in the inside pocket along with a handful of cash and her driver's license. Car lights brightened as Fr. Geoffrey's white jeep wagon turned into the driveway, then dimmed to off. Rennie could hear him and Bonita making their way up the stairs to the front door on the street side of the house. Bonita's familiar cackle and shouts began before she saw her.

"Why you white women so slow? Quit your lollygagging! Damn, it didn't take me this long to get down here from New York. Come on out here and give me some home grown Summerlea love!"

"Boneeeeetaaaa!!! Hey, girl! Aint no lollygagging going on! Just us women getting ready to get our groove on! Get on over here with your bad self!"

Best friends greeted each other in celebration, happy to be together after the lengthy separation. Rennie marveled at Bonita's continued transformation to a sleek and sophisticated professional. Her afro was still there, but longer and softer, with the front pulled back into a smooth, sleek look beneath a paisley print headband. A worn brown leather jacket and peach colored shirt accented the embroidery in her blue jeans. Meticulously placed classic gold bangle jewelry made her ebony skin shine.

"Where's my future bride, the lovely and talented Miss Josie Easter? I miss her!"

"Whoa!" Bonita froze, holding up a hand as if to stop traffic and stared at the priest, then back at Rennie. "What did he say? Did he say what I think he said? Fr. Geoffrey and Josie? Engaged? Oh, my God! Finally, it's about damn time! I always wondered when you two would realize this was a heaven-made match!"

The screaming and hysterics reignited as Josie emerged, her radiant blue eyes only enhanced by the azure sweater she wore atop faded denim bellbottoms and boots. She gave a demure smile to Fr. Geoffrey, who was enjoying the display of love among those who were like family. He thought of Ray and Catherine. Rennie reveled in Josie's contentment, relishing the newfound sense of peace in her sister. It was as if the anger she had once held toward her mother for the strange sickness and the agony of the deaths of both parents had finally been laid aside.

"I still can't believe it's happening!" Bonita threw her hands in the air in a gesture of delight as she hugged Josie. "Rennie, why you didn't tell me this!"

"She didn't know until today, either." Fr. Geoffrey kissed the cheek of a blushing Josie and held her hand in both of his. "We wanted to see your faces when we shared our news. Bonita, we have a special request for you if it fits in with your erratic schedule, now that you are becoming a Broadway star."

"'I wish! Please!" Bonita laughed, "I hardly think being an ensemble girl and a leper in Jesus Christ Superstar qualifies me for fame and fortune! But, I do have a little bit of good news, too. I have been selected to be an understudy for Miss Clamma Dale for the role of Bess, in the Houston Grand Opera production of *Porgy and Bess*."

"Oh, Bonita!" Rennie wiped tears from her eyes, remembering the day she watched an angry and defiant young girl grow into the person of beauty that she had come to cherish as her best friend. "I always knew you were destined to sing 'Summertime' on the big stage one day. You gave me chills the first time I heard you do it. This is just the beginning for you! I will make the trip to see that, if you get to do it!"

Bonita smiled, tears also trying to gather in the corners of her eyes as she quickly brushed them aside. "Lawd, please, don't get me all emotional, Ren. I spent time and money on this blasted makeup just for y'all. But, yes, you'd better bring it on to Houston when I perform. So, where were we? A request? Hope it ain't for money. I'm just a struggling artist underneath all this magnificent black beauty."

"Here we go," Fr. Geoffrey made the sign of the cross in the air. "Lord, please deliver us."

Josie placed a hand on his shoulder and waited for the levity to ease. "Bonita, what Geoffrey and I would cherish more than anything is if you would sing at our wedding. We would be so honored. That is, if it can fit with your schedule. We haven't set a date, and we are very flexible, as it will be a simple ceremony and done at St. Jude's, of course. Do you think it'd be possible?"

"Ok, now you've done it." Bonita flapped her hands wildly in front of her face, trying to control the pools of emotional tears that refused to be quelled. "I can't think of anything I'd rather do more. Yes, of course I'll sing. Let me get in a quick practice right now!" As if on stage underneath the burning lights of Broadway, Bonita bent her knees, eyes closed as if in prayer, and began a low hum. Her hands swayed in a rhythmic lull, then clenched into tight fists as she crescendoed to belt out the bluesy bars of Percy Sledge's "When a Man Loves a Woman."

In the midst of all the merriment, Fr. Geoffrey motioned to the door, grinning and gesturing to Rennie. "I hear you have agreed to be the maid of the highest honor and might even entertain an attempt to paint your sister's bridal portrait?"

More excited utterances and wild dancing about the warmly lit family room ensued. It had been a long time since this house had seen such laughter.

"Yes, to the first part of that, still negotiable on the second, as I'm sure Josie wants quality. I would be happy to give it a shot. Actually, I'd like to paint you both, to preserve you in time forever!"

Fr. Geoffrey smiled, squeezing his fiance' once more and rolling his eyes to the ceiling. "Dear Lord, pray the rest of the evening is calm and sane. After all, what else could possibly be in store?"

Chapter Forty-Four

Isle of Palms, South Carolina
The Citadel Beach House
October, 1975

The grand old two-story beach house had been seasoned over the years with unforgiving summer suns and relentless waves of salt mist and cadet revelry. Mounding dunes, recently damp with foamy remnants of high tide, boasted of plentiful sea oats standing tall in the chilly air, now rife with the smell of fresh seafood. Steamed shrimp and oysters adorned the picnic tables on the front porch that stretched seaside across the entirety of the building. An array of saltine crackers, cocktail sauce, and oyster knives lay scattered about the tabletops, while the thudding sound of shucked shells, pitched into large metal buckets underneath, punctuated the feasting. Inside, the open fireplace added an ambiance of warmth and merriment as people meandered in and out, stopping for drink refills and offering up best wishes to the guests of honor. Rennie sipped on a gingerale, coaxing the last few drops out of the chilled can and holding it high in the air before her friend, as they leaned against the outside porch railing.

"I've come to learn, through a few years of personal training experience with alcohol, that pacing is everything. Tonight, I'm already a few glasses of wine ahead of you, courtesy of Josie. Hence, the gingerale. Mama and Daddy used to always give it to us for whatever ailed, and it's still my go-to remedy and de-tox. Now I think I'm finally ready to transition on over to cold beer to go with those oysters I'm getting ready to sling down! You ready to eat yet?"

Bonita didn't make a move toward the tables but took another slow sip of wine. "Not quite. You still have some explaining to do. Girl, what happened last year that kept you out of touch and away from Summerlea, especially during the holidays? I was working my tail off in New York, between waitressing and trying to get established as a singer, so at least I had an excuse. I wanted to be here and couldn't. But you, on the other hand, could come home and didn't. Why not?"

Rennie stared into the vast ocean, searching past the horizon for an answer to the painful question that she had wanted to avoid but knew better than to patronize her friend. Crushing the gingerale can, she tossed it into a nearby garbage can and took a deep breath. "I was pretty messed up for awhile, Bo. After I broke up with the guy I thought I might marry, I started on this downward spiral. He always said I competed with him in everything, and I guess that was probably true. A sidenote: Never date someone in your field of work, at least not until you're comfortable in your own skin. We began to argue all the time about every possible aspect of work, and it spilled over into our social lives. He said I was trying to channel my father and be an instant expert critic. I accused him of being an ass-kisser and not being forthright when delivering a critique. I was devastated when he eventually decided to accept an offer in London that did not include me. I threw myself into fast-forward and refused to look back. Traded sex for love. Lots of sex. But no love. Then, one of my grad professors became interested in me romantically. He was handsome, brilliant, and thought I was everything I wanted to be. It was the affirmation I craved, and again I thought I'd met my soul mate. Sadly, turns out there was a Mrs. Professor that he eventually said he had no intention of divorcing, despite their being separated, and I was crushed beyond humiliation. How could I be so stupid? I just lost it. I started drinking more just like Mama sometimes did. I let it all go. My faith, my drive, my self-confidence, and worst of all, my self-respect."

"Oh, Rennie. Damnit, you should have told me! I'm so sorry." Bonita shook her head back and forth as if to erase what she had just heard. She faced Rennie, her jaw clenched, as she growled underneath her breath. "I'm also pissed, damn it! Why didn't you tell me? You were hurting all that time and I had no clue, and might have helped you agonize through it."

"I know, I know. It's my fault. Hell, all of it was my fault, and I was drowning in my own self-pity. I could not rid myself of the tremendous guilt I felt over the poor choices I'd made. I became defined by my mistakes and an overwhelming sense of sadness I could not identify, much less shake. Truth is, I was too ashamed to let you or Josie or Fr. Geoffrey know what was happening. You were all so successful at what you were doing and I was trying like crazy to achieve those goals, too, or so I thought. I kept digging that hole deeper until one early morning, I woke up in a strange place with an even stranger man. I sneaked out, walking in downtown Atlanta, looking like ten miles of bad road, crying, and feeling even worse than I looked, if that were possible."

"What happened?" Bonita demanded.

"A young priest was walking into a nearby Catholic church. I must've appeared pretty desperate, as he invited me to come inside. He listened, encouraged me to stop lying to myself and closing everyone out of my life. He gave me the name of someone competent to talk with. He said God would help me unravel the mess I'd made. Of course, I was given the spiel about going back to church, to start taking care of my own emotional needs first, rather than relying on a guy to do that, and to start by giving back to the community in some way. He never came across as proselytizing, just caring. You know, like Fr. Geoffrey. Geoffrey, that is, if I can remember to call him that now. He advised me to see my doctor, too. Thankfully, I managed to stay healthy in the middle of it all."

Rennie smiled, laughing aloud and brushing the chestnut hair out of her eyes. "Wanna hear the best part? I immersed myself in reading, attending the theatre, concerts, new art projects, sports, volunteering, either by myself or with friends. No sex or romantic relationships for several months while I was on this soul-searching pilgrimage of sorts. And shortly into counseling, I discovered I was seething with unresolved grief that kept piling on with each setback. I was still a kid when it all started, not understanding what was happening with Mama, then losing her and Daddy, then Josie leaving for college only two months after they died. I thought I was handling it all just great, you know? I was happy, or so I thought. St. Jude's became my family, followed by my own college experience. I was fine. Then, somehow, when those first vestiges of adulthood appeared *a real job, being responsible for my own bills and life_* it was like I hit a brick wall or something. The pain and the loss all came screaming back, and it caught me totally offguard."

"Rennie." Bonita grabbed her hand and spoke with authority. "You were the person who pulled me out of a despairing life. You were the first person to like me for me, to see beyond the lost, raging black girl that had every reason to be angry at the world. You reached out to me despite the pain you were in, not to mention the pain I tried to inflict on you. Because of you, I finally had a friend. You will always be the strongest person I know and my best damn friend, and don't ever forget it! To me, you and I are sisters as much as you and Josie are."

Rennie grinned broadly, squeezing Bonita's hand. "I don't know, you were pretty upset with me on spring break that time I dragged you to a shooting range, just so I could impress a guy that dared me to go shoot with him."

"Oh, Jesus take the wheel!" Bonita exclaimed, her eyes narrowing with false disdain. "Yes, I was ready to stomp your lily white ass for that. I saw and heard enough violence and gunfire in my neighborhood as a kid, and to this day, I never want to see another gun. I was a nervous wreck just being there, and you were the only one shooting!"

"Hey, those oysters are going fast." Rennie pointed to the crowded tables. "Let's go eat. I'm starved. More late night urban history when we get home. You're staying at the house with Josie and me for the entire weekend, right?" The October night air was crisp. Those outside had begun to don jackets, scarves, and more work gloves to tackle the oysters. The girls slid into a space at the end of a large table and dug into the delicacies from the sea.

"Now this is what I call good eating." Rennie laughed, wiping the juice that ran down her chin as she slurped up the oyster scraped out of a steaming shell and immersed it in horseradish and cocktail sauce. She closed her eyes and raised both hands in mock appreciation of the salty morsels. Bonita leaned close to whisper.

"If you enjoy those oysters any more than you are now, I think the guys at the end of the table are going to explode. They've been watching you eat since you started. They're looking at you like you're having an orgasm or something."

"What on earth are you talking about?" Rennie shoved another oyster into her mouth, chasing it with a swig of beer, and licked her lips, as she raised her brows at Bonita, who nodded her head toward the opposite end of the table. A small bevy of men, huddled around a haul of seafood, smiled at Rennie with lascivious delight. One of them raised a bottle of beer in a mock toast. Rennie stopped chewing and gave a vigorous wipe across her mouth with the back of the gloved hand that held her oyster knife. Another round of laughter and undiscernable comments erupted from the male end of the table. She reached for yet another oyster.

"Well, they're just gonna have to suck it up. I haven't had oysters in so long I can't remember, and I'm going to enjoy myself, men be damned! After all, I paid good money for this new attitude."

Bonita bubbled over the hum of noise. "Uh, girl, I think it's you sucking it up that they are enjoying. You know a damn man can make anything be about sex, especially when they congregate like that."

A burst of laughter from the feminine side of the table now drew the attention from the men, as Fr. Geoffrey and Josie made their way to Rennie and Bonita and motioned for the men at the other end to join them.

"We're so glad you two are here," Fr. Geoffrey put a respective arm around Bonita and Rennie. "I'd like to introduce you to some of the folks who are helping us with security this weekend."

"Of course it would be them," Rennie winced through gritted teeth.

Fr. Geoffrey greeted each of the four off-duty law enforcement officers from Charleston and Summerlea by name, stopping momentarily for the last of them. "You're the visiting one from Savannah, right? The narcotics guy?" The man, a few inches taller than the others, was handsome in a classic rebellious kind of way, with thick brown hair tousled in rugged abandon about an intense face and the deepest of green eyes. He took a hand from the pocket of his denim jacket to extend to Fr. Geoffrey, then Josie, but saved his slow, lazy smile for Rennie, his stare boring a hole into her as he grasped her hand.

"I'm Aidan Cross," he said, with a decidedly southern drawl in the smooth baritone voice.

"The beer saluter," Bonita whispered to her, as the men nodded and laughed.

"I know who he is," Rennie hissed, giving the most gracious return of smile that she could muster. What was so unsettling about him, besides the obvious physical good looks and a voice like butter? Was it the way he regarded her, the way he made her feel as if he could see inside her soul, or the manner in which he seemed to command the crowd with his southern boy self-assurance? Whatever it was, Aidan Cross was both intriguing and disarming. She motioned for Bonita to go with her for a beer. As they waited at the bar, she saw him approaching and felt her heartbeat quicken as he stood next to her.

"Now this isn't a proposal, just an observation. You know if you were married to me, your name would be Rennie Easter Cross." Aidan's hands were once again shoved deep into the pockets of his denim jacket as he smiled down at her. Rennie supposed him to be at least six feet tall or more. He leaned in closer to whisper, his unrelenting green eyes bearing down on hers as a wicked grin spread across his face. "Could be divine intervention, what do you think?"

Rennie stared at him, waiting to respond, as she gathered composure. "Why, Officer Cross, I think you might be on some of those narcotics you've no doubt confiscated from some poor unsuspecting college kid. I don't even know you." She spun on him abruptly to face her friend, but he stepped to her side, angling between her and Bonita.

"I'm Aidan Cross," he said with resolve, his eyes burning into hers with no trace of a smile. "Both a lover and a fighter, when that which I cherish is threatened. An advocate of justice and loyal to a fault. A connoisseur of well-prepared food, fine whiskey, and an occasional smooth cigar. A music and sports enthusiast, I'm most comfortable in old blue jeans but can work a tux on demand. Above all, a purveyor of laughter that makes life fun every damn day. Who are you, Rennie Easter?"

"Lawd have mercy." Bonita fanned her own face with both hands. "Cuff me now, Officer," she sputtered aloud, then whispered to Rennie. "I could get disorderly with that. Too much sexual tension for me, though, I think I'll grab my cold drink elsewhere." Bonita scurried to the other side of the bar, leaving Rennie to consider the bold intrusion.

"Okay. I'll bite." She took a sip of beer and turned to face him. "I'm Rennie Easter. A believer in honesty, even when it hurts. Lover of art and history, haunter of museums, appreciator of good champagne, hot blues, cold beer, and of course, fresh steamed oysters on a night like this. Fiercely dedicated to family and friends, ridiculously passionate about Halloween, autumn walks on the beach and in the mountains. Rabid about my Carolina Gamecocks. An occasional tennis player, but never a game player."

Aidan Cross smiled, shifting side to side as he folded his arms and regarded her with obvious approval. "Halloween, the night when people get to be something they are not. I like it, too. I think we can work with most of that. Well, with the exception of your college team choice. I'm a Bulldog, but we won't let your being a Gamecock get in the way."

"A Citadel Bulldog?" Rennie asked, as two of the other officers and Bonita joined them and handed a beer to Aidan. "You went here to The Citadel in Charleston?"

"Hell, no!" Aidan smiled, slightly raising his voice. "Vince Dooley and the Georgia Dawgs, baby!" Motioning for one of the officers to join him, they began to chant, "Bulldog born, Bulldog bred, and when I die I'll be Bulldog dead!"

"Lord have mercy, I'm in college football hell." Rennie flashed a coquette smile. "At least on the bright side you didn't say

'Clemson', thank goodness! Bonita! I need reinforcements here. Let's show 'em how it's done." Rennie put an arm around Bonita's neck and raised the other to the ceiling yelling, 'Game!' and waited for Bonita to finish with the requisite, 'Cocks!"

"What did she just say?" One of the out-of-town guests stared wide-eyed at Bonita. "Is that really what they say here?"

"Short for 'Gamecocks'," another replied, "and, yes, they say it a lot, so get used to it." The phrase was repeated several times to the delight of the officers, followed by a Citadel cadet rendition of the "Citadel Ramble," to which the crowd roared their delight as Fr. Geoffrey and Josie watched in amusement. With the food consumed and camaraderie established, the merriment and dancing went on for a few more hours until Fr. Geoffrey thanked everyone for attending and reminded them all of the anniversary celebration.

"It is getting late and tomorrow is a big day for us, so Josie and I unfortunately must take our leave now. Until tomorrow, everyone! Thank you again for making this a special evening for us."

"That's our cue," Rennie smiled at Aidan, who reached for her arm.

"Do you have to go? We can give you and Bonita a ride. Please stay just a little longer. One more spin around the dance floor at least? My shagging gets better each time out there, you know. Or maybe it's just the dancing ability of my partner." His green eyes held her gaze. There was a time when she would have stayed with him through the night, if he'd asked.

"As tempting as that is, I just can't. It's a big day at St. Jude's and I need to be on deck early to help. We've already stayed longer than we should, which means I really need some rest. It was great to meet you, Aidan. I do hope I will see you tomorrow."

"Count on it," he said, smiling, "but you're not quite done with me yet. I'm walking you to your car. Remember, I'm from the

South, too, and it's what we do, even us rogue types. After you, ladies." Aidan motioned for Rennie and Bonita to move first. Bonita giggled like a smitten schoolgirl and grinned sideways at Rennie, who shook her head as they descended the stairs and turned toward the direction of Fr. Geoffrey's car.

"Ren, look!" Bonita grabbed her shoulder and nodded toward the van parked at the end of a line of cars.

"What is it?" Aidan demanded.

"The greenish van at the end of that row. It was parked at our house before we left and now it's there. The same man is sitting in it, I think."

"I didn't see it follow us here. I don't know, maybe its just coincidence." Rennie said, staring at the car. "It sat near the front of the house for a long time. I think Josie thought it might be following me, but that makes no sense at all."

"Let's err on the side of caution. I want you two to walk to your car while I watch. Tell Fr. Geoffrey to stay put for a few minutes to give me time to get the tags and check it out. If he follows you, don't get out of the car. Drive to the police station. I'll be close by. Rennie, I need your number and address, just in case, to be sure you all get back alright." Aidan smiled. "At least this way I have the important information, right?"

"I love a man who takes charge." Bonita playfully punched his shoulder. "However, you are seriously slowing down on the job, Officer, if you don't have her number already. You really think that van could be following us?"

"I don't know," Aidan replied. "Any reason they might be tailing you?"

"No, what in the world could anyone want with us?" Rennie offered.

"Well, it may be nothing. But let's be sure. I'll be in touch. Be safe."

Aidan Cross smiled, squeezed Rennie's shoulder, and waved as she and Bonita walked to their car. Making a stealth circle behind the van, he saw clear windows only in the front seats as he memorized a Virginia tag number. There was a lone male driver, muscular and big, who flicked ashes from a smouldering cigarette through the barely open window and tapped his fingers on the dashboard in time to the faint radio sound of The Doobie Brothers' *Long Train Running*. Aidan crept closer. The man's hands were white as alabaster. He was wearing gloves, the heavy latex kind that prevented fingerprint encryption. Aidan felt the familiar onslaught of adrenaline that signaled possible danger as the headlights of Father Geoffrey's jeep blinked on and sent a ripple of light down the length of the Citadel Beach House and over nearby homes as they moved down the parking area. Making a right turn onto Palm Boulevard and heading toward the route to Summerlea, the party began the drive home. Before he could reach the car, the mysterious van cranked into life and began a slow roll into the street along the same route as the jeep. Aidan headed to the closest phone booth and waited for the voice on the other end to retrieve the requested information.

"Yeah, man, thanks for running it for me. Contact the sheriff in Summerlea and let him know. Fr. Geoffrey Radcliffe from St. Jude's is driving the jeep we need to intercept. I'm headed to the Easter home in about five minutes."

In his rush to get back to the beach house, he made no attempt to recradle the receiver as it fell and bounced against the glass wall of the booth. His mind raced ahead to Rennie as he took the stairs two at a time and looked for any of the local deputies he had met who would accompany him to the Easter home, then dashed toward his

Mustang. The information he had been given kept playing in his head.

Stolen car. Involved in the commission of an unsolved, likely racially motivated crime in Mississippi. Murder.

Chapter Forty-Five

Summerlea, South Carolina
The Easter Home
October, 1975

Climbing the stairs to the house, Rennie moved in silence along with the others, wondering when Aidan would arrive and clarify what had been discovered. She knew he had notified the local police, who stopped them as they were going through the town of Mt. Pleasant and provided an escort home. Now the deputies combed the perimeter of the house, checking every possible hiding place as well as the area of the dunes on the beach side. An officer had entered the house before them and scanned each room for signs of intrusion. Finding none, he had motioned them inside. Bonita took off her jacket and sat on the leather sofa in front of the fireplace, fluffing her hair with her fingers.

"Well, this little visit down south sure has been exciting so far! I haven't seen this much drama lately even in New York. You all sure know how to show a girl a good time."

Fr. Geoffrey, who usually responded to quips from Bonita with more levity, remained stonefaced, peering out the window to observe the officers below. The sound of the screen door opening followed by the loud rapping of the door- knocker announced the arrival of Aidan Cross. His eyes went straight to Rennie.

"Everyone okay here?"

"Yes, we're fine." Rennie folded her arms across her shoulders. "Thank you, Aidan, for all you did. What's going on? Were all of these officers necessary?"

"The truthful answer is that I'm not sure just yet." He looked at each, then again at Rennie. "Someone once told me that honesty is important, even if it hurts. So, let me tell you what I know. The vehicle tags are stolen. Last registered to a Jason Browner in Virginia. Anyone recognize the name, assuming it's even legitimate?"

"Never heard of him," Fr. Geoffrey replied, as others shook their heads in the negative.

"The van was found abandoned in the Shem Creek area down the road aways. No sign of the driver."

"Well, at least we are all safe now." Josie offered.

"I'm not so sure about that." Aidan stopped momentarily. "According to our data from the National Crime Information Center, the van may have been involved in a 1968 unsolved crime in Mississippi."

"A crime? What kind of crime?" Rennie pressed.

Aidan ran his fingers through his hair before answering. "A homicide. Racially motivated, likely in response to the Voting Rights Act of '65 that helped minorities exercise their constitutional right to vote. A white man was kidnapped and later found hanged and burned. He was a known sympathizer to the black community and had worked hard to help them register to vote."

"My God," Rennie breathed. "How in the world could that possibly involve any of us here in Summerlea, South Carolina?"

"I'm fairly sure it doesn't," Aidan said, "but stolen tags often have a way of circulating amongst criminals and being involved in more than one crime. And, I should tell you one more thing," he added quietly. "The driver of the car was wearing gloves. Surgical gloves, to be exact. No fingerprints left anywhere, but they found a few possible footprints to check. The bigger question is why was this individual following Rennie and possibly Josie, too?"

Fr. Geoffrey instinctively put an arm around Josie as all considered the question. "What do you suggest we do?" he asked.

"Well, the sheriff here has already begun an investigation and will have a patrol in the area through the weekend at least. If I may be so bold, I'd like to suggest that Fr. Geoffrey and I both stay here tonight, just in case. I've slept on lots worse than a sofa or floor and I'd feel better providing some more security."

"Aidan, I think it's a good idea. There is an extra bedroom upstairs, if you'd like," Josie offered.

Bonita cut her eyes at Rennie, the faintest glimmer of a smile tugging at the corners of her mouth. Rennie remained stoic and focused on Aidan.

"Actually, I'd like to stay downstairs, if that's all right with everyone. On the outside chance that if anyone were to attempt to get in, I'd be who he met first."

"Josie's room is the master bedroom downstairs. It opens onto the deck, too. Should she stay upstairs with us?" Rennie asked.

"Ladies," Fr. Geoffrey smiled. "I'd like to think I've curried a small bit of favor from the Almighty. I'm not leaving the future Mrs. Radcliffe alone. She's stuck with me this evening, with sleep being the sole agenda for the night."

Bonita pointed a finger at him, raised her other hand high in the air, and closed her eyes in mock prayer. Rennie smiled at Aidan, glad for the normal moment of comic relief.

"Brothers and Sisters," Bonita announced, "please pray for this priest, that he not succumb to the temptations of the flesh as he submits himself to the guardianship of your precious child, Miss Josie Easter. Pray also that our newfound friend, Mr. Aidan Cross, will kick some devil butt if he tries to enter this blessed house of your humble servants. Amen, Sweet Baby Jesus!"

Aidan could not contain his amusement. Seeing every line on his face as he laughed, Rennie felt the chemistry between them. She would proceed with caution, but there was no denying the attraction she felt for him. The others said their goodnights and drifted off to respective rooms.

"Let me get you some blankets and a pillow, Aidan." Rennie blushed under his intense gaze, aware of him staring as she gathered two heavy blankets and a bedsize pillow from the top shelf of the cedar-paneled closet. As she turned to deliver them he was there beside her, his eyes searching hers as he lifted a hand to touch her arm. He looked at her with an expression she could not fathom, but she was sure that he also felt the synergy. Raising his hand from her arm, he braced it against the edge of the closet door above her head and bent low so that his lips barely brushed against her cheek and his breath, warm and sensual, whispered in her ear.

"Goodnight, Rennie Easter. Sleep well."

Bonita was waiting in the upstairs room they would share, sitting on one of the iron double beds in an over-sized white t-shirt with the face of Jimi Hendrix. Rennie closed the door and stretched out on the soft quilted top of the other, her mind racing. "So?" She motioned for more information. "Spill it, girl!"

Rennie raised her head from the bed just enough to reply. "I can't even breathe right now."

Chapter Forty-Six

Summerlea, South Carolina
The Easter Home
October, 1975

Rennie donned a pair of weathered jeans and buttoned a long-sleeved red plaid flannel shirt over her pajama top as she glanced at the clock by her bed. It was just past seven in the morning. The smell of fresh perked coffee beckoned as she shut the door on a sleeping Bonita and crept down the stairs, her bare feet sliding against the smoothness of the wood. There was something about bare feet on wood floors that brought back comforting memories of childhood and her parents. Voices from the kitchen told her Fr. Geoffrey and Josie had beat her to the first cups of hot goodness. She smoothed disheveled hair away from her face and rubbed her eyes, yawning and waving a greeting.

"Good Friday morning, Rennie," Fr. Geoffrey raised his mug to her. "We made it through the night safe and sound, and now our weekend can officially begin with your interview and then our big luncheon."

"What's this about an interview, Rennie?" Aidan wiped his feet against the mat at the open sliding glass door and entered from the deck. His smooth baritone voice rose just above the sound of waves lapping against the shore. He held an empty coffee cup in one hand and tried to finish buttoning the rumpled shirt that was secured only at his waist. He was even more handsome in the light of day, his dark hair tossed about by the ocean air and a smile that was highlighted by a whisper of a yet unshaven shadow. Rennie subconsciously straightened the lace on her pajama top that peeked from beneath her flannel shirt.

"Oh, the interview is our small-town thing for the anniversary celebration of St. Jude's." She took a sip from the cup of coffee that Josie handed to her. "I'm going to share some of the history of the home and where things are now. By the way, Fr. Geoffrey, what time is the interview and where?"

"You know, Rennie, it's okay to start calling me just 'Geoffrey'. We can save the 'Father' part for around the kids or at a St. Jude's function. What do you say?"

"I know, I know," Rennie mused. "It just seems so different. You've been 'Father' for as long as I've known you. But, I guess time marches on and I need to step up. Besides," she grinned, "I could not be more thrilled to have you as a brother. So, Geoffrey," she emphasized the name, "I need some details on that interview, please."

"Eleven o'clock sharp in the courtyard, my dear. Very casual, your best jeans are fine."

"Rennie, may I drive you there?" Aidan offered. "That way, I can keep an eye on you and your car can be left here. There will be patrols in this area, also." Rennie nodded, noting the smiles on the faces of both Geoffrey and Josie.

"I'd love a second cup of coffee, which I'll be glad to make, and a quick walk on the beach. Anybody game?" Aidan asked.

Geoffrey and Josie elected to stay in the house while Bonita continued to sleep, leaving Rennie more than willing to accept Aidan's offer. She grabbed a jacket out of the closet, along with an old pair of beach moccasins that had long since been retired from sand detail. Aidan reached for the overnight bag that he had retrieved from his car and laced up a pair of old running shoes before following Rennie down the walkway to the ocean.

"Did you grow up in this house?" he inquired. "If I may ask, where are your folks now?" Rennie stopped walking and regarded him with care. He did not know.

"Okay, the 'honesty hurts' thing is coming into play here again, so I guess now is as good a time as any. Yes, I grew up here in this house until I was twelve. My father and mother met and married in Finland during World War II, where they lived, worked, and attended school. As the war was in its final days, they managed to leave Finland and brought many orphan children with them. With the help of the people in Summerlea, they started St. Jude's. Of course we grew up with the kids in the Home, too, and were thrilled when my dad and mom decided to take a trip back to Europe with the Atlanta Art Association and left us at the Home for the duration of their trip. It was June of 1962. Josie was eighteen and getting ready to attend the College of Charleston where my father had been a tenured art professor and considered an expert in his field of restoration and art history. Sadly, my parents never returned home. Their plane crashed on takeoff. Only two stewardesses survived."

Rennie took a long sip of coffee and an even longer breath of air as she gazed out over the great Atlantic. She could feel Aidan staring at her, deep in thought.

"My God, Rennie. You mean the Orly Crash, don't you? I remember it. I'm so sorry. I didn't know. Please forgive me. All I knew was I was coming here to visit a police buddy and got recruited to help him with an event at the Home. How terrible that must have been for you."

Rennie studied him, watching the dark furrows of his brow and the most serious of expressions on his face. "It's okay, Aidan. Actually, I'm glad you asked. Talking about them is something I used to be afraid to do. I spent a good bit of my hard earned cash in an Atlanta therapy office to understand just how sad and angry I was deep inside. It's weird, as I always thought I'd had a pretty happy childhood despite their tragic deaths and the demons my mom secretly battled, no doubt left over from stuff she must have seen during the war. Adulthood brought out the unresolved issues, I suppose." She smiled, briefly touching his shoulder and taking in the clean smell of fresh salt air and masculinity as he walked close to her. "More on me, later. It's your turn, now."

"So, I guess you're going to hold me to the honesty thing again, aren't you?" He grabbed her hand and assisted her down the rickety steps to the beach. They began walking against the morning breeze.

"I'm from Stone Mountain, Georgia, originally. I was the quintessential middle child, the bad boy, so there is the disclaimer," he smiled. "But I did finally outgrow most of it, so don't hold it against me. Anyway, my parents divorced when I was thirteen, and my brother went with my dad, while my mother took my sister and me to Savannah. In one day, I lost my dad and my brother. Admittedly, I was a handful of trouble. I think the only thing that kept me out of jail at the time was my athleticism and dedication to football. When I turned eighteen, I realized I should go ahead and volunteer for service or I would be drafted anyway, based on my number. So, I took up with Uncle Sam. I think my mother was actually relieved, even though she cried like hell when I signed up. They had me take some tests after basic training. After that, I was stationed for awhile at Ft. Benning, where it turns out they decided I wasn't as stupid as some might have initially thought. I eventually ended up as a Special Forces Medical Sergeant."

"You mean a Green Beret medic?" Silently impressed, Rennie now understood where the quiet self-confidence and extreme fitness regimen must have originated. He came across as laid back and easy going, but there was more to this intriguing man underneath the surface.

266

"Aidan, I can't even imagine what it took to achieve that level of competency and grit. You must have nerves of steel."

"Yeah, it was one of those things you'd never do again but wouldn't take a million bucks for the experience either, you know? In Special Forces one cross-trains, so in addition to a rigorous medical background, I became fairly proficient with communications also. Did some time in Thailand and Viet Nam. Lost my best friend there. Even though the military saved me in all kinds of ways, as odd as that sounds, I eventually was honorably discharged due to an injury I received. I still periodically entertain the idea of further medical schooling, since that type of training is quite thorough in Special Forces and I could piggyback off that. The combination of narcotics knowledge combined with some communications and military expertise also gave me a unique background and skill set, and I liked the idea of a job to walk into while I was in school. So I made it past a biology degree at Georgia with a minor in partying, got some additional law enforcement training, and here I am working in narcotics, at least for now. Mine was a kind of a roundabout journey to get to where things are today. So, that's the short version."

Aidan looked at her with warm attention, brushing hair out of his eyes and engaging her with his smile as they traded pages and an occasional painful chapter from their respective lives. With every story, every confidence, Rennie felt the desire to know as much about him as she could. There was no denying the attraction that was growing with every minute she spent with him.

"We should get back. I could do this all day, Aidan, if we didn't both have to be on duty. Thank you for walking with me and for being here last night." As they mounted the stairs to the boardwalk, Aidan turned to face her.

"Rennie. I hope you can tell that I want to get to know you even more. I know you are pretty committed to all that is happening at St. Jude's this weekend, and I don't want to intrude or stop you from doing what you need to do. Having said that, I would love nothing more than to be able to spend some time with you alone. Let me know when you are free. I'm going to take my cues and invitations from you." His green eyes were penetrating as he waited for her response.

"Thank you for the consideration of space, Aidan. I do have a few responsibilities and need to spend some time with folks from the Home. But I will have free time, too, and would love to get to know you more, as well. An invitation will come soon." Rennie smiled, happy that he had at last voiced feelings that matched her own. Aidan placed his hand on the small of her back and guided her down the steps on the other side of the walkway as they made their way back to the house.

"Let's get you safely to that interview."

Chapter Forty-Seven

Summerlea, South Carolina
St. Jude's Home
October, 1975

Fr. Geoffrey greeted the small gathering congregated in the green courtyard that was just beginning to show hints of seasonal color. All was going as planned thus far, as the last of the tables were added to the outside area for the community lunch. Rennie had done an exemplary job of outlining the history of the Home and her parent's involvement in its inception, while the now veteran priest had provided the outline for the events of the anniversary weekend. The day was bright and crisp, full of promise, as former residents, the art community from varying cities and the town of Summerlea had all begun to arrive. Rennie scanned the growing crowd for any signs of Aidan. He was likely helping new arrivals park and find their way around the campus and church and make their way to the dining hall for the pick up lunches to be shared picnic-style outside.

Fumbling with her crossbody bag, she excavated a tube of lipgloss and massaged a tiny bit of cocoa butter over her hands. That was enough gussying up with conflicting scents for now, she surmised, not wanting to overpower the freshness of her cologne. Glancing around once more for a glimpse of Aidan, she caught sight of Fr. Geoffrey and Bonita coming across the far side of the courtyard with a tall blonde man garbed in jeans and a V-neck sweater over a white dress shirt. With him was a striking brunette with a modern close-cropped pixie haircut and bangle earrings that accentuated her casual chic look. Rennie recognized Ethan Werner just by the easy way he strolled across the grass. The three years or so since she had seen him appeared to have been good ones for him as he looked just the same, only with a hint of age-appropriate refinement. It was hard to believe he had settled into life as a financial consultant, had a steady girl, and a small house in the upstate Greenville area.

"Rennie! Rennie Easter, is that you?" Ethan beamed, the prankster in his eyes returning to revel in the reunion.

"Lord, have mercy! Ethan Werner, live and in the flesh! Hey, did you bring any gum for us?"

Laughter ensued as Rennie grabbed her former classmate around the neck and hugged him with the ferocity of memories and friendship renewed. It felt good to be here once more, among her friends that had become family. Ethan placed an arm around the girl beside.

"It seems that wedding announcements are all over the place, so I'm going to add to the fun. This is Anna, my fiancé."

After the greetings had subsided the group began to move toward the dining hall, where Fr. Geoffrey presided over the blessing and words of welcome. He extended an invitation to tour the campus in the afternoon and drop in on Friday classes in the school. Saturday promised more tours, another picnic and a slide show, with resident children and staff providing the narration. They would also have time to view the archive area set up in the back of the small auditorium. Dinner each night was on your own, and all were invited to attend the Sunday morning service at the church and the requisite photos before returning home. Rennie commented to Bonita on the commendable job that the planners of the celebration had done in utilizing the afforded time, with large chunks of unscheduled activity for all to relax, drive into Charleston, or make the quick drive to the beach.

"Perfect," Bonita whispered, pointing to the door. "Look at him. Rennie, I think he's for real. And speaking of, check out that solid hunk of black beauty in a uniform standing with them. Where was he the other night? Inquiring minds want to know!"

Rennie smiled as Aidan and the other members of the security detail entered the dining hall after Fr. Geoffrey's announcements and blessing, and now waited patiently at the back of the room for guests to get their food first. She managed not to laugh aloud at Bonita, noting the lone black Summerlea police officer amidst the seven men.

"What's the matter, you don't like white men?" Ethan teased.

"Nothing wrong with a little sweet cream, but I like my chocolate strong and hot," Bonita shot back.

Rennie shook her head, trying in vain to smother another round of laughter that threatened to make a volcanic eruption.

"Here we go. You two at least try to hold it down, please." Fr. Geoffrey made the announcement for the security detail to get their plates first. On their way out of the cafeteria to the courtyard, Aidan met Rennie's gaze with a wink and his trademark lazy grin.

"So, when are you going to see him again?" Bonita demanded.

"I don't know. He's been really considerate. He told me I should let him know when it was a good time. You know, he said he didn't want to monopolize my time but wanted to see me again. Thoughtful, isn't he? You really think he's for real?" Fr. Geoffrey made his way over to Rennie before Bonita could answer.

"Josie is tied up with classes and kids most of the day, but we made an executive decision. How about tonight for dinner we grill out down at the house? Keep it easy, everybody bring meat of their choosing for the grill and a beverage. I'll spring for some baked potatoes and salad. It will be a small crowd, just us, Ethan and his girl, and maybe Sean and his family if they get here in time. Oh, and

Rennie?" Fr. Geoffrey smiled. "I think we ought to invite the security guys. After all, they really are working hard to help us." He nudged Rennie's shoulder as he headed toward the exit to the courtyard. Bonita could scarcely contain her excitement.

"That does include Hot Chocolate, right? I don't see a ring, so I'm hoping that's a good sign. This could be another wild night in Summerlea, if he doesn't have a wife. Lawd, I think the earth just moved. Be still, my heart."

Fr. Geoffrey smiled, shaking his head as he continued walking toward the festivities outside. He sensed the weekend celebration would be monumental in more ways than anyone thought possible.

Chapter Forty-Eight

Rennie smiled at the scene before her this night, remembering how much her parents had enjoyed the merriment of good friends and family. If only Ray and Catherine could be with them now, enjoying cold beers, barbeque chicken on the grill, and the sound of October waves crashing on the beach. They would have been so proud of the growth of St. Judes, of the accomplishments of its original residents, and of the engagement of Fr. Geoffrey and Josie. She wondered, as her eyes met Aidan's, if they would approve of him also. He moved toward her with quiet confidence, taking a seat on the ledge of the fireplace beside her.

"That dinner was fantastic. I'd say all seem to be having fun. Especially Bonita and T. Rex."

"T. Rex? You mean Theodore?"

Aidan nodded toward the striking black officer that had Bonita's full attention. "His name is Theodore Rex. But the guys all call him 'T. Rex'. A great guy, usually pretty quiet at first. When you get to know him though, he's funny as hell. I'd love to hear what he and Bonita are talking about. I'm not sure which one I'd put my money on for the most laughs. Together, they'd be quite the show. But, Miss Easter, I'd like to know a little more about you, please, while we have a moment of solitude."

"What would you like to know specifically, Mr. Cross?" Rennie smiled, enjoying the flirtatious exchange and the reassuring sound of his deep voice.

"You said you were passionate about art and history. Because of your father?"

"Yes, mostly him," Rennie paused. "I was a daddy's girl in many ways. He taught me to paint, to know the great artists, to understand their techniques. When I wasn't in school, I often went with him to his lectures and classes at The College of Charleston. I was like a tiny mascot of sorts, you know, absorbing everything he taught his students while being the professor's cute little kid. I suppose his love of art in its many forms was contagious simply because of his immense passion. He saw beauty and design in everything, and of course, being near the sea nurtured his creativity even more. He talked incessantly about the artists during World War II who were considered degenerate, how the Nazis had destroyed many of their great works and stolen the work of other artists they deemed superior. He always talked about art as a deep expression of the human story, and he was very connected to the works impacted during this time period. It was his dream to be able to one day see stolen art restored to rightful families and descendants or donated to museums."

"So you inherited his artistic passion. Your parents must have endured a great deal while in Europe during those times. What about their families there? Did any survive?"

"No, none. I was told that my mother was an only child and my father had an older sibling who was killed in battle. My parents said many times that they felt compelled to rescue as many orphans as they could. So, since Josie and I have no real relatives left, all at St. Judes became our family in every possible way. We are both inextricably tied to the Home our parents started."

A brief clatter of noise at the front door interrupted their conversation. An older, slightly heavier Sean Bennett emerged from the hallway flanked by his wife and a tiny boy and girl, likely twins.

Rennie guessed them to be about three years of age. Though it had been at least eight years since she had last seen him, she could not help but smile, noting the black shirt that was reminiscent of the somber attire in their teen years. As soon as introductions were made, Sean directed his attention to Rennie.

"Hey, you're becoming world famous, apparently. A guy pulled up beside us outside at St Judes, when we stopped for information about the celebration. He said he'd overheard us say that we were headed to your house. Said it was a matter of grave importance that he speaks with you tomorrow about your father. He said he believed you might have information he needed."

"Was he a big burly kind of guy?" Aidan asked, his eyes narrowing with concern.

"Yeah. He talked to you, too?" Sean replied, before his wife distracted him with plates of food.

Aidan motioned for Rennie to follow him outside. She grabbed a denim jacket from the closet as they made their way to the vacant side of the deck. "Rennie, I need you to think about any possible connection your father might have had that would be of interest to this guy. We now have the first indicator that it's you someone is interested in and not Josie. This has something to do with art. It's the best connection we can make right now."

"Aidan, my father was an art professor, that's all. He had expertise in restoration and knowledge of art history. He would sometimes go out of town on consulting trips to various museums around the region, but that's all I know about what he did. Nothing more than that, until he went to Europe with my mom. He would never be involved in anything illegal."

Aidan was undeterred. "I need a phone in a quiet room. Can we do that?"

"Of course. Let's go to Josie's room. The phone is by her bed. We can let Josie and Geoffrey know later if we find out anything."

As she sat on the bed next to Aidan, who was laser focused on the phone conversation, Rennie tried to remember any discussions she might have had with her father or mother that might pertain to what was happening now.

"Yeah, I'm looking for anything pertaining to renegade or supremacist groups interested in stolen art, maybe, especially from the World War II era. Any activity at all from anyone pursuing anything connected to art, or Professor Easter at The College of Charleston, or his daughter Rennie at the High Museum in Atlanta? Yeah, I'll hang on."

"My father never had any stolen art or ever said anything about being involved with recovered art. It was only an interest of his, as far as I know," Rennie offered again. Could Aidan think that her father was involved in something illicit? Aidan held up a hand to signal for silence, as he listened to the voice on the other end of the line.

"You sure? Is that the specific one in this region? So, their sole mission is to restore Nazi glory by recovering works of art and materials from that time period? Any other known operatives other than Jason Sneed, aka Jason Browner, that owned the tags? Think he could be our guy? Okay, yeah man, thanks." Aidan placed the phone back on the hook and stared at Rennie. "Have you ever heard of Jason Sneed or a group called 'Wulfsreich'?"

"No, never heard of them. Is Jason Browner or Jason Sneed the same person who's been following us in the green van? What could he possibly want from me?"

"I don't know just yet," Aidan offered. "I'm not sure how it's all connected to you and your father, but I believe it is. If he just wanted to talk to you, he could do that without all the efforts to tail you. This guy wants something else." Rennie heard the concern in Aidan's voice and felt a tremor of fear rush through her body. What could anyone possibly want from her, or her family?

"Aidan, I know the sofa is not the most comfortable and there is a vacant room here, but I was hoping you would stay again tonight?"

"Yes, ma'am." His smile widened. "No way I'm leaving now. You've got me through the weekend, if it's all right with everyone else. We can talk with your sister and Fr. Geoffrey about all this tonight or tomorrow after lunch. Didn't he say earlier that he wanted you to come by his office then? For now, we enjoy the night and stay vigilant and safe." Aidan lowered his voice and whispered in her ear. "I'm sticking close by you tomorrow, girl. I'll clear it with the sheriff and the head of the security detail and make sure that all the officers know what's going on."

Rennie relished the safety and security of Aidan's confidence. She was falling hard for this man.

Chapter Forty-Nine

Summerlea, South Carolina
Easter Home
October, 1975

After the last of the guests had departed and the remnants of cleanup had been completed, Bonita offered her goodnights and turned only once to wink as she ascended the stairs to the bedroom. "Don't you two do anything I wouldn't do," she drawled, shaking a finger at Rennie and Aidan and smiling. "But then again, that should leave you some room to improvise."

Aidan shook his head, laughing, as she disappeared upstairs. "You and Bonita have an amazing friendship. Not many like that. Hey, want to go outside?" He tapped her shoulder, as if in afterthought. "Maybe go sit on the steps out there or stay out front on the beach? We can stay close to the house and at least get outside a little."

"Yes, that would be nice," Rennie replied. "I'm going to leave a note, if anyone comes back out here so they won't worry. Maybe we should take a key and leave the doors locked, anyway. How about turn on some outside lights in the front, too?"

She quickly gathered a house key, shoes for the beach, and a hearty tan woven cardigan from the nearby closet. Adjusting it underneath the chestnut hair that fell in thick waves around her face, she pushed the sleeves up on her forearms. The night air was brisk as they made their way down the dark walkway. Rennie noted the open storage cabinet at the top of the stairs that lead downward to the beach.

"Someone must have left this open, with all of the Home's nets and flashlights for sandcrabbing."

"Sandcrabbing?" Aidan asked. "What do you mean?"

"Oh, my gosh, you've never been sandcrabbing, or ghostcrabbing?" She smiled up at him.

"I've done a lot of things in my life, but pretty sure I've not done that." Aidan smiled back.

"You'll need a net and a flashlight," Rennie instructed as she handed him one of each and procured her own, and then grabbed a large bucket. "Don't turn the light on until I tell you. You'll shine it across the beach, looking for crabs. When you find one, you run to shine the light directly into their eyes. That immobilizes them and they look kind of haunted, with glowing eyes. Then, you pounce with the net, or holler for whoever has the net to come scoop them up." Rennie walked ahead of him onto the beach, holding the net in her right hand and the flashlight in her left. "Watch and learn, Mr. Green Beret. Look there!"

Aidan chuckled as Rennie immediately found an unsuspecting tiny crab to hypnotize with the beam of light and almost simultaneously swooped the net down with no mercy. She shook the crab out over the bucket, as it dropped in with a thud. Aiden nodded his head, laughing.

"I see you folks are easily entertained in these parts. Wish I'd known about this capture tactic with the Viet Cong."

"C'mon, we do this with the kids from the Home. They love it! Give it a try. Unless you're scared." Aidan smiled, going into attack mode and laughing aloud as they filled the bottom of the bucket within minutes.

"Now what?" He demanded, still grinning. "I know you don't eat these little ones." Rennie dropped her net and flashlight and grabbed one of his hands. She stared at him with an expression of mock urgency.

"Now," she whispered, "we run for our lives!" With a quick frontward kick of her foot, the bucket toppled over as the sea-going creatures spread across the sand and scurried toward the sanctuary of the ocean. Aidan jumped with surprise, running to catch up with Rennie, as if chased by demons. Without warning, she felt her foot catch on a sizable divet in the solid-packed sand, falling hard on her side and rolling onto her back. Aidan, who still held her hand, came crashing down against her. Rennie could scarcely catch her breath from laughing as she looked over at him. Her soft hair sprawled across the sand in waves and her eyes sparkled. Aidan growled at her, laughing and making opening and closing clawing motions with his fingers, as if his hands were crab claws, and began to inch them toward her.

"The monster crab is coming for you, Rennie Easter!"

"Oh, no!" Rennie howled with delight as Aidan grabbed her arms and pretended to be attacking her. Watching her laugh, he suddenly pushed himself up on his hands and silently stared into the green eyes beneath him, studying her with the intensity of one on a hunt. Rennie had never had a man look at her with such raw, almost feral expression. Her lips barely parted to draw the deepest of breaths. Aidan never took his eyes off hers as he touched the fullness of her bottom lip with his fingers and stared deep into her eyes, far beyond the past. Searching her face once more, he bent low to kiss her; soft, gentle kisses at first. He pushed into the sand against his own weight to keep from crushing her. Rennie placed her hands on his shoulders, feeling the muscles grind beneath his shirt and felt herself drawn into his fervor, her mouth working with his almost as if they breathed for one another. Kissing him was the singular most sensual experience she had ever had. Aidan pushed himself upward again, his lips brushing her forehead with a light kiss. He searched her eyes once more.

"Rennie," he breathed her name with a reverent pause, "I should get you back to the house now." She did not question why. She knew what he meant. Grabbing his hand once more, Aidan pulled her to her feet and smiled as he wrapped both arms around her and held her close. She could feel the rise and fall of his chest with every breath and found herself wishing they could remain in that moment until daybreak. Releasing her, he brushed the hair out of his eyes and gestured toward the sandcrabbing equipment that had been abandoned on the beach.

"I don't think those are going to get back into storage by themselves." When all had been had been stored and locked, Aidan reached to take her hand. "I hope I didn't scare you, Rennie. The truth is, I'm pretty crazy about you, if you haven't figured it out already." She held her breath and prepared to bare her soul. The honesty thing, again. This man was worth the risk.

"The truth, Aidan Cross," she stopped to look into his eyes, "is that I find you the most intriguing man I've ever met. What scares me more than anything is that I feel like I can't get close enough to you."

This time, there was no hesitation as Aidan raised her hands over her head and pinned her body against the storage wall, kissing her lips, her ear, her neck, then back to her lips once more. Rennie succumbed to the symbiotic dance, drawing her breaths from his as his mouth moved over hers one last time. Aidan wrapped an arm around her shoulders as they walked back to the house in silence, enjoying the quiet moment. Bonita stood in her sock feet by an open refrigerator door, a small container of chocolate milk in one hand and an oatmeal cookie in the other. A wide grin spread across her face as she took notice of the windblown hair, the bits of sand that still clung to clothing, and the giddy smile on the face of her friend.

"We were sandcrabbing. Aidan had never been," Rennie offered. Bonita straightened the oversized t-shirt emblazoned with the image of Jimi Hendrix and bold letters that said, "Let Jimi Take Over", and finished chewing her cookie, the crumbs dribbling down her chin.

"That's the story you two are going with?" She shook her head and held up one hand. "Yeah, okay. Goodnight, I'm out of here."

"Goodnight, Bonita. You're not hiding T-Rex upstairs are you?" Aidan asked. Bonita turned and raised her eyebrows as she trudged back up the stairs.

"No," she mumbled, grinning. "Not yet. I'm letting him rest up first."

"I guess we should get some rest, too. We're going to need it," Rennie smiled. Aidan pulled her close to him once more and whispered into her ear before she went upstairs.

"Rennie, I won't let anything happen to you. That's a promise."

The eyes that watched them through night goggles squinted as the focus was adjusted. It appeared that Aidan Cross was not going to leave that night. There was always tomorrow.

Chapter Fifty

Saturday morning buzzed with excitement as former residents mingled with current occupants, congregants, and staff. The nuns hustled children to and from the many planned activities of the day. Rennie facilitated several tours for guests and took pride in the legacy her parents had left at St. Jude's. There were people from the High Museum and from The College of Charleston, as well as many former students of her father's and local dignitaries in attendance. Throughout the day, wherever she was Aidan was always close by, watching with unfettered admiration and perusing the attendees for anything that appeared unusual. As the mid-day luncheon came to an end, Fr. Geoffery dismissed the crowd for the day. Rennie and Aidan walked across the courtyard toward the parking lot, when an older woman approached them from the opposite direction. .

"Miss Easter? Rennie? I hope you will forgive my intrusion. May I have a moment? I knew your mother well." The woman shifted her purse from one arm to the other. "I was Catherine's therapist." Rennie froze, taking in the grandmotherly figure before her. "I want you to know that she was the strongest woman I have ever known," the woman continued. "You resemble her in many ways."

"My mother, strong? How so?" Rennie winced, thinking about Catherine and the crazy eating disorder, whatever that was about, that she couldn't save herself from. She must have struggled with depression and God knows what else. Though she seemed to get better before that fateful trip to Europe, she had also regressed again just days before the trip. Likely it was this therapist that had at least helped her to begin achieving peace. The woman smiled.

"There's something I want you to have." She bent a head of thick gray hair over the satchel purse and fumbled with the contents, finally extracting a piece of paper that was twice-folded and handed it to Rennie. The rough drawing resembled a Venn diagram done with color pencils, with strange and dark images on the left side. A syringe. A rotund cartoon face with round black spectacles. A plate of food with a fork and knife that looked more like instruments of torture. A swastika. On the right side, the images were more positive, with lighter and brighter colors. Faces of many women, but none were smiling. A heart with the letter 'C' emblazoned in the middle. Another with the letters 'RJR'. A fireplace with a blazing fire. Then there were two tiny hearts in the middle section, each labeled with the letters 'J' and 'R', respectively.

"What is this?" Rennie demanded, as she passed it to Aidan.

"I asked your mother to make it just before she left for Europe, with only images and not words. The left side represents her deepest fears. The right, her greatest joys. And in the middle, her greatest accomplishments. As you can see, you and your sister were deeply loved."

"I don't understand. Can you tell me what all of these drawings mean?"

I think Fr. Geoffrey holds the key for you. Rennie, your parents were the most incredible people. Don't stop until you know it all. Good day to you both." Without explanation, the woman turned her back to them and walked, without looking back, toward the large areas of parked cars.

"That was cryptic," Rennie murmured. "What could it possibly mean?"

"Rennie, I think she knows some of it, whatever it is, and she wants to be sure that you know, too."

"So why didn't she just tell me? Why all of the mystery? Do you think Geoffrey really knows anything about any of this?" Aidan hesitated only for a moment.

"What I know for sure is that therapists are always held to a certain level of confidentiality, even for the dead. It was important enough for her to come to you. There are answers out there somewhere, Rennie. We just have to find them. Start with Fr. Geoffrey. If he knows anything, I'd have to believe he'd tell you. Do you want me to go with you to his office now? By the way, he and Josie have offered to keep Sean's children so that you and I, Bonita, T-Rex, and Ethan and his wife can grab dinner and perhaps some music and let you guys reminisce a bit, if you are up for that. Ethan seems to be the music connoisseur and said you used to go clubbing at all the good places in Columbia and Charleston to hear great bands. We will have to compare notes on preferred music."

"That sounds like fun," she mused, trying not to sound worried. "We definitely did some travelling to see shows and concerts. But, yes, I'd like to find Geoffrey before I leave here for the day and yes, I'd appreciate your coming with me."

"Look at me, Rennie." Aidan reached out to take her hand. "This is all good. The answers are going to come. We're going to find out what all of this is about." Rennie found herself staring at the bench where her mother used to sit, where news of her parents' deaths had first been shared. She hoped Aidan was right, but unspoken fear gnawed deep inside.

Chapter Fifty-One

Summerlea, South Carolina
Office of Fr. Geoffrey Radcliffe
St. Jude's Home
October, 1975

Fr. Geoffrey Radcliffe sat in a leather chair in front of his desk across from Rennie and Aidan, who were seated on a matching sofa. He studied the drawing that Rennie gave him. After a thorough perusal, he handed it back to her.

"I knew that Catherine had an eating disorder and that she was seeing a competent therapist. I was the one that recommended her. I know that she and your father both thought the return trip to Europe would do her good. Your parents had not been back there since the war, you know."

"Geoffrey, the woman said that she thought you held the key. Do you have any idea what that might mean?" Aidan asked, leaning forward in his seat on the couch next to Rennie. "Could it have to do with the art this man, or group of people, might be after?"

"Well, yes to to both questions, actually," the priest replied, much to their surprise. "Quite literally, I have a key for you, Rennie. Two keys, in fact. I can only assume that Catherine must have told her therapist of her and Ray's intentions to give them to me." Fr. Geoffrey rose from his seat and took a set of ringed keys out of the top drawer in the desk and handed them to Rennie. "These are keys to the bell tower that your father had built years ago. I'm sure you remember climbing to the top as a child. Ray had a special circular room built in the middle, just for him, high enough to withstand floods and hurricanes, with no windows and specially regulated climate controlled conditions. He said he kept all of his old art restoration materials and artifacts in there."

"I never knew," Rennie said. "Was it always a secret?"

"I knew of the room," Fr. Geoffrey offered, rubbing his collar as he resumed his seat in the leather chair, "but to this day, I do not know all of its contents, only some. I believe that your father left some valuable artifacts there. My personal belief is that he might have been consulting with those working to return stolen art works. He took great pains to not involve anyone else in whatever was going on. Your father did not plan for anyone except for your mother and me to know about the room until you and Josie were both older. I go periodically to check on the temperature and humidity controls in there, but it remains largely untouched, as per Ray's instructions, until you girls were into adulthood. You, specifically, as your father was well aware of your artistic leanings, even at age twelve."

"So the man who has been following Rennie could very well be after art items that he believes Ray Easter had and that he thinks Ray's art professional daughter might still have?" Aidan asked.

"I think that theory makes the most sense." Fr. Geoffrey looked at Rennie. "The day your parents drove to Atlanta to go to Europe, your father left letters that he and Catherine wrote for you and Josie. It was his plan for you both to see them specifically at this time for this event. That was their wish, and I have honored it as best I could. It was my intention to let you and Josie have the extra set of keys I made you and some quiet time on Sunday, after the event was over and before your flight back to Atlanta. I can tell you that there is a sizable amount of art stored in there, and I think Ray wanted to be sure that, in the event of his death, someone with specific knowledge would take over for him. There is also a large file cabinet with a locked drawer for you and Josie. I added the sealed letters to the few personal items in them. I can tell you that in your drawer, there is a locked box from your mother with your name on it. That is what the second key will open. There was not one for Josie. I don't know why. Nor do I have any idea what it is specifically that the man who followed us wants, but I agree with Aidan that whoever it is believes that Ray had, or knew about, valuable art somewhere, and that he believes you know of it now. He may want it now."

Rennie looked first at Aidan, who sat next to her with arms folded across his chest, and then back at Fr. Geoffrey, who ran his fingers through the thatches of lightly graying hair. "Does Josie know about any of this?"

"As of today, she knows there are works of art and that letters are there, per your parents' wishes. That's all." Fr. Geoffrey leaned forward in his chair, elbows resting on his thighs and his fingers interlocked. "Rennie, Josie wants to know more but is also reluctant to reopen that past hurt, or to make potentially new and difficult discoveries. As a teenager, she was angry with Catherine for a long time. She felt Catherine robbed the family of normalcy, so to speak, and that you two never got the chance to know why. Of course, we all know there is strife and struggle in the best of families, but we are only beginning to understand the dynamics and psychology of eating disorders and the specialized treatment they require. I suspect Catherine may have had significant events in her past that were relative to her unusual type of disorder. She preferred meats to vegetables, and would often attempt to regurgitate what she'd eaten, as I'm sure you remember. Your father always maintained that she carried many memories of the orphaned children and the depravity from the Nazi regime. But, God love her, Catherine did not want whatever it was to be known by anyone, especially by her children. She adamantly refused to go to any type of residential group treatment. She was terrified of confinement. However, she loved you two more than anything, and she fought hard to make the progress she did with her therapist, a nutritionist, and Ray's loving care, of course. I sincerely believe she could have eventually overcome it had she lived longer."

Rennie surveyed the strange drawings once more. "I feel like I didn't really know her. I really want to see what is in there. Do you think Josie would be angry if I looked first, without her?"

"Truthfully, I think she would prefer it. There is still a part of her that does not want to know and is afraid to know. Your being willing to go first might be the buffer and encouragement that she could use. I tell you what. Let's be sure. You talk with her as soon as she finishes speaking to a group of teachers and board members. If she wants to come with you, it will be okay, or you can have some alone time to look, if you want. I think many answers will be there."

"Rennie," Aidan offered, "I hope I'm not being too intrusive here, but I think it might be a good idea to have someone nearby when you do this, especially if it is this evening after dark.

"I should at least ask Josie how she feels. We could go in a few minutes, if she can, or wait until later. I also think that someone standing close by, given all that has gone on, might not be a bad idea either."

Aidan glanced at Fr. Geoffrey, then back at Rennie. "You know I'm offering, only if you want." Rennie stood and walked to the window that overlooked the courtyard at St. Jude's. The bench where her mother used to sit was visible underneath a swirl of falling leaves. What was it she felt? Fear? Confusion? Perhaps apprehension? Longing for the family that would never be again? She felt trapped, as the tears rose, and she rushed to the door.

"I need to think about this for a minute. Alone. I just need to think. I'm going outside for a moment."

"Rennie, wait!" Aidan stood to go after her, but Fr. Geoffrey intervened.

"It's fine, Aidan, I know where she is going. It's right outside, the place where her mother used to sit. It's also where I had to tell her and Josie about the death of their parents. Rennie's overwhelmed. Let her go. Besides, you can see her from the window. She's strong and stubborn as hell. She will be okay."

Aidan stared through the large glass window at the bench below. *But would she be safe?*

Chapter Fifty-Two

Summerlea, South Carolina
St. Jude's Home Courtyard
October, 1975

The bench seemed smaller somehow than her memory of it that terrible day. The coldness of the cement seemed to infiltrate her body and work its way through every muscle. Rennie felt as if she were standing on the edge of a cliff, looking into the deep waters below and not knowing if the jump would save or destroy her. Either way, she knew she had to know. What she remembered of her father underscored the belief that he could never be involved in the heinous act of stealing and smuggling stolen art. Did he possess priceless works that were in the act of being restituted after provenance gaps were complete? With whom was he working, and who might be attempting to discover and steal the hidden art? Was it this Wulfsreich that Aiden had discovered? Was any of this even real?

"Excuse me, miss. You're Rennie Easter, aren't you? I didn't mean to intrude." Rennie attempted a smile at the man standing before her. Somewhat disheveled in appearance, his face was craggy with a beard that needed trimming beneath an uneven haircut. He wore an older dark blue suit that she imagined could have easily belonged to a homeless man, except that this man was a heavier build, well fed.

"Yes, I am. Can I help you?"

"I hope so," he replied, sitting next to her on the bench without an invitation to do so. "It is important, I assure you. I came by your house one evening, but it appeared that you had company, so I did not stop."

Rennie felt every nerve in her body fire at once. Was this the man that had spoken to Sean? She made a nervous glance around the courtyard. It was vacant, as most were now enjoying an afternoon elsewhere, although a staff member or parishioner could be seen periodically meandering across the way. At the opposite end of the courtyard, she saw Bonita and T-Rex sprawled on a blanket on the soft lawn. With a measure of reassurance, she faced the man.

"What exactly is it that you want with me?"

"I represent a group of folks in South Carolina that are interested in art from the period during World War II. Your father spoke to us once about recovering such works. We saw you interviewed on television and had no idea that he had children, much less one that followed in his footsteps. We would love to have you come and speak with us. Did he talk about the pieces he had recovered? Do you know if he still has works to be returned to their rightful owners?" Rennie's eyes narrowed, her courage returning with the presence of her friends nearby. Something wasn't right.

"Art was my father's life's work. Yes, the last piece he returned was a Van Gogh, a self-portrait. *Painter on the Road to Tarascon*, it was. He was thrilled to be able to return it to the Netherlands."

"Ah, yes, what an extraordinary piece!" The man clasped his hands together. "I'm surprised we haven't heard about that, but I'm sure the Dutch were glad to have it once again. Are all of the works he had kept here at St. Jude's or elsewhere?" Rennie stood, crossing her arms, as she glared at the stranger.

"You need to leave now. If you knew anything about art from that period, you would know that *Painter on the Road to Tarascon* was burned, forever lost. I don't know who you are, but you are an imposter of the highest order. Do not ever come back here." The man stood as well. He made an aggressive reach for her arm, his sleeve riding up to reveal a tattoo of a large "W" on the inside of his left wrist, as he gripped her forearm. His facial expression was angry, despite the words he chose.

"Please, Miss Easter, I'm only trying to help right a wrong here, like your father!" Rennie tried to pull away, but he would not release her. "Please, Miss Easter, I only want to help."

Before Rennie could respond, the man was spun around and pinned, face forward, against the rough bark of the great oak tree beside them. An enraged Aidan, eyes glazed over with singular purpose, had the man by the throat with one hand and searched for a weapon with the other as he braced himself against the man's back. Fr. Geoffrey had caught up with him, and wiped his brow with his shirtsleeve.

"Who are you and what do you want with this woman?" Aidan demanded, his baritone voice sounding even deeper with a tone that was frightening as he pushed harder on the man's throat. "Tell me now, before I break every bone in your body!"

"Aidan, it's okay, I'm not hurt," Rennie whispered, looking wildly about, as Bonita, seeing the melee, rushed to her side. T-Rex assisted in patting the man down before facing Aidan.

"Aidan. Hey man, stand down! Everything is fine. Aidan!" Without removing his hands from the man, Aidan turned to look at T-Rex, his eyes still filled with anger. He turned toward Rennie.

"You okay? Did he hurt you?"

"I'm fine, Aidan." Rennie whispered, her eyes pleading with him. "Are you all right?"

"Yeah. I'm good." Aidan ran his fingers through his hair, as he took slow and deliberate breaths before returning his focus to the man who now stood between him and T-Rex. "I'm good now. Who are you?" he demanded, a hint of threat returning to his voice. The man withdrew a card from his front coat pocket and handed it to Aidan, who read it aloud. "Summerville Art Association. David

Adler. What do you want, David Adler? That's a nice German name, by the way, if it's really your name."

"I _I wanted Miss Easter to come speak, to come talk with our group, is all." The man stammered, ignoring the rest of Aidan's comment and taking a step away.

"So you are not a member of Wulfsreich?" Aidan took a half step closer to him.

"Never heard of it," the man murmured, shaking his head, but returning Aidan's stare.

"I think you're lying," Rennie spoke up. "You don't know enough to be a member of a bonafide group. And there is a "W" tattooed on your left wrist." Before the man could speak, Aidan had twisted his arm in front of his face to reveal the tattoo. The man grimaced.

"You're hurting me!"

"Well, well. Let me guess. Wulfsreich." Aidan snapped at him. David Adler, if that was his name, yanked his arm from Aidan's grasp.

"I can see I've overstayed my welcome. Miss Easter, please forgive me for the misunderstanding. You have my card, if you decide to use it. We would really love to have you."

"Leaving us, Mr. Adler? Please allow me to walk you to your car." Aidan offered, glaring at the man.

"Not necessary," the man returned, "and I've done nothing wrong. You cowboys have active imaginations."

"Let Fr. Geoffrey and I do the honors, Aidan. That way, you can stay with Rennie while I check the tags on his ride." T-Rex smirked at the man, who now returned his gaze as he shook his head. Bonita hugged Rennie mouthing the words, "talk later" and scurried away with them.

"Adler!" Aidan called out, clenching and unclenching his fists though his voice was controlled and firm. "You touch this woman again and I'll keep that promise." The man never turned around, but Rennie was sure he heard every word. Aidan sat on the bench and leaned forward, resting his elbows on his knees and burying his forehead in his hands. "I'm sorry, Rennie. I didn't mean to scare you. I saw him grab you like that and I went on automatic, I guess." Rennie sat beside him and touched his arm.

"Thank you for being there, Aidan. It caught me offguard, is all." For a moment they sat in silence. Aidan reached for her hand, but did not look at her. His gaze went to difficult memories instead.

"I spent some time in a bad place during Viet Nam, and saw some things. When I came home, it was to people who thought we were the monsters. Let's just say I spent a little time in therapy when I got out. That was almost as grueling as battle, I might add. Romantic relationships were never part of the picture when I got back. In fact, most of my relationships suffered a bit. It was almost as if the war continued for me, somehow. Believing you to be in danger just pushed me over the edge and back there. I'm sorry." Rennie reached up to kiss his cheek.

"It's okay, Aidan. You know, in all the excitement I momentarily forgot about the keys Geoffrey gave me, and the bell tower room, too. I never made it to talk with Josie. She's probably left by now."

"How about I take you home so you and Josie can have some private time before tonight? T. Rex and I can go run the tags on the car driven by David Adler, or whoever he is and hopefully have enough info to wrap that up. He and I might even be able to grab a happy hour drink with the other security guys and local police over at the Windjammer. I think everyone still wants to go out for dinner, if you feel up for that, then to one of those places in Charleston that

Ethan was raving about for some music and dancing. Miss Ken's Tavern, I think he said?" Rennie giggled, shaking her head.

"What? What'd I say?" Aidan grinned back, grateful for the return of lightness to their conversation and for the ease with which Rennie Easter made him feel alive.

"Not 'Miss Ken's'. The place is called, 'Myskyns'. M-y-s-k-y-n-s. Like 'Miss Ken's' but accent on the first syllable. I was always told it meant 'magic' but I don't know for sure. It's a great laid-back venue for music."

"Magic," Aidan repeated, taking her hand. "I think I can feel it."

Chapter Fifty-Three

Charleston, South Carolina
Myskyns Tavern
October, 1975

Rennie took in the ambiance of one of her favorite places. The weathered brick walls, the funky artwork of dogs playing pool, the John Carroll Doyle paintings of jazz musicians, and the nudes evoked the unencumbered late days of college and visits back to Charleston. The music was rock and blues fusion that permeated the bar with blazing guitar riffs and hot, raw vocals. Aidan slipped an arm around her shoulder and took a sip of beer.

"I agree, it's magic. This place is really cool and the music is unbelievable. I could get lost in here, especially tonight, now that we have also arrested that David Adler guy for possession of stolen goods and connected him to Wulfsreich. Hopefully, we can uncover more about whoever his associates are."

"Here, here," T-Rex raised his glass, "To putting away the bad guys!"

"Speaking of getting lost in here, I'm afraid we did, many times," Rennie laughed, making another toast with Ethan, Sean, and Bonita. "Myskyns, it's legend! The place feels like home to me. This band used to be called 'Osmosis', I think, but now they are 'Hydra'. See the guitarist there, the one that did the crazy solo just then? He made Guitar Player Magazine's list of those nominated for 'Guitar Player of the Year,' right up there with Clapton, Beck, and Page."

Aidan took another sip of beer and shook his head, tapping his fingers to the beat of the bass. "She knows her music, too. Damn, girl, no wonder I like you. So, you should know 'Mother's Finest,' out of Atlanta?"

"Absolutely." Rennie preened like a peacock. "I've seen them there and once or twice even in Columbia at a place called, 'The Left Guard.' I don't think you were there, Sean, but Bonita and I went with Ethan. They put on an amazing show. Hey, remember that time we ran into Murdock, Wyzard, and Baby Jean in the parking lot and they let us take a promo picture with them?"

Bonita jumped out of her chair, waving her arms in the air and screeching. "I almost forgot, oh my gosh, Rennie! Who's your buddy, who's your friend? Bonita, the black goddess of love, that's who!" T-Rex feigned sudden interest and winked at Rennie. Bonita grabbed her shoulder bag and dug out a folded envelope. Without speaking, she handed it to Rennie. "Watch her now," Bonita smiled, wide-eyed at the others. "I predict an eruption!"

Rennie scanned the unfolded paper inside and smiled at Bonita. "Is this what I think it is? A setlist from Deep Purple's '73 New York show? You went?"

"No, but the one you love was hanging out with some of the cast after one of our shows when they were in New York. I guess because he sang the lead part on the original Jesus Christ Superstar studio album. Read the rest, girl! Go ahead, read it and weep." Rennie turned the paper sideways and read aloud the scribbled comment at the bottom.

"Rennie, I hate you couldn't be here for the show! Much love and kisses, Ian Gillan." She screamed with delight as Bonita raised her arms skyward, proclaiming her newly minted status as the queen of all time. Rennie passed the cherished autograph around the group and turned to Aidan.

"You like Deep Purple and Mother's Finest? Maybe you and I can go see them sometime. Even if Gillan isn't with them now."

Aidan set his beer on the small table in front of them and leaned close to whisper. "Nothing would make me happier, Rennie. Well," he hesitated, "maybe taking you to a Georgia football game would make me pretty happy."

"Losing to my Gamecocks maybe," Rennie shot him an evil grin. "Sure, I'll go with you. But then you have to go to one of ours, too." Aidan leaned in to whisper.

"Hey, this is changing the subject a bit," he started, "but since the band is getting ready to take a break, I've been wanting to ask what you and Josie decided about viewing your parents' letters and your father's room." Rennie ran slender fingers through the mound of chestnut waves and shook her head.

"You're probably going to think this sounds like alcohol talking, but I'm ready to do it now," she smiled. "Josie wants to read her letter alone or with Geoffrey after I see what's up there and give her a preview of my letter."

Aidan squinted his eyes and lips in a puzzled expression. "Why would I think that? I think it's great that you are going to do it."

"No, you don't understand. I want to do it now. Tonight."

"Tonight," Aidan repeated. "Tonight, as in after we leave here?"

"Yes, tonight. Since I have the keys, I can go whenever I want. Bonita offered to go with me. I don't want this all hanging over my head on Sunday when I have to leave. If you must know, Aidan Cross, I've been feeling a bit teary anyway about having to say good-bye to you."

"Whoa, wait." Aidan squeezed both of her hands, his brows knitted together. "Who the hell said anything about 'good-bye'? Girl, if you can't see by now that I've got this thing for you, then you are a blind woman in the dark! What's that we Southerners say? I'm on you like white on rice, baby."

Aidan held her cheeks in both hands and kissed her. "Look, Ren, I don't know exactly how we will negotiate the location gap between us, but I'm not leaving until you throw me out. When I imagine days ahead, you are in them. We will figure it out." He smiled his grin that stirred every fiber in her body. "You and Bonita are going to need a couple of lookouts at the belltower, don't you think?"

Chapter Fifty-Four

Summerlea, South Carolina
The St. Jude's Home Bell Tower
October, 1975

The midnight October air was brisk but comfortable, as it most always was this time of year in South Carolina. Rennie felt an electric shiver of anticipation travel the length of her spine as she remembered the day her parents left for Europe, full of hopes and eager to create new memories. She and Josie, too, had been looking forward to time spent with their friends at the Home. If only it had not gone so horribly wrong then. She took solace in the sentiments shared by all that there was no way her father could be involved in stealing art. Yet works of some kind had been left up there along with whatever revelations her parents had saved to share, and the lingering aura of mystery warned of secrets yet unknown. Somehow it felt right coming here at night while all others slept in the safety of the Home. She found herself wondering how this night might change all that she had believed about her family.

"Listen." Bonita tugged at the sleeve of her friend's denim jacket as Rennie pulled the keys from an inside pocket. "I never had the honor of knowing your folks, Ray and Catherine. But I know, Rennie, I just know deep down that there is no way they would be involved in anything but good works." Rennie smiled and felt the emotion well up from an old familiar place.

"It feels like I'm getting to talk to them again. Thirteen damn years it's been. Thirteen years since they died and I am shaking, just wondering what they are going to say to me now that had to wait until I was an adult to hear it."

"Rennie, T and I are right here," Aidan smiled down at her and kissed her cheek. "We're right here, and we can stay all night if you want."

"Yeah," T-Rex offered. "We guys can find all kinds of bathroom spots out here to go with the massive amounts of coffee we're getting ready to consume on top of the beer we've already had. Maybe some pizza delivery, too." Rennie smothered a giggle, glad for the reassuring humor of friends.

"If we pull the all nighter, I'm buying breakfast in Mt. Pleasant," she offered.

"Yeah, now we're talking. Say it with bacon, baby." Aidan put a hand on her shoulder. "You two get going. Great discoveries are in store. We'll be right here if you need us. Open the door and holler down at us. We'll run up."

Rennie stared at the door to the realm of secrets past. It was time. The stairs were dark and steep in the massive bell tower with the expected chill, but surprisingly without the normal humidity of the area. She knew the atmospheric conditions for maximal storage benefits would be something her father would have considered. The tower was built with stairs that were attached to the inside of the exterior walls, rather than in a stairwell in the middle so that the room on the third flight of stairs in which the artifacts were kept would be windowless with a solid protective surrounding wall so there would be no damage over time by sunlight or floods. Rennie thought it genius that there was so much attention to detail. Had her father been working behind the scenes to restore stolen art all these years? If so, how did he acquire it, what exactly did he have, and with whom was he working? Why had he kept the secrets all these years?

"This is the door," Rennie announced as she shone her flashlight on the lock. "There is no window in this door, like Geoffrey said, so this has to be it. We need to close it behind us." Bonita held the light as Rennie inserted the key in the lock. She pushed the heavy door open, listening as it creaked and groaned exposing the interior of the small circular room. Lights in the high ceiling flickered on, appearing to work automatically. They were shielded by protective glass that filtered out detrimental light for precious works of art. Large vertical rectangular-shaped cabinets designed to store valuable art were angled and spaced a few inches apart and appeared to line most of the circumference of the room. A drying rack was folded and stored to one side next to a few old cans of paints and artist chemicals, while a large file cabinet stood conspicuously alone. From where she stood, she could see that her name and Josie's were scribbled in deep masculine strokes on the top two drawers. The bottom three were unlabeled.

"Perfect temperature," Rennie murmured, "about seventy-three degrees and maybe fifty-five percent humidity. This is unbelievable. Dad must have installed a generator and a backup around here somewhere for Geoffrey to maintain these conditions. Do you see any gloves?" She looked around the room and saw a box of thin white cotton gloves, specially designed for handling art.

"The gloves keep the oils in your skin from damaging the work," she explained.

"Okay, then I'm not touching any of this stuff. Besides, I wouldn't really know what I'm looking at. But I will open a cabinet and take a peek," Bonita smiled. Rennie put a hand on the drawer with her name on the masking tape on the outside. It had come down to this moment. Her eyes closed in a brief second of preparation. Without warning, Bonita threw an arm in the air and burst into tune to a soft rendition of, "The Twelve Days of Christmas".

"My true love gave to me: Five dan-cing ladies!"

Rennie shook her head, grinning. "Goofball, I think you mean, 'Five Golden Rings'." She smiled as she pulled the drawer open.

"Nope."Bonita was adamant. "Five dancing chicks, right here. Look like ballerinas, maybe, with white fluffy tutus. Kind of ghostly looking. Don't worry, I'm not touching them."

Rennie felt the blood drain from her face as her pulse quickened. Releasing the drawer handle she grabbed a pair of the gloves and rushed to Bonita's side. There it was.

"My God," she whispered aloud, her voice shaking, as her fingers felt the edges of the piece. "This is an original Degas. 'Five Dancing Women.' The pastel was presumed lost, like tens of thousands of other works. I can't even tell you what this is worth. What else could be in here and why did my father have them? Bo, we have to look at each piece in here! Each one, and carefully!"

"I think you should look in the drawer first," Bonita urged. "There has to be an explanation for all of this." Rennie stared at the drawer with her name and pulled the handle til it rested against her chest. Two letters lay on top of a medium sized lock box. Both had her name on them, one, saying "read first" written underneath. She recognized her father's handwriting.

"Open it," Bonita said. Rennie began to read aloud.

"My Dearest Rennie,
If you are reading this, your mother and I are not there to tell you ourselves how much we love you or answer the questions you must surely have. We are always the parents who will love you through eternity, but we were not always Ray and Catherine Easter. My real name is Rainer von Bauchelle, from Colmar, France, and your mother is Cotterena Becker, from Rastenburg in East Prussia. Everyone called her 'Sonne,' which was short for the German word "sonnenschein," or "sunshine." You were named for your mother,

304

and also for my Mother, so your family name is Cotterena Marthe von Bauchelle and we derived "Rennie" from the first name. Your sister's name, Josefine Alsa von Bauchelle, was in honor of my best friend Josef, a Jew who fought and died as part of the Resistance, and also in recognition of your maternal grandmother."

"What the hell is going on?" Rennie stared at the letter, at Bonita, and at the letter once more. "My parents' are not who I thought they were?" Bonita urged her to keep reading and stood motionless as Rennie continued.

"I met and married your mother in Konigsberg where I was recruited from the University of Strasbourg to work, quite against my will, to help restore the Amber Room for Nazi Germany. Your mother has written about it all for you and Josie in a journal that she expressly wanted you to read first. I am certain that she explains, better than I ever could, about her frightening past and her forced endurance of atrocity. I have suspected she carries more secrets still unknown to even myself. We were lucky to escape to America with the help of Albert Goering, the brother of the brutal Nazi Hermann Goering. Albert helped thousands of Jews, much as he helped us secure safe passage with war orphans, valuable works of art to be restored over time to their rightful owners, and a large sum of Nazi money that he obtained for us. We had to change our identities and build new lives here, as there are those who will do anything to secure these valuables, even now. We will be forever indebted to Albert and have begun the work of determining provenance gaps and such, while we maintain St. Jude's Home.

I know you must be confused and for that, I am so sorry. My precious Rennie, I hope you know that your love of art is rooted in a rich tapestry of history. Perhaps one day, you and Josie will visit the beautiful places that your mother and I called home and know that they, too, are a part of who you both are. I pray you will understand all of this and forgive your mother and I for having to do all that we did in the way that we felt best.

Love always,
Daddy"

Rennie released the letter and watched it drop back into the metal drawer, and faced her friend. "What's my name, again?" Her lips quivered. "Von Bauchelle?"

"Oh, Rennie. Oh, God, Rennie. Are you okay?"

"I'm not sure. I mean, I don't know. All these years I never knew who they were, what they've been through. God, they had lives people never knew, lives I could have never imagined! I have families I never knew, maybe never will know! I don't know who I really am now. Who the hell am I?" Bonita rushed to her, grabbing her by the shoulders and frowning.

"Now, wait. Wait a minute! Get a grip here for a moment. You are the same incredible person you've always been. You once reminded me about my parents choosing a name of beauty for me, remember, so now it's my turn. You are a tower of strength and a force to be reckoned with, girl, and it is not only what your parents instilled in you, but because you made the choice to be strong. Our genes are one thing, but you get to choose who you are, always. Right? Tell me I'm right, damn it, you know I am!" A smile crept across Rennie's lips, through the tears that streaked her face.

"I love you, my friend. You're one of a kind, Bo."

"Well," Bonita rested her hands on her hips, "ain't that the damn truth! Glad you admit it! Ren, your mother's letter, you have to read it. I think your father may have been right and there is still more. You ready for it?" Rennie opened the remaining letter and held it against her chest, closing her eyes to take a deep breath, wondering if more knowledge would crush her. She imagined her mother there beside her, in the lurking shadows of the revelations that waited in the darkness.

"Dear Rennie,

Since you've read your father's letter, you know that my given name is Sonne Becker. You must have wondered all these years why I behaved the way I did. I'm so sorry that I put you all through part of my hell and that I am laying a heavy burden on you even now. I thought I was making the better choice to have my family not know the secret I have carried for as long as I could.

I was a young girl on the brink of adulthood when I was tricked into service at the Wolf's Lair, which was a Nazi secret fortress in the Masurian Woods. I was forced to become a food tester, along with other young women, for the Fuhrer of the Third Reich, Adolf Hitler. He was vegetarian, so he did not eat meat. We had to eat the food he would be served and then wait to see if it had been poisoned. We never knew who would get sick or die. There were days when I didn't much care, either way."

"Mama," Rennie breathed just above a whisper, the tears rising. "Now it all makes sense. She would eat mostly meat. She was terrified of being confined anywhere. She hated any discussion of that period in time, and would often leave the room when one would speak about anything from those horrendous years. My God." Rennie could feel her hands shaking as she read once again.

"One day, I was taken from the other women to a medical room at the Wolf's Lair, where I was used in a secret experiment. I was restrained, given drugs, and then an insemination procedure was done. I escaped with the help of an SS soldier named Conrad, but he

307

was killed in the attempt, sacrificing his life for mine. I found out that I was pregnant when I met your father."

Rennie paused to look at Bonita, raising a hand to cover her face as understanding began to seep in. Bonita put a hand on her arm.

"My sweet Jesus," she whispered. "Go on, Rennie."

"I'm not sure I want to find out more," Rennie whispered, taking a deep breath. "All those years I doubted her, thought her weak. Why didn't she tell us? Why?" She fought back more tears and continued reading.

"I have written most of the details about our lives in the journal left here. Doing so was part of therapy for me. There is something that I have never shared with another living soul, including your father and my therapist, although I think she was beginning to put it together. I don't know why I share it now, as it has been most important to me to be able to shield my family from the incomprehensible pain. I know I paid a high price for keeping it inside, and perhaps my secret has cost us all. I hope that you and Josie, if she ever finds out, can forgive me. My dear Rennie, somehow I know that you will know what to do for your sister and when. Someone who loves her needs to know. Love your sister. None of this was ever her fault. She did not choose a Nazi birth father, and God knows, I felt sick with guilt for wishing many times that I was not pregnant with her. After the experimental procedure was done, I was alone for a moment in the room with just the doctor and another person. It was very quiet. My eyes were closed. I dared not open them, so they did not know that I heard all they said. The Lebensborn project had been instituted by the Nazis to create a superior race, or ubermensch, by having German women breed with Nazi soldiers. Often times, the children from such arrangements were raised by the Third Reich, instead of by their own mothers.

Such was to be the case for my child. I heard a man say that he loved children but would never raise this child, if I became pregnant. He said he wanted the child to be groomed as a superior Nazi, but could not bear the thought of such a child ever being a failure, or risk that the mother would ever reveal what had been done to her in secret. Therefore the plan was to eliminate me at some point and keep the identity of the child a secret if his expectations were not eventually met. I did not look at the man's face then, although I knew his voice. I could never forget it. Then I heard Dr. Clauberg confirming what I already knew. He said that this child would be destined for greatness because the father was none other than Adolf Hitler."

Rennie felt a gut slug of nausea reel her body backward as she looked up from the letter. The expression of horror on her friend's face mirrored her own. "No! God, no! No, no! This can't be happening! No, no!" Rennie muffled another sob as she crumbled to the floor beside the table. Bonita rushed to her side, wrapping arms around her.

"Oh, my God, Rennie! Oh, my God, oh God! I can't believe this! Come on, just breathe, take deep breaths. Dear God in heaven, help us!" Without warning the lock in the door rattled as someone shoved a key inside, and pushed the heavy door ajar. A police officer stepped cautiously inside. He wore a standard-type uniform and a thick bomber-style tactical jacket, but not exactly like the Summerlea police uniforms.

"Hey, what's going on in here? Are you okay? What are you two doing in here this time of night?" Rennie's heart began to pound even harder, and her head ached with the knowledge of what she had just discovered. Something was wrong. She shoved the letter underneath the rack on the bottom of the table with her foot, as she and Bonita stood to face him.

"We're fine. What are you doing here? Where are Aidan and T-Rex?" The man let the door close on its own, the lock sounding ominous as it sealed them off from the outside, encapsulated in an almost soundproof circle of two layers of stone. He made a slow glance around the room, resting his hands on his hips.

"I'm on duty tonight. When I was making my rounds, I thought I saw something in the top of the bell tower and must have been on my way up the stairs to check it out when you all arrived. I took a smoke break up there and then I heard a noise down here, so I decided to come back down. I haven't seen any one else."

"How did you get a key to this room?" Rennie demanded. "And we didn't see a squad car anywhere."

"Fr. Geoffrey gave the Summerlea police chief a key so we could check it out on our rounds. My car is parked out of the way a bit. I like to walk this campus when I'm here. So what are you doing here this time of night?"

"No," Rennie said softly, her voice growing angry with insistance. "He didn't give you a key, not to this room!"

"Rennie, what are you doing?" Bonita whispered. Rennie felt her fingers tighten around Bonita's arms, as the man moved to retrieve the pistol that was holstered at his side.

"Oh, my God," Bonita cried out, gripping Rennie's arms in return as her eyebrows knit together in fear.

"You might have a key to the bell tower but not to this room. You stole it out of Fr. Geoffrey's office, didn't you?"

"Well, Rennie Easter," the man sneered, raising the weapon. "Congratulations, you got it all figured out. Yeah, I'm more than just a local cop. But I'll be long gone before anyone ever even attempts to find me. Just a mere slide down the rope I left at the top of the other side of the bell tower. I won't hurt you unless you make me." With one quick motion, he pointed the gun at Bonita and grinned.

"But I'll kill this black bitch in a heartbeat if you give me a reason to." Bonita whimpered, terrified, as her eyes searched Rennie's.

"Turn around both of you. Put your hands where I can see them. Now!" Rennie faced the table with deliberate slowness. She fought the rising panic in her body. He could never know all that they had discovered. Making a rapid scan of the items on top of the table for any possible means of stopping him, she saw an oversized box cutter that was perched on top of a roll of duct tape. Sliding her hand up over the side of the smooth surface, she felt for the handle and inched the knife as close to the edge of the table as possible. The man moved toward Bonita, reaching for the pair of handcuffs that dangled from his side.

"You know you'll never get away with this. What do you want?" Rennie asked again, trying to distract him. "You're really from that ignorant Wulfsreich group that is foolish enough to try to reincarnate the Nazis, aren't you? How pathetic."

In an instant he was upon her, thrusting the tip of the gun to the side of her head with his right hand and gripping her neck with the left. He made menacing hissing sounds in her ear, the tiny droplets of saliva spraying her neck.

"As you've now discovered, Miss Easter, your father has stolen much from the Third Reich that we intend to take back. Let's start by having your worthless nigra friend here make herself useful and get me whatever it was you tried to shove under the table. Didn't think I saw it, did you?"

"What are you waiting for, bitch, move!" He glared at a frozen Bonita and pressed the gun harder against Rennie's head. Bonita bent low to retrieve the letter, her hands visibly shaking. "Read it! Out loud!"

Bonita winced as she began to read, her words barely discernable at first. When Rennie was certain the man was focused on listening to Bonita, she slid the knife off the table and held it close by her side. Bonita tried to rush through the last part of the letter, but the man missed nothing. His face contorted into a ghoulish grin with eyes that were crazed with evil as he breathed hard against Rennie's cheek.

"Damn, this is better than I thought possible! Let's talk about resurrecting the Nazi party, shall we, since your sister is living blood of the Fuhrer himself! Sweet, noble Josie will deliver us strong and pure Aryan children. She's worth as much as anything in here. The motherlode." Heil Hitler!" He whispered the words next to her cheek. She could feel his lips touching her ear and smell the stench of tobacco on him. Rennie felt the same sensation of nausea threaten to overcome once more as her fingers gripped the box cutter. There was no other choice. She had to do it now. With one quick sweep, she plunged the blade into his lower abdomen as deep as she could, then pushed it up toward his chest before tossing the weapon as far away as she could manage. The man dropped to his knees, howling in pain and cursing as the gun fell and bounced to the floor at the feet of a stunned Bonita. The man grabbed Rennie's ankle.

"You fucking bitch!"

"Bonita, the gun!" Rennie screamed, fighting to shake him off. "Get the gun!" Bonita reached for the pistol, holding it like lit dynamite in shaking hands and wimpering with fright. The man held Rennie's leg with one hand, but could not reach with the other, as blood spread through the side of his shirt and onto the floor in small pools of crimson.

"Shoot him, Bonita!" Rennie pleaded, kicking as he tried to pull her to the floor. "Shoot him!" She screamed again, sensing her friend's hesitation and fear. With all the strength she could muster, Rennie kicked underneath the man's chin, snapping his head backward. Breaking free she rushed for Bonita, grabbing the pistol from her hands and shoving it toward the man, who tried to lunge toward them. Without stopping she fired three rapid rounds into the center of his body. The echoing sound of gunfire was deafening. The man's shirt burst into a soaking vivid crimson and his wild eyes dulled as life drained from his body. Bonita began to wail, the hysteria mounting as she held her head in her hands.

"Oh God, Rennie, he's dead! He's dead! Oh my God!"

Rennie gripped the shoulders of her friend and stared into her frightened eyes. "Stop, Bonita! Look at me! Look at me!" She lowered her voice to an almost indiscernable whisper. "You couldn't kill him. Better that I shoot him instead of you, for all kinds of reasons. Besides, I'm the one who wanted to. I had to. Do you hear me? I had to do this. You know I had no choice! He was going to hurt us, and then the rest of Wulfsreich were going to take Josie and do horrific things to her! They would force her to have their children for their demented plan to create NeoNazis! There's no way I could let him do that, or tell the world her birth father was the most demented monster the world has ever known!" Bonita shook her head, as sobs wracked her body. She held onto Rennie, who continued to whisper.

"Everyone will be here soon. No one can know what we have discovered about Josie. It's going to be all right, I promise!" Rennie bent to scoop up the dropped letter and stuffed it inside her jeans pocket. Grabbing her mother's journal and shoving it into her shoulder bag by the door, she thought she could hear the faintest sounds as Aidan and T-Rex yelled and pounded their way toward the secret room. Aidan's voice sounded terrified as he called out for her, and she knew the sirens would arrive soon enough.

"Remember, Bonita, no one can ever know! Not ever."

313

Epilogue

Summerlea, South Carolina
St. Jude's Home; The Ray and Catherine Easter Monument
Easter Sunday, 1976

My name is Cotterena Marthe von Bauchelle Easter. It is a long
name, to be sure, like royalty. Indeed I am that _born of the most
noble and courageous of humanity. I know everything now, having
read my mother's journal in its entirety and traveled to pay homage
in all of the places in Europe that were a part of their history. As I
stand before the St. Jude's memorial to my parents on this perfect
spring day of resurrection, I trace their newly added birth names on
the memorial stone with my fingers and reflect on all that has
happened.

The coastal city of Konigsberg, now the Russian city of
Kaliningrad, is beautiful with an old-world feel. Some of Klaus
Ludwig's relatives came back to the area years later, and say that he
died in the attack on the city that leveled the Konigsberg Castle. I
could scarcely take in the wretched remains of the Wolf's Lair, still
wrapped in unspeakable horror, and I could not fight the flood of
tears that refused to stop flowing. I stood by the remnants of railroad
tracks there that carried my mother to freedom, thanks to Conrad
Dietrich, a brave young SS officer who risked his life for hers, and I
am profoundly grateful for his love and courage.

The Becker family home in Rastenburg, now Ketyrzyn, Poland,
is no longer there, but some of the older buildings remain. There are
a few older folk who remember the family, with special fondness for
the girl they knew as 'Sonne'. I was inconsolable at The Natzweiler-
Struthof Concentration Camp, where Josef Taffel was killed prior to

314

the attempt at inclusion in part of what history will know as the Jewish Skeleton Collection. I found his memorial in the Cronenbourg-Strasbourg Jewish Cemetery, where I left another gold necklace that bore both a cross and a Star of David. Josie now wears the necklace Josef gave to our father, and it is more than fitting that she does so.

Colmar proved to be as magical as I had envisioned, with cobblestone streets and beautiful canal, half-timbered homes, shops, and quaint little bistros. One might imagine my surprise to discover that the von Bauchelle winery and home were still in existence. How I wish my parents could have seen the faces of my Aunt Gisela and her good friend Elena Taffel when I arrived unannounced at the winery. I suppose it was a rapturous second coming, of sorts. Unbeknown to my father, both had survived the war, living in England until they decided to restore the winery. They never knew that Rainer von Bauchelle had survived but believed he had perished all those years ago. We spent a few days filling in the torn spaces of all the lives lost and of those that remained. I treasure them all, my family and new friends, and will spend a portion of each year in Colmar, helping them maintain the winery and small café. I, too, will learn the winemaking craft and become proficient in the art of making Alsatian spice bread just the way my grandmother used to do. I intend to carry out my father's legacy of restoring lost art, books, and jewelry, of which there is a good amount still left, and transforming the von Bauchelle winery into a haven of culture and beauty. There are plans for an area of remembrance there to honor those who lived through the atrocity. I will make sure that the presence of my parents and their families_my family_ Josef, and the women who never escaped, are forever there as well, with painted portraits and plaques.

My final excursion was to the Eglise St. Martin, where I met with a kindly priest to share my father's boyhood experience with the judensaues. With me were my newly adopted uncles, Ben and Ian Taffel, who were once hidden at the church and then the old winery. They were smuggled back to the church before the Nazis raided the von Bauchelle home and winery, and thus their lives were miraculously spared. The remaining Taffel family members are also partners in the winery today and helped to build the added "Maman Café," where kosher foods are served in addition to selections of breads and jams, all made with my grandmother's recipes. I am beyond overjoyed that the priest was amenable to further discussion about the creation of two sculpted pieces to add to the great gothic cathedral; of Jew and Christian clasping hands, that would be donated in honor of the Taffel, Becker, von Bauchelle, and Easter families, respectfully.

And so my mind wanders now, as thoughts often do, to Aidan Cross, whom I hope will be present in my life always, and to that day in Fr. Geoffrey Radcliffe's class when I first learned about the center of gravity. In my young life, I have lost a family I loved beyond measure, discovered a family and an identity I never knew I had, and unearthed a secret so monstrous that I was willing to kill a man to prevent it from ever being shared. In this moment, I don't know if there will ever be a reason to tell my sister who her birth father is. I know the truth, in the event it must be made known. Like my mother, who I admire with growing devotion for her towering strength and love for her husband and children, I will sacrifice a portion of my own piece of mind to ensure that Josie is protected from the people and the knowledge that would do her harm. My center of gravity and the essence of who I am in this world are forever changed. I will travel the rest of my life's journey in the orbital path where I now exist, in which all rests precariously in a place of balance and contentment. At least for now.

Memento Mori.

Made in the
USA
Columbia, SC